THE WINTER CRASH

THE WINTER CRASH

BOOK 1 IN THE DEAN INVESTIGATIONS PI MYSTERY SERIES

K.W. BENNETT

__Acknowledgements.__
Many thanks to I. H. and G. de G. - my first two readers -
for their invaluable feedback and encouragement.

ISBN-13: 9789493241015

Cover Design: K.W. Bennett
Cover Image: Pexels / Erik McLean

For my parents

CHAPTER ONE

Caitlyn stood outside the police station, her shoulders slumped, her mood perfectly fitting the grim, gray sky. She was shivering in the icy wind that seemed to cut straight through all layers of clothing, and tried to use the side of the building to shield herself from the worst of it. She jumped at the sound of a loud honk, and saw her mom idling the car in the middle of the street in front of her, with the window cracked open.

"I'm here! Come on, get in!"

Caitlyn eased herself onto the passenger seat.

"They closed the case."

"They, what? Was that why it took so long? Do you mean they caught him?"

"No." Caitlyn slammed the car door shut. "It means they are done. I didn't expect this either, but they're closing the case. They don't have enough evidence, or leads, or whatever they said." She was fighting back tears. "The officer said they can reopen the case when new information comes to light. But for now, this is it."

For a few seconds her mother stared at her without moving, then she shut off the engine. "I'm going in."

"No, mom, no! Please, don't. It's no use. It's done, they...
You can't change this."

Caitlyn let out a long sigh. "I already tried. Let's just go home."

She gestured at the waiting cars behind them.

"We're blocking the street. And it's cold, and I'm tired."

Anne studied her daughter's face. "You do look a little pale."

Caitlyn leaned her head back.

"First the crash, then Todd, then that letter from school, now this! I thought these things were supposed to come in threes." Anne scowled. "I never liked Todd."

"Not the time, mom."

Where am I? Dashboard lights...
My car. It's black and white outside.
Caitlyn blinked at the snow that was floating down, illuminated by the beam of her headlights. *I'm dizzy. My leg hurts. Don't puke.*
She tried to lift her hands.
What the hell is this white thing?! Oh, airbag.
Caitlyn pushed it to the side and reached up to straighten her glasses. Something sticky was covering her face.
Am I bleeding? What happened? Did I crash?

"Caitlyn, are you upstairs?"
Caitlyn shot up in bed, winced and in a quick reflex grabbed the top of her Thinkpad to keep it from sliding off the duvet. She tried to slow down her breathing.
Why is this stupid nightmare still happening?!
"Yes, I'm here!" Caitlyn shouted back. "Hang on, I'm coming down!" She closed an open code editor and a few command line windows, then tapped the touch pad on her laptop. The blue dragon wallpaper vanished and was replaced by a picture of two white Persian cats. The cats, Newton and Volta – named by her high school physics teacher dad – were currently keeping her company. Volta was curled up at the foot end of her bed, and Newton was sitting on the windowsill in front of her bedroom window. Intently staring at nothing.
Caitlyn had recognized Michelle's voice instantly, and smiled as she slid out from under the covers. Michelle Laveaux lived across the street from Caitlyn's parents with her daughter Sophie. They had moved in eight years ago when Michelle inherited the house from her aunt. Michelle had no family living close by and Caitlyn's parents, Martin and Anne, had quickly become surrogate grandparents to Sophie.

Caitlyn and Michelle had been running buddies from the start. When Caitlyn had gone off to college, one of the things she had missed most was their early morning loop-around-the-lake runs. When the world was just waking up. When the birds and the soft thumping of their footsteps on the sand were the only things you could hear. Whenever she was home, she always tried to go for a run with Michelle. But Caitlyn wouldn't be running for a long time to come. At the moment, even normal walking was impossible.

Caitlyn shook her head to snap herself out of her train of thought and reached for the black forearm crutches that were leaning against the desk beside her bed.

Almost two months ago, she was a med-school student. One close to failing out of her second year, but still. It had been the end of December, and she had driven the three and a half hours from Washington to Oregon, to spend Christmas and New Year's with her family. She never made it home. Someone had crashed into her car, had T-boned her, and then left her on the side of the road. Alone.

She had eventually managed to stay conscious long enough to dial 911. The cops had found her about thirty minutes from home, close to Haweville's city center, and close to bleeding to death with the front of the car wrapped around her, and a pole.

Caitlyn didn't remember any of this, nor did she remember emergency services cutting her out of the car and strapping her to a stretcher.

Two days after the crash she had woken up in the hospital, in the ICU. With a big forty-eight-hour gap in her memory in between leaving for home and the beeping of the hospital machines. The brain's built-in protection system against trauma. Or the result of the concussion. Who knew.

The deep gash on the side of her head had required seventeen stitches – thankfully the scar was now hidden underneath her hair – but most of the blood loss had been from her severely damaged right leg. Turns out that, if you're really unlucky, you can bleed out internally just as badly as from an open wound.

The car's pedals had fractured her ankle and lower leg, and the impact of her knee smashing into the bottom of the dashboard had snapped her femur in half. It had taken an excellent orthopedic surgeon three attempts and an impressive collection of screws, plates and staples to piece her Humpty Dumpty leg back together again.

Caitlyn slowly hopped down the stairs with the crutches in one hand, and gave Michelle a quick hug when she arrived at the bottom.

"Sorry," Caitlyn said, "I dozed off."

"Oh no, I didn't mean to wake you up!"

"It's fine," Caitlyn said. "Thanks for coming."

Michelle followed her into the living room.

"Do you want something to drink, or some food? You'll have to get it yourself though, I can't carry anything."

"No, no thanks. I have to leave again soon; Sophie will be home in a bit."

Caitlyn sat down on the couch and lifted her leg onto it.

"How are you doing? Does it still hurt?"

"It's getting better, thanks. My energy level is a lot better too."

"Good. New crutches?"

"Yes, much better than the ones I got from the hospital."

"Your dad just told me that the police closed the case, but they didn't find who did it?"

"Yeah. Hit-and-run. Apparently, whoever did this is as good at the running part as they are at the hitting part."

Michelle didn't laugh.

"Caitlyn, you almost died."

"Sorry, I know. I didn't though. And as soon as these stupid femur pieces decide to finally glue themselves back together like they're supposed to, I'll be as good as new."

If you don't count the nightmares.

"One of the detectives talked to me when I was still in the hospital, and we talked a few times over the phone, but the concussion and the drugs made me pretty incoherent."

Caitlyn tapped a finger against her head and made a face.

Michelle gave a small shrug.

"I was called into the station yesterday, and they told me they were closing the case. It was a bit of a shock, actually. I thought I was coming in to sign a statement or something. Or that maybe they had caught him and were ready to throw him in jail. Ugh, if only I could remember!"

"Hey, that's not your fault," Michelle said.

"I know, I know. It's just frustrating."

"You don't remember anything at all?"

"I remember putting Christmas gifts in my trunk, and getting into the car. I know I called home to say I was on my way. I remember waving goodbye to Meagan, and I think there are bits and pieces of the journey home. And some brief flashes of me waking up in the car and passing out again... Then nothing until the ICU," Caitlyn shook her head, "but it's fine."

"Really?" Michelle raised her eyebrows.

Caitlyn shrugged. "I don't know. I've been so focused on getting better, it didn't even occur to me that not finding who did it was an option. I don't really know how I feel about it yet."

"Hmmm," Michelle said, "I'd want to know." She took a quick glance at her watch. "So, how's everything else?"

An angry frown flashed across Caitlyn's face, "Did my dad also tell you about the letter?"

Michelle shook her head.

"I got a letter from the whoever of the whatever of the scholarship program. Dear Ms. Caitlyn Doreen Harrison. We are cutting you off. Can't run, can't give you money. Oh, and we know you won't be attending any of your classes for a while, but no backsies. Pay up. Good luck, and goodbye."

"Gosh, that's... pretty bad. Can you fight it?"

"I don't know if it's even worth trying to fight it at this point." Caitlyn sighed. "I mean, walking should be fine, eventually, hopefully. But I'm not even sure if this leg will heal to the point where I can run and compete again. And if I can't compete, I can't get the scholarship back anyway. So even though I hate those sticklers-for-rules administrators, the laws and the school rules are probably on their side. Fighting this would just be a pointless waste of time and energy. Did I mention that if I go back, I will have to redo this entire year because I missed too much these past few months? I mean, it's not like my grades were anything to write home about, so a do-over might actually help me get my GPA up, but still, the whole year?!"

"Wow..." Michelle was a little overwhelmed. "When it rains it pours, eh?"

"I'm sorry to dump all this on you. It's just - I don't know. Maybe I'll have to get a job once I'm back on my feet. Work for a year or two and save up enough money to go back. But then I'd be practically forty by the time I'm a real doctor."

"Hey, missy! I'm... Well, let's say I'm a lot closer to forty than you are, and it's not that old." Michelle said. "But, I see your point."

"Any chance you need an apprentice?" Caitlyn joked.

"Maybe you could pay me to–"

Michelle interrupted her and laughed. "No thanks. Poor starving artist-slash-waitress here. And I've seen your art skills! I'd hire Sophie before I'd hire you."

Caitlyn smiled. "Fair point. Sophie could actually do it, though, if you were willing to bypass some child labor laws."

"Hard pass." Michelle said. Then she added: "Don't worry, I'm sure you'll figure something out. Just take things one step at a time."

"Literally." Caitlyn shot a gloomy glance at her leg.

"Anyway, it's good to have you home again, I really have to go now, but I'll come by later this week with Sophie." Michelle leaned forward to give her a big hug, and Caitlyn was partially blinded by her huge mass of black curls.

Caitlyn looked at her parent's living room. At the black Yamaha upright piano that was standing on the far side, near the kitchen. At the wooden floors that still showed all the dents, scuffs and scratches from her childhood.

The wall the piano stood against was painted in a neutral light gray. It always held two of Michelle's paintings; she swapped them out for new ones every couple of months. The one on the left depicted a fall landscape, precisely rendered with light blue foggy mountains in the distance, next to it a female dancer was spinning around in a red dress, with bold and colorful paint strokes representing the movement.

There was a cozy nook in the other corner, with two couches opposite each other, a TV, and a fireplace. The low glass table in between the couches had a fluffy white area rug underneath, something hand woven from goat or sheep wool, that her mom had brought back from a trip to South Africa.

It was strange to be back home, Caitlyn thought. Not only after all those weeks in hospital but also because, at twenty-three, this was not at all where she had planned to be. Back in the house she had grown up in, back to sleeping in her old bedroom.

But she was happy to at least be in a place where all the smells and sounds were familiar. Happy to get some home-cooked meals after all the hospital food, and happy to be surrounded by friends and family.

Her dad walked in and seconds later Volta jumped up on the couch next to her and loudly started purring. Caitlyn stroked her soft fur and gently tucked on a black-tipped ear.

"Hey, dad, do you know where mom is? She said she'd take me to my hospital appointment. We have to leave in about twenty minutes."

"She's in the garden, doing something to the fruit trees, I think. Hold on."

He walked out again, and Caitlyn heard him shout, "Anne, my dear, the wounded kid needs a ride!"

Her dad walked back in and sat down at the kitchen table. "Between the scarf and the distance, I couldn't tell what she was saying, but she waved her arms around. I'm pretty sure that means she remembered."

Caitlyn nodded.

"Did you check on the bees just now?"

Most of the large backyard behind her parent's house was taken up by her mom's garden. There was a small strip of grass in between the back porch and the vegetable and herb beds. In summer all the big planter pots would be filled with strawberries. Further back were a large shed, and a dozen fruit trees and berry shrubs. At the moment almost everything was bare sticks and twigs, and her mom was doing the last of the winter pruning.

Caitlyn's dad kept his bees all the way in the back, in a neat row of hives on concrete blocks. From early spring to late summer the back of the garden would be full of wildflowers and clovers. He had started with one hive a few years ago and had recently added a fourth one. Three hives were painted a uniform light blue with a white top super. The fourth was painted using several shades of red from the "oops" buckets that were available at a steep discount at the local hardware store. A small purchasing error her dad didn't like to be reminded of.

"They're starting to get more active." Martin said, "I'll have to suit up again soon, but so far, so good. All hives look healthy. I'm guessing you don't want to see for yourself?"

Caitlyn shook her head and waved a hand in a half apology. "I'll take your word for it, thanks."

Caitlyn liked bees, but – just like her mom and sister – only from a safe distance, where there was no risk of getting stung.

Her dad had given up on getting the rest of his family involved. He occasionally gave Bee Talks to groups of students from his high school, and Caitlyn was happy to help him when the slideshow needed updating, but if her dad needed any actual hands-on help, he had to call on one of his many beekeeper friends.

Anne came in, shook off her coat and gloves and put her dirty boots against the outside wall.

"I'll go clean up, are you ready to go?"

CHAPTER TWO

Caitlyn was crutching through the hospital hallways. Exercise and sports normally gave her energy, but she found rehab mostly very draining. She was grumpy from the nagging pain in her leg and annoyed because of the long wait between her first appointment – still no sign of bone regrowth – and the physical therapy. She wanted to go home, crash on the couch, and binge watch something on Netflix.

"I'll see you in the parking garage. I'm taking the stairs."

Caitlyn smiled. Her mom got claustrophobic just putting on a turtleneck sweater. She *always* took the stairs.

Caitlyn pressed the elevator call button and politely made a little extra room when a man in a wheelchair stopped to wait next to her.

"Caitlyn Harrison?"

She looked down at the man in surprise, then recognition.

"Officer Dean!

"Hi! I thought that was you! And, it's just Thomas these days."

"What hap–?"

"How come...?"

They both stopped talking and Thomas laughed.

"Don't you hate it when people ask that question?"

Thomas Dean was the police officer who had been called in to deal with "the incident". Caitlyn had figured out a way to bypass the password on her high school's main computer, and was waiting for the perfect moment to sneak in and change the grades of the class bully, Kaden.

Not by a lot, that would be too obvious. Just enough so his GPA would drop to where he would be held back and couldn't torment her and her friends anymore. But what should have been a permanent solution to the bullying problem, had almost become a permanent consequence for her.

Caitlyn had made the mistake of telling her friends what she was about to do. They had told others, who had told others, and pretty soon the whole school was abuzz. It didn't take long for Caitlyn to be dragged into the principal's office, and she still vividly remembered the anxious half-an-hour wait before her parents and the police arrived.

Officer Dean had initially come down on her hard, and she had found him very intimidating. But after Caitlyn and her parents explained the lack of measures the school had taken to stop the bullying, he had become more lenient.

In the end he had been the one who had talked the school out of expelling her. And after Caitlyn pointed out that she hadn't actually changed any grades (yet), her school's administrators couldn't do much more than to give her an 'official warning' and a seven-day suspension.

They also made Officer Dean promise he would check in with her regularly for the rest of the school year, to 'make sure Caitlyn kept on the straight and narrow'.

In reality, this meant they had met for lunch every Friday to talk about how her life was going. Thomas had given her some helpful advice on how to deal with Kaden, and had been a mentor figure in Caitlyn's life during that time.

They had lost touch after those six months were over, but Caitlyn knew things could have easily turned out differently for her, had it not been for Officer Dean.

When she was applying for medical school scholarships, she had sent a whole bunch of silent thank-you thoughts in his direction, every time she did not have to check the box that asked if she had ever been arrested for a crime. The elevator arrived, and Caitlyn followed Thomas inside.

He turned his wheelchair around, careful not to bump into a crutch. She studied him in the dull metal of the elevator wall.

When she had first met him, he had been a muscular but lean man with light blue eyes, and short dark hair in a military buzz-cut. His hair was longer now, and turning gray in places. His legs were skinny, and his upper body was much broader with strong arms and shoulders, but the calm friendly eyes were still the same.

"Parking garage?"

Caitlyn nodded. "Car crash," she said when she saw he was looking at her knee brace. "Spent about a month in a wheelchair then upgraded to these."

She lifted the crutches up a little. "Few more months to go, hopefully."

"Gunshot. The chair is permanent."

"Oh...! I'm s–"

Thomas waved a hand at her. "Don't worry about it."

The elevator dinged, and the doors opened.

Thomas reached into his pocket and handed Caitlyn a business card. "I'm visiting newly injured people about once a month here. Let me know if you ever want to grab a coffee and catch up. You know, like the good old days."

"Thanks, I would love to!" Caitlyn smiled and looked at the card. "Hey, cool, you're a PI now?"

"Started my own firm recently. It's not very busy, yet."

"I hope it picks up soon. It's really good to see you again!"

"You too, Harry, good luck with the leg!"

Caitlyn smiled. It had been a long time since she had been called Harry.

Caitlyn threw her crutches onto the back seat and held on to the grab handle above the door as she got in. With the seat pushed all the way back, she could just about fit her non-bending leg in.

"You'll never guess who I ran in to!"

Her mom looked at her questioningly and Caitlyn showed her the business card.

"Oh, Officer Dean!"

"He's a private investigator now."

"Good for him. He was such a nice man!"

Caitlyn grinned. "You mean back when he was threatening me with years and years of juvey? I mean, in the end –"

Anne's cell phone rang, and she kindly shushed Caitlyn. "Sorry, I've been waiting for this call. I have to take this, it's OCD."

Anne, Annelies Harrison-van Dam, was on the board of a large nonprofit called the Organization to Combat Desertification. They funded various projects all over the world, employing locals to dig shallow wells to capture and hold rainwater, plant seeds and maintain the land as it started to flourish again.

Caitlyn pushed Thomas' business card back into her pocket, closed her eyes, and leaned her shoulder against the car door. She half listened to her mom talking on the phone, but was asleep by the time Anne started the car and headed for home.

Martin inhaled deeply when he walked into the kitchen later that afternoon and gave Caitlyn a quick hug and a kiss on the top of her head. His beard prickled her cheek, and she shied away a little. "Kid, it's not under ideal circumstances, but the house sure smells great when you're back home. I'm glad you're feeling up to it again. What's baking?"

"Two loaves of sourdough bread, and this is for waffles," Caitlyn was sitting on a tall chair close to the granite counter-top and stirred some milk into the batter that was happily bubbling away. She checked the oven timer. "The bread should be ready in a few minutes if you want to wait, but the waffles are for tomorrow for when the Blues Crew stops by."

"That's nice of them," Martin said. "What time?"

"Subtle, dad." Caitlyn grinned and poked him with her elbow. She changed her voice into a bad English accent, just like her dad had always done when he put food on the table when Caitlyn and her sister Jessica were little.

"Waffles will be served around twelve-thirty."

"Excellent, I'll be there. I'll check if there's some alfalfa honey left."

"You know you can always bake some bread yourself, right?"

"Nah, I'll stick to cooking bee food in the shed."

Anne had permanently banned Martin from mixing up bee supplements in the kitchen, after his first attempt had transformed all nearby surfaces into one big instant sticky fly trap of a mess. Caitlyn grinned at the memory. Her dad was a good cook, but definitely not a neat one.

The shed in the backyard was her dad's domain, a well-lit man cave that to anyone else seemed a hopelessly disorganized mess. But to Martin it was a place of organized chaos where he could hammer away at various DIY projects, or talk to fellow HAM radio operators.

When Caitlyn was little, she had often joined her dad. They had sat together, with a thermos of hot chocolate, all huddled up in warm blankets on dark winter days. She had loved transmitting and decoding the Morse code, as her dad connected with people from all over the world. It was pretty similar to what she did on IRC these days, she thought, except with a bit less secrecy and a lot more nostalgia.

The oven beeped and Caitlyn slid off the chair, using the counter for support. She handed her dad a pair of purple neoprene oven mitts and watched as he pulled the two cast iron bread pans out of the oven for her. Both loaves tipped right out, and Caitlyn put them on a wire rack to cool. She re-greased the pans so they would be ready for use next time, careful not to burn her fingers. She liked to watch the Crisco melt. With no oven in the dorms, she had really missed baking her own bread.

Anne walked into the kitchen and put a small stack of mail on the counter. "Did I hear the beep? Are they ready?"

"Sheesh! What do you guys normally do when I'm not home?" Caitlyn laughed.

"We starve," her dad replied, already holding a large serrated knife. "Anne, could you get the butter?"

"Dad! You're supposed to let them cool off first. And that one is for Michelle, I'm going over after dinner, so leave that one alone, please."

Moments later they all enjoyed a slice of steaming, fresh-out-of-the-oven fluffy and mild sourdough bread, with a thick layer of melting butter on top.

Caitlyn flipped through the stack of mail and pulled out an envelope. "Insurance? I thought that was already settled."

"Uh, not exactly." Anne replied. "We didn't want to tell you yet, but they're not covering all of the medical bills, and car insurance won't pay out at all, until they can confirm who was at fault."

Caitlyn was quiet for a few seconds. "So how much do we have to cough up?"

Anne told her, and Caitlyn paled a little.

When she was getting ready for bed, Caitlyn took Thomas' card out of her pocket and studied it before putting it on her desk.

```
THOMAS J. DEAN
Private Investigator
thomas@deaninvestigations.com
555-24046
"To verify what you don't trust."
```

Caitlyn's parents had told her not to worry about the bills, or their finances, but Caitlyn knew they would struggle to come up with all of it. They weren't poor by any means, and had been very comfortable financially until a few years ago, when her mom had quit her old business and taken a position at OCD. It had come with a big pay cut, one her dad's teaching salary couldn't compensate for, and Caitlyn knew her parents were regularly dipping into their savings. But her mom, and her family as a whole, were a lot happier, so the change had been well worth it.

Caitlyn wondered if the career she had planned for herself would bring her the same happiness, or if maybe she liked the idea of being a doctor more than actually being one? Because if the last few months had taught her one thing, it was that she had more than enough of hospitals for a while. And she wasn't sure if studying for ten more years to spend the rest of her days locked up in one, surrounded by sick people, would be worth it.

Caitlyn undid the Velcro on her knee brace and put on her pajamas. She gently but firmly directed Volta to the foot end of the bed before she got in herself. Volta had a tendency to relocate during the night, inching closer and closer until she was right on top of Caitlyn's face. Caitlyn hoped she would stay put tonight; her sleep quality was bad enough these days without a cat smothering her.

As soon as she laid down, her mind filled with thoughts.
The crash, her future, the bills her parents had to pay.

She wondered if she would wake up again tonight with her heart racing and some horrible crash image stuck on a loop in her head. She wondered if these recurring nightmares were her brain's way of telling her that she should try harder to remember, or her brain's way of telling her she shouldn't.

It was a very strange feeling to have this gap in her memory, to have this nothingness of missing days. Especially since her memory had always been the one thing she could rely on.

She had resisted remembering until now, choosing to see the fear as a protective warning against a memory best left forgotten.

But in the back of her mind there was also a voice that whispered a counter argument; *what if that's just an excuse so you don't have to find out you caused the accident yourself? What if you only have yourself to thank for all of this? What if this is just the easy option?*

But, Caitlyn thought, if she had somehow brought all this on herself, why had the other person fled the scene? That didn't make any sense! So, it probably hadn't been her fault?

Only one way to find out.

Then another thought hit her; what if finding out what happened could make insurance cover all medical costs, or make the cops reopen the case?

The more she thought about it, the more she thought Michelle had a point.

I'd want to know.

Yes, Caitlyn thought. The only way forward is to fix this first.

I do want to know. And this whole anxiety thing needs to be fixed too, it is getting very annoying.

She reached over and picked up the business card.

Dammit, this is a puzzle. Puzzles can be solved!

Just because the cops found nothing, doesn't mean there is nothing to be found. Officer Dean isn't a cop anymore, and he is still investigating things.

"What do you think,Volta?" she asked out loud. "Should I try to do some investigating of my own?"

The cat ignored her.

It was true, Caitlyn thought, that the cops had gotten nowhere, but they were bound by laws and available time and resources. She had more... options available. And online friends she could turn to for help.

She took her laptop off the nightstand and felt the start of butterflies in her stomach, a familiar mix of nervous excitement and determination. She started typing.

CHAPTER THREE

After a restless night Caitlyn took a long hot shower. She was sitting on a plastic fold-up lawn chair and tried to let the warm water relax her, slow down her heart rate, and wash away the last remaining fragments of nightmare.

When she was done, she held on to the sink for balance and toweled off. She sighed as she looked at her reflection in the mirror. She used to be fit. A runner, an athlete. Her body a well-oiled supple machine. Now whatever muscle she had left was covered by a nice layer of extra... insulation.

She poked at her belly and felt flabby. Oh well, she thought with a shrug. It'll hopefully all go back to normal once I can run again. She looked at her leg, at the still swollen knee, and all the barely healed surgical scars.

If I can truly run again.

Caitlyn carefully tried to bend and straighten her leg. It was not going well. She sighed again, sent some bone-fusing thoughts to her femur, some healing thoughts to her knee, put on a robe and crutched to her bedroom. Volta followed her and jumped on the bed where she curled up and promptly fell asleep. Caitlyn felt a pang of jealousy.

She stopped in front of her closet, and tried to decide what to wear. She had never really been into fashion or makeup, but she wanted to at least not show up in sweatpants and a hoodie today, when the Blues Crew came to visit.

Caitlyn always jokingly said her sister Jessica was the one who had inherited all the fancy beauty genes.

They were polar opposites in most respects; Jess was a shorter extroverted blue-eyed-blonde version of her mom, while Caitlyn had her dad's taller, darker features.

Caitlyn picked some stretchy dark blue jeans that weren't too annoying to wear under the knee brace, a white woolen sweater with a long-sleeved shirt underneath to combat the itchiness, and one of her dark brown leather ankle boots. Shoes still bothered her ankle, so she only put an extra thick sock on that foot. She quickly ran a comb through her hair, tied it back into a ponytail, and swiped on some mascara for good measure.

After a breakfast of sourdough bread with last summer's strawberry jam, she went back upstairs and worked on a letter and a gift for Sophie.

Sophie had learned to write last year, and to Caitlyn's surprise and joy had started sending her hand painted postcards. Caitlyn always wrote back and when school work and time allowed, added word puzzles for Sophie to solve. This was going to be a good one.

When Caitlyn was done, she jumped on IRC for a while.

```
[10:06] <panicked_kernel> Morning. Anyone online?
[10:18] <foxx78> hi pk.im here.hows the leg.
[10:18] <panicked_kernel> Still attached. Doing
better.
[10:18] <panicked_kernel> Thinking about looking into
who hit me.
[10:20] <NiNjAZZ> Umm. Thought cops were looking into
that?
[10:20] <panicked_kernel> They were. Got nowhere.
Gave up.
[10:20] <NiNjAZZ> Suckss dude, good luck! Let me know
if I can help.
[10:20] <panicked_kernel>Thanks! I will.
```

Caitlyn had never corrected NiNjAZZ' assumption that she was male. To be honest, she assumed all the others were male too. It was a small group of about fifteen regulars that frequented this private IRC room. They had met online years ago on a message board and, among other things, liked to discuss all forms of hacking. White hat, black hat, hardware, firmware, and everything in between. Not all of them were very active, but the core group had kept in touch over the years. They were bonded by a mutual love for learning, and an aversion to boundaries put in place where they felt there shouldn't be any. Occasionally new people were invited to join, but the group remained small and private. Over the years Caitlyn had gotten to know most of them pretty well – or at least their online identities.

Caitlyn had stumbled onto the board when she was trying to learn more about programming, a few years before she got caught at school. Someone who called himself T00R had helped her out with the basics. He later took her under his wing and taught her some 'scripting for information gathering purposes'. It had been the best primer a young scriptkiddie could have hoped for. For a long time, she had been by far the youngest member of the group, but she was pretty sure she wasn't anymore.

When the original board went down over a moderator argument, their small group had moved to a private server, managed by Foxx78 and NiNjAZZ, that ran a heavily customized version of IRC. Caitlyn had recently written a script that sent a weekly encrypted summary of the chat room log to anyone who wanted it, before it got erased. There were a few bugs that she still had to work out, where it didn't remove all useless banter, but it was a quick and easy way to keep up with everything if you didn't have a lot of time.

```
[10:21] <foxx78> hey did you see that thing about the
  latest CIA leaks?
[10:21] <panicked_kernel> Fox - no, where?
[10:21] <foxx78> pastebin link. and i will help 2 if
i can, and will let the others know.
```

Most members of the group had a sort of specialty, a main area of interest they focused on. Their levels of expertise varied, but everyone's input was valued, and they always helped each other learn.

They were not true hacktivists, but together, with a little effort – and often trial and error – they usually could get any information they wanted to get. No matter where it was stored.

Foxx78 was excellent at soldering bits and wires to all types of electronics, changing out board chips or adjusting firmware to make a device do things it wasn't originally intended to do. A true modern-day MacGyver. Caitlyn had various devices of his design in the gadget drawer at the bottom of her desk.

Whenever you needed access to a database, or needed one created, NiNjAZZ was your go-to guy.

After getting caught, Caitlyn had switched her focus from gaining system access to web scraping. Much safer, and just as much fun. Using some popular scraping and natural language processing packages, you could quickly collect information from various online sources and compile it all into a single document with one command.

It was a big time saver, and a skill that had served her well whenever she had to do research for a school paper, or had to find medical articles about a certain topic. It was not necessarily a hacking skill, but – like any other programming language – Python too could be used for more nefarious purposes, if she chose to do so. These days she mainly wrote or optimized scripts for others, in whatever spare time she had left between medical school, her track training and music. It had been a long time since she had crossed that legal line herself.

But, she thought, maybe that was about to change.

The conversation continued, and Foxx78 linked to a few other pages where more of the CIA dumps could be found. When NiNjAZZ and Foxx78 went into a long discussion about creating cheat codes for one of the PS4 games they played, something about checking memory addresses for changes, Caitlyn lost interest. She thanked them both for their offer to help and closed the chat window. It was fun to be connected to people this way, she thought.

They had never met in real life, but she still considered them her friends. She knew most of the group's members lived in the US, but suspected Foxx78 to be somewhere in Eastern Europe or the Middle East because of the times he logged on, and the way he typed. Of course, his lack of capital use could also just be laziness, but she always read his voice in a foreign accent in her mind.

She knew NiNjAZZ was on the east coast somewhere, and T00R was in Florida. He had turned his hobby into his work and was a professional penetration tester. The only professional in their group, as far as she knew. They always made sure to keep the conversation in the main chat room completely legal – or vague enough – so as to not get T00R into trouble in case some alphabet soup authority ever intercepted their logs. As an extra security measure the main chat was reset every Sunday, but whenever something needed to be discussed and not logged at all, they used private back-channels.

Caitlyn thought for a while, then opened a code editor. It was often her almost automatic first step whenever she needed information that went beyond a simple Google search. The problem was that, if you want to run a script to collect information, you have to know exactly what you were searching for. And when it came to figuring out what happened the night of the crash, her mind was still drawing a giant blank.

Caitlyn muttered something under her breath as she stared at the screen for a few more seconds before slamming the laptop lid shut.

CHAPTER FOUR

Caitlyn sat on a high stool in the kitchen and was toasting the waffles she had made the day before. By the time the Blues Crew trickled in, she had a full stack of still warm waffles covered by a dishtowel, ready to be served.

The Blues Crew was a group of musicians from Jimmy's Steakhouse. It was no longer owned by Jimmy, but they did still serve excellent steak. It was also the best place to go to for live music. Almost every night of the week there was a different live band.

Steakhouse guests were encouraged to jam or sing along, be it local diner guests who knew a few chords or – increasingly common – professional musicians passing through nearby Haweville, looking to play at a small, intimate venue for a friendly crowd.

In summer, people had to book a table at Jimmy's weeks in advance. In winter it was still relatively busy, but most of the time you could just drop in and be seated.

Friday night was Blues Night. The Blues Crew that Caitlyn was part of played a mix of blues, rock, country and occasionally their own version of a current pop hit to keep the younger clientele happy. She hadn't convinced the others to play any musical showtunes, yet.

The crew arrived in three cars.

"Hey doc," some of them greeted Caitlyn as they shook the raindrops of their coats.

"Man, it was foggy this morning, I couldn't see a thing!"

They came into the living room and gathered around the wood-burning fireplace that was radiating a soul-and-body-temperature restoring heat.

"I think you all know my parents?" Caitlyn asked. "This is my mom Anne, and that big tall Viking looking guy is my dad, Martin. Some people find him a little intimidating, and I know with the beard he looks like he should be all tattooed up and in a biker gang, but he's a physics teacher. Totally harmless."

A few people laughed.

Anne served everyone drinks and put the huge bouquet of flowers in a glass vase in the center of the table. Caitlyn answered all the standard questions about the crash, her leg and how she was doing, then leaned back and looked around the happily chatting circle of people in her parent's living room.

There was Fred MacLain, an energetic middle-aged guitar player with a haircut that belonged in a boyband. He had been the one who years ago had started recruiting fellow musicians for a weekly jam session at Jimmy's. He was also the one who had immediately called Caitlyn's parents as soon as he heard about the accident and had visited her in the hospital as soon as visitors were allowed.

Next to him sat fellow guitar player Webber Michaels. A true blues man in his early seventies with a face where every wrinkle told a story, and a short gray beard. Depending on his mood he either wore a dark brown felt fedora hat, or a lighter colored panama hat. Today was a fedora day.

Howard Booker was a gangly, pale guy in his late twenties with zero athletic abilities, and a killer harmonica riff. Caitlyn remembered the night he asked to join them on stage. He had been a nervous wreck back then, but he had blossomed and grown confident in the years since.

Ayana Soliz, the short and curvy lead vocalist sat to Howard's left. She had joined the group two years ago. Caitlyn suspected they were dating.

"You know, normally we evenly distribute the music tips

amongst the regular musicians at the end of the night", Fred explained to Martin, "But last week we had to give the whole tip jar to Noah again. The poor kid is practically living out of his car!"

Noah Watterston was the newest member of their group. At only eighteen he'd hopped over from the Gold Coast in Australia to finish his last year of college in the US. He was an excellent bluegrass and classical violinist.

"You still haven't found a job?" Howard asked him.

"Nah mate, not a lot of job openings in the marine conservation field. At least not a lot of paying ones. So it's helping me out massively that you all are willing to donate those tips. Really, I can't thank you all enough."

"Oeh! Marine Biologist? Wat interessant!" Anne stood up and sat down next to Noah, who looked very confused.

"Mom, wrong language," Caitlyn said. She turned to the group. "My mom's Dutch, born and raised. She sometimes switches languages when she gets excited. Or," she added with a grin," when she's mad, or surprised, or... You get the idea."

"Do you know any Dutch yourself?" Ayana asked her.

"I can understand everything, but I don't speak it enough, so I'm a little rusty," Caitlyn said with a slightly guilty and apologetic glance in her mother's direction. "My mom also speaks the local dialect of the region she grew up in, up north, but I can't understand any of that at all."

"It's what I speak with my own mother," Anne said. "Regional dialects are dying out, sadly."

Anne turned to Caitlyn. "I don't understand why you have so much trouble with it though, it's not that different from regular Dutch."

"Mom, it is totally different!" Caitlyn said.

Anne shook her head with a smile and turned to Noah.

"So, you're finishing school here?"

"Yes. It's more of a strategic decision, really. The school you finish at is the school name you get on your diploma. The one I picked here in the States is much better known than the one I went to in Oz, and I've saved heaps on tuition. But, although that's a good thing in theory, it's not making my job search any easier, so far."

Soon Noah and Anne were deep in conversation about the differences and similarities between rebuilding coral reefs on the ocean floor, and re-greening deserts on land.

There were two members of the blues crew missing; Lucy Song and Hugo Rosefield.

Hugo had replaced Caitlyn as the group's lead pianist. He was an easy-going man in his mid-thirties, a redhead with a neatly trimmed beard, who worked as a veterinarian in Haweville.

Lucy was the youngest of the group and still in high school. She was trying to find a balance between freedom and her stereotypically strict Chinese upbringing and in a brief rebellious moment had chosen drums when she was told to pick an instrument. As it turned out, she was really good at it, and – more importantly – she really enjoyed it.

Her parents still would have preferred piano or violin, but as long as she maintained her 4.0 GPA, they couldn't object. Caitlyn had often seen them smile proudly at each other when they came to Jimmy's to eat and watch their daughter on stage.

Martin got the waffles from the kitchen, and soon everyone was adding the toppings of their choice. Caitlyn accepted all the compliments, poured a little maple syrup on the melting butter, and took a big bite of hers.

She listened in on Webber talking to her dad and chewed slowly. She had always liked Webber's calm deep voice and southern accent.

"Back when we started out, we just called it Blues Night. Every Friday was Blues Night, and strictly blues. They were very particular about that back then. Anyway, there was this fella you see, and I think he may have had something wrong with his hearing. Because when someone invited him to eat at Jimmy's on Friday, on Blues Night, apparently he misunderstood and didn't hear the S at the end of the word blues. The poor man showed up dressed in a light blue suit. Head to toe. Looked like a goddamn smurf! Excuse my French. And everybody was laughing at him so hard when he walked through the door." Webber chuckled.

"And then he explained why he was dressed like that, and they laughed and laughed at him even more. And then, of course, they all bought him drinks. So that's how it all started. That when you wear something blue to Jimmy's on Fridays, you'll get one drink on the house."

Martin's deep rumbling laugh filled the living room.

"That's brilliant, I never knew!"

When the group got ready to leave, Fred turned to Caitlyn.

"Oh, before I forget, do you think you could play the sixteenth? Hugo can't make it. We've got a big fundraiser for the MacCowan Middle School Library and no one on keys. Even if it's only for an hour or two, it would be really great if you could make it."

"Sure, no problem!", Caitlyn replied, "Or, wait, can you drive me, mom, dad?"

Martin nodded.

"Great!" Fred let out a deep sigh and was visibly relieved. "And if you don't have a ride, call me and we'll get someone to pick you up."

Caitlyn had started piano lessons when she was seven, and despite her teacher's best efforts she'd had an instant and permanent aversion to classical music. At fifteen she had switched teachers, and with that she had learned to play the blues. She had loved it. When she was seventeen, her then boyfriend had taken her to Jimmy's, and he had encouraged her to join the band on stage for a song. They had asked her back, and soon she was playing most Friday nights, making decent pocket money. When Caitlyn moved away to college all that had ended, but she always tried to drop by whenever she was back home.

Later that evening Caitlyn watched as her mom and dad cleaned up after dinner.

"Good visit with the Blues Crew, right?" her mom asked. "And Noah is such a nice young man! I think it's great that they're all helping him out financially."

Caitlyn nodded and briefly hesitated.

"Talking about finances… I think that when my leg is better, I should get a job for a while. Maybe as a programmer, or webdev or something. And, if I can work things out with Hugo, a regular thing at Jimmy's again. That way I can save up for medical school and pay you back for the car, and perhaps some of the medical bills too. It will take me a few years, but I think it's what I should do."

"Don't worry about it kid," her dad said. "It's only money, we will figure something out. Just focus on getting better. Go back to school as soon as you can."

Her mom agreed. "Don't throw away your whole future because of this. Don't make an already bad situation even worse. Listen to your dad, don't worry about the money, that's our job. We'll wait it out, if nothing changes with the insurance company, we'll just hire a lawyer to fight them."

Anne changed the topic. "Hey, have you heard from any of your medical school friends?"

"No…, nothing." Caitlyn felt a little sad. She had spent almost two years with these people thinking they were her friends. But the only ones she had heard from when she was in the hospital were her roommate Meagan - who called once - and Todd, the fling-slash-boyfriend who promptly broke up with her.

"I guess they're all moving on with their own lives", Caitlyn continued. "And, I mean, of course they should! I know how busy the bubble of medical school is, and how it can isolate you somewhat from the rest of the world. It's also a three-hour drive, and that's one way, so I understand why they're not visiting."

She paused. "It's such a big difference with how my life is now, that even though it has only been a few months, it already feels like half a lifetime ago. And of course, I could reach out to them as well. It's not all on them. But I think it would just be too weird: Hey, remember me? I know you're having a great time, here's how my life sucks at the moment".

"'t Komt wel goed meisje", her mom reassured her.

Her dad walked over and gave her a big bear hug. "Thanks, dad." Caitlyn hugged him back, then crutched to her mom, and hugged her too.

"Just think about it Caitlyn, don't decide on finances alone." Anne gently pushed the hair out of Caitlyn's face.

"Thanks mom, I will," Caitlyn said. "Later. Right now, I'm going upstairs. I've got computer stuff I need to finish, and I'll probably go to bed after that. And mom? You were right. Today was a good day."

Ann smiled at her. "Weltrusten, slaap lekker".

"Sweet dreams Caitlyn," her dad said.

I hope so, she thought, as she made her way up the stairs.

Caitlyn checked her email and pushed an updated script for the IRC bot to a private GitHub repo so Sayid could take a look at it. She got in bed and tried to sleep, but as soon as she closed her eyes her brain pushed on the gas pedal. Finances, car crash, future life choices, and the newest addition to the ever growing list of things that kept her awake, the one possible solution to it all: *I need to find out what happened.*

Frustrated and restless she got out of bed again and hopped to the chair behind her desk. She reached behind her to grab a sheet of paper from the printer, took a random fountain pen from the large Sequoia National Park mug on her desk, and started to write.

December 21st: Crash.
Investigate

- Where to start?
- What do the cops have?
- How to get a copy of the case file?

She thought for a while and added

The 911 call would give her a timestamp, so that would probably be a good starting point. Except she really didn't want to listen to it.

Her eye landed on the business card on the corner of her desk, still laying where she had put it down the night before. Without giving it another thought she got her cell phone and dialed the number.

"Dean Investigations, this is Thomas."

"Officer Dean? It's Caitlyn Harrison. Sorry, I know it's, uh, a little late. Is this a good time to talk?"

"Please call me Thomas. And sure, go ahead."

"Right. Thomas. So, I was wondering...." Caitlyn took a deep breath and then let it all out. "Two months ago, a car hit me, and the driver fled the scene. The police looked into it but got nowhere. Overworked, understaffed, bunch of murders to solve... I don't know. They closed the case two days ago."

"I'm sorry to hear that."

"Well... I want to know... I need to know what happened. Who did it. Why they left. Could you help me get a copy of the police file, and the 911 recording?"

Thomas was silent for a moment, and she heard the rustling sound of papers being shuffled around. "Let's meet up to discuss this, let me check my calendar. Hang on... Where is that thing?!"

Caitlyn heard him mutter and suppressed a giggle. So he still was one of those low-tech old school guys, and apparently didn't use the calendar on his cellphone.

"Got it. When do you have to be at the hospital again?"

"Um, I have PT on Monday, then a doctor's appointment on Thursday, I may transfer to do PT somewhere else soon, though."

"I can do Monday. Let's meet for lunch at twelve in the hospital cafeteria and talk about your case then. Does that work for you?"

"Yes, that's great! I guess I'll see you then!" Caitlyn was surprised at how quick and easy this had been. "And thanks!", she quickly added.

But Thomas had already hung up.

CHAPTER FIVE

Sophie came bouncing into the living room. She had her mom's dark curly hair and the same slender frame.

"My mom sold a painting, so she had to go to the gallery, but she said I could come on my own. I made you a drawing." Sophie held out a rolled-up piece of paper with a blue piece of ribbon tied around it, and looked at Caitlyn with her big brown eyes, eagerly awaiting her reaction.

Caitlyn had been snoozing on the couch with Volta asleep on her stomach. Her knee and ankle were acting up and she was tired, and feeling more than a little bit sorry for herself. She half sat up and patted on the seat next to her on the couch.

Sophie sat down and Caitlyn carefully untied the ribbon. Sophie had very much inherited her mom's talent for art. The drawing showed a hospital room in pretty decent perspective, with Caitlyn in a hospital bed with a big cast around her leg. In letters that glittered in shades of neon, Sophie had written "GET WELL SOON" across the top.

"Wow. Another masterpiece Sophie, thank you very much!"

Sophie's face lit up.

Caitlyn looked at her phone. "What time is it? Did you just get home from school?"

"Yes." Sophie nodded. "I had some apple juice and a sandwich at home." Sophie was eying the small box with chocolates that was sitting on the table.

"Go ahead, you can have one if you like," Caitlyn said.

Sophie studied them all carefully before carefully picking one out and continued talking. "My mom said we can go skating when she's back, but I can't use the trampoline until spring."

Michelle had bought Sophie a large trampoline for in their backyard a few years ago. It was a great way for Sophie to burn off some energy, but Michelle didn't like her to jump on it unsupervised. Sophie tended to get a little over-enthusiastic, and in general she often wasn't aware of any possible dangers, or the risks she was taking. It was one of the reasons Michelle had signed her up for dance classes and not gymnastics classes. Michelle always stored the trampoline in the garage over winter, and Caitlyn wasn't sure what had made Sophie think of playing on it this time of year.

"It's a bum-", Caitlyn yawned, feeling a little groggy, "bummer you have to wait for spring, eh?"

Sophie giggled. "You said bum! And it's OK, skating is sooo much fun too. And maybe Elise is coming, if her mom says it's OK." She hesitated. "You can come too, when your leg is better?"

"That would be nice." Caitlyn agreed.

Martin poked his head around the door. "There you are, I thought I heard my little neighbor!"

"Hi Mr. Martin!"

Michelle had grown up in Louisiana and had instilled some of her Southernism courtesies into her daughter. Caitlyn's parents had quickly grown to like and appreciate it, and much preferred it to being called something akin to grandpa or grandma.

Martin took a quick glance at Caitlyn, saw her suppress another yawn, and turned to Sophie again. "Do you want to help me paint some bee boxes? I'm building a new house for them in case one hive swarms. That's when their current home gets too full, and some of them start looking for a new one."

Sophie jumped up, then looked at Caitlyn, hesitating.

"Go ahead, Soph, I'll come look at what you painted later, surprise me."

Sophie bounced off. "Can we do a rainbow?"

"A rainbow?" Martin said. "Ooh, Sophie, I don't know about

that one. It would be a bit of an unconventional color scheme for bee boxes. Let's see what paint colors I have left."

"Maybe there's some red left." Caitlyn quipped.

Martin turned his head away. "I didn't hear that, did you hear anything Sophie?"

"I learned about rainbows in school when I was little," Sophie said, as if her being little was ages ago. "ROYGBIV, Red, Orange, Yellow, Green…" Sophie rattled off all the colors.

"Very nice. First let's find you one of those big old T-shirts to put on over your sweater, so your mom won't get mad at me for ruining your clothes."

Caitlyn mouthed a silent thank you to her dad as he led Sophie out of the room, and tried to get more comfortable on the couch. She felt exhausted.

Volta, annoyed by all the moving around, swished her tail and gave a little growl of protest.

"You and me both Volta." Caitlyn muttered.

On Monday morning Caitlyn felt a lot better. She put some oatmeal in a pan, and added dried cranberries, chunks of half a cut up apple, and a handful of pecan nuts. She added water and waited for her breakfast to cook before stirring in a small chunk of butter. It was a bit more work than putting a slightly stale leftover waffle in the toaster, but it was also much more filling, and she had rehab, and the meeting with Thomas later that afternoon. She took the sourdough starter out of the fridge and sniffed. It had a fruity pleasant smell and looked very active and bubbly. She added some fresh flour and water before putting it back, so it would be ready to use the next morning.

A few hours later she was sitting at a table in the hospital cafeteria, close to the entrance. It was brightly lit by cold LED ceiling spotlights that gave the place a sterile atmosphere that was only mildly countered by the two-story high glass wall that looked out onto the parking lot.

It was starting to get busier, and Caitlyn knew the large space would fill to capacity within an hour. At the tables sat patients and visitors, as well as hospital staff who were easily identifiable by their scrubs and white coats. Caitlyn had gotten lunch here multiple times as a patient. She wondered if she'd one day be one of the doctors here too.

Some of the staff were talking, most were eating or drinking alone. Working in a hospital, Caitlyn knew, you ate when you could.

Caitlyn had bought a salad with pasta that a helpful man had carried to the table for her. She was pushing lettuce leaves around with her fork, too nervous to eat.

Am I really doing this? Am I starting my own investigation?

She checked the large clock on the wall, 12:50PM, she was early.

But so was Thomas.

She saw him come in and scan the room. She waved and he rolled up, pushed a chair out of his way, and put the tray with a sandwich and coffee from his lap on to the table. He was wearing jeans, a black sweater and a slightly faded dark gray baseball cap.

He took the lid off the cup and took a careful sip. "Aahh, this is surprisingly good coffee." He looked at her. "So, let's talk."

Caitlyn's mouth turned up at the corner. Straight to the point, just like he always had been.

"I'm not sure how much I can pay you," Caitlyn started. "What's your hourly rate?"

"Don't worry about the money. Your mom has sent me Christmas cards every year since… that thing at your school. They helped after…" He gestured at his wheelchair. "It was a part of my life that was still normal. Still the same. Think of this as me owing your family a favor. I'm repaying it."

"My mom met up with you?"

"Of course! Can't have your kid talk with some random cop without checking him out. But we're not here to talk about all that."

"Right. So. Someone hit my car and then left the scene. At

least that's what we think happened... Insurance is putting up a fight because they need to figure out who is to blame, and they'd rather have the other guy's insurance pay out either way, so I need to find him. I also hate having this hole in my memory. I want to know what happened. I mean, if he wasn't guilty, why didn't he stay to make sure I was OK? The police didn't get anywhere though, and they closed the case last week. Do you think you could get me a copy of the case file and maybe take a look at it? See what's in it, see if the cops missed anything?" Thomas hesitated, then took a bite from his sandwich. Caitlyn waited impatiently for him to finish chewing.

"I could try, but I think it's better if you ask for a copy yourself first. I didn't exactly leave the force on good terms."

"Oh... OK.", Caitlyn poked at a tomato, and waited for more, but Thomas didn't elaborate.

None of my business, she told herself.

"I think you can request them online now," Thomas added. "They were changing the system when I left. It was a bit of a mess. It might take a while for you to get an answer back. In fact, by the time they get around to it, we may have solved this case already." He grinned and made a face at the memory.

"Right," Caitlyn said. "Also... The 911 recording? I know I can request a copy of that myself too, but I ...uhm.. I don't really want to listen to it. I mean, I don't remember much from the accident itself, but I do know that I almost died and I kept passing out.

So it's not exactly something I want to ask my family or any of my friends to listen to either. I think the recording would give me at least a timeline, a place to start, and hopefully some clues. I know it's a lot to ask, but could you...?

"Not a problem, this I can definitely do for you. That's no problem at all. It normally takes a few months for them to process your request, and there's a small fee involved, but I've got a friend I can ask – he'll be much faster, and he's free."

Thomas looked at her. "And yes, I will listen to it for you."

Caitlyn let out a big sigh of relief.

"Thank you so much!" She paused.

"Are you sure about me not paying you?"

"I'm sure. Thank your mom for me."

"I will. Wait, if you got all the family Christmas cards since high school, that means you also got the one with the antlers?!"

"Oh yes, I remember that one." Thomas chuckled. "Really hard not to notice."

Caitlyn felt her cheeks flush. "That was supposed to come with an explanation in the Christmas letter. I'm a lot less gullible now, at least I like to think I am. My dad told me it was a *test photo*." Caitlyn made air-quotes with her fingers. "And then when he ordered the cards he apparently *uploaded the wrong file*." More air quotes. "Man, I got so many presents with reindeer on them that whole year."

They both laughed.

"It was pretty memorable," Thomas said.

Caitlyn finally relaxed and took a bite of her salad. "So, you're a PI now?"

"Yes, I started my own PI firm a little over... Huh, almost a year ago already. I always had the plan to retire a little early and start my own PI business. My injury moved everything up by a decade or so. Business is a bit slower than I hoped. Some clients turn right around as soon as they see the wheelchair." Thomas half shrugged, half grinned. "Thankfully I'm excellent at surveillance work, you know, sitting around and taking pictures. Some PI colleagues who hate that type of work refer clients to me. I also teach a wheelchair self-defense class once a week, play on a basketball team, and volunteer here as a mentor to newly injured SCI patients."

"SCI?"

"Spinal cord injury, paralyzed."

Caitlyn nodded. "Do you have a family? I never asked before."

Thomas blue eyes lit up. "Yes, I'm married now and we have a four-year-old son, Bradley." Thomas reached his arm behind him and put a small bag on the table. He took out his cellphone and flipped through a few photos until he found the one he was looking for. He held up the screen so Caitlyn could see.

"Oh man, your kid looks just like you!"

Thomas smiled. "Yes, Bradley's a little mini me, but thankfully he has a lot of his mom's traits too. What about you?"

"Medical school student."

"Congrats," Thomas said.

Caitlyn shrugged half heartedly. "I've been single since the crash because my kind-of boyfriend broke up with me in the hospital. And as far as med school goes, my grades aren't all that good. I had a partial athletic scholarship, track and field, and well," she gestured at her leg, "they kind of broke up with me too. I'm not sure when I can go back. It will be a long time before I can even walk normally again–"

Caitlyn stopped talking abruptly and gasped. "Oh, I'm sorry! I mean…"

She felt guilty for complaining about her leg to someone who couldn't walk at all.

"No need to apologize. Sounds like you've got some ways to go with the leg?"

"My ankle and lower leg are healing fine, they're starting to get back to normal now, but the two parts of my femur are not growing back together yet. It's called a non-union, it happens sometimes, apparently. Lot more fun to learn about when it's not happening to you. Plus there was some knee damage that's not exactly helping things. I might need more surgery later, or it might be fine. We'll see. I'm not allowed to put any weight on it yet, but I hope to get the OK in a few weeks."

"Yikes, sounds painful."

"Hmmm. It's OK now, as long as I don't move around too much."

Thomas looked at the knee brace. "And that thing helps keep it straight?"

"Limits range of motion, but I can bend it a little."

Caitlyn unlocked the brace to show him and grimaced.

"Yeah, I can tell," Thomas said, with more than a hint of sarcasm.

He finished his coffee, and the last of his sandwich.

"So, you'll send me a copy of the case file when you get it, I'll get the 911 recording and I'll listen to it." He paused for a beat. "You don't remember anything at all about your crash?"

"No. Or, maybe. I don't know. I remember some parts right after. And I get some small fragments of memories in my... dreams, but not enough to form a clear mental picture. I'm not even sure if they are real memories or not."

"Mine were," Thomas said, and for a short moment he seemed lost in thought. "You know, most hit-and-run perpetrators are drunk or in a blind panic when they run. There are some who have, in their minds at least, a very good reason to not want to be there. When you find whoever did this, you need to be careful about how you approach him or her."

Her?

Caitlyn had never once thought of the person who did this as female, but of course that was a possibility.

"Thanks. I will," she said.

Thomas checked his watch. "Look, I've gotta go. I'll let you know when I find something."

He took a small pump bottle with hand sanitizer out of his bag and, after using it, wiped his hands on some paper napkins. He put everything back in the bag and slightly turned so he could clip it to the back of his chair again. He winced a little as he repositioned himself, then turned back and smiled at her.

"It's really good to see you, Harry. And, hey, the nightmares? They will get better. Give it some time."

When Caitlyn got home, she went straight upstairs and searched Google for "how to request a copy of your police case file". It led her to the Haweville Police Bureau's website, and ten minutes later it became clear to her that the mess Thomas had mentioned had either not been fixed, or had been made worse by someone attempting to fix it.

She had created an account, clicked on pretty much every available link in the menu, and even went back to Google to try and get to a different landing page. No matter what she did, she couldn't find the right request form.

She glared at the banner ad that was staring her in the face.

Become a police officer. Join us. We're hiring!

Better hire some people to improve this stupid user interface, she thought. She gave up for now, closed all open browser tabs, and crutched downstairs to go look for her dad.

Martin was in the back of the garden, peering into the Blue hive, fully geared up in a beekeeping suit. Caitlyn kept a comfortable distance and leaned on her crutches. She was pretty out of breath from crutching the long distance over grass, but at least the ground was hard enough for her crutches not to sink in.

"Better stay there kid. I've got to work quickly here. Although they're pretty docile in winter, they're never too happy about me disturbing them this time of year. Protect the honey at all costs. Never mind biting the hand that feeds ya."

Caitlyn could smell the smoker, but was far enough away so that there were no bees coming to see if they needed to chase her off. "They all OK?" she asked.

Martin pointed at the ground in front of the first hive. "They've been throwing the dead ones out, and there haven't been too many. And I can tell there's a pretty active bunch inside here. Not a lot of mites either. They're doing pretty good, I'd say."

He put some sugary fondant patties on top and watched the bees for a few seconds as they came hurrying up to check out the food. He carefully put the top cover back on and adjusted something inside the smoker.

"Hey, dad? Got a minute to talk?"

"Sure, what's up?"

"I am... I think I am going to look into who hit my car that day." Martin straightened up, secured the strap around the hive and walked towards her, small puffs of smoke trailing behind him. "I see." He gently brushed some stray bees off his suit and unzipped the hood when he was far enough away.

"At the very least I hope to get enough information for the

insurance company so they will pay for the car. And maybe it will give me some closure too."

"That would be good. Are you sure though?"

"Yes. I need to know."

Her dad nodded, and they slowly headed towards the house.

"Do you think you could drive me to the police office sometime this week? I'd like to get a copy of my case file. I just tried to get to a request form on their website, but their website absolutely sucks."

"I can drive you, sure. There's some kind of school outing on Wednesday so I won't have to start until third period. But, you know, I also have the email address of Officer Stewart, couldn't you ask him?"

If she hadn't been holding on to the crutches, Caitlyn would have slapped a hand against her forehead. How stupid not to think of that herself!

"Yes!" Caitlyn's mood instantly lifted. "That's much easier. Thanks dad. He's the one who came to see me in the hospital, right?"

Martin nodded. "My laptop is on the dining room table, you know what to do. The password is still the same."

"You really should change that sometime, beeman1962."

"No use, haven't you heard what Snowden and Assange say? The Feds are reading everything anyway."

"I thought you told me that was the NSA?"

"I knew you were paying attention! They all are though."

"Ugh! Dad, you're a nut job!"

Martin stopped in front of the door of the shed. "I'm right though."

"Probably." Caitlyn teased. "If you want to level up, you could turn into one of those prepper guys though."

"Into what?"

"Preppers, you know, with the food and the bunkers..."

Her dad gave her a blank stare.

"Never mind. I'll go email the detective."

Caitlyn headed for the back door but stopped and half turned around when her dad spoke again.

"Are you gonna tell your mother, or should I?"

Caitlyn thought for a few seconds. Caitlyn's mom had a tendency to focus on all possible problems in her initial reaction. It could be pretty discouraging, even if it wasn't meant that way. It had led to more than a few shouting matches and hurt feelings in the past. But, Caitlyn decided, this was something that should come from her. And she was learning to see it more as concern than discouragement, anyway.

"I'll tell her myself, later."

CHAPTER SIX

Anne poked her head around the door of the living room. "Caitlyn, there's a package for you. I think you have to sign."

"Jeez, mom, you scared me!"

Caitlyn paused Netflix, got up from the couch and made her way to the front door.

"Oooh, nice! I've been waiting for that!"

A few weeks ago, Foxx78 had submitted a wiring diagram to the group complete with accompanying video instructions for how to turn a certain model of baby monitor into a portable signal scanner. The resulting device would allow someone to intercept the signal from any unsecured wireless camera, or anything else that transmitted on the same bands. The parts and the monitor itself were cheap, and Caitlyn had plenty of time to put it together and add yet another device to her ever-growing collection of useful gadgets, so she had ordered them.

Caitlyn had learned to solder when, back in high school, a boy she wanted to impress had asked her if she could modify his gaming console. She had found that she had both the steady hands and the patience that were needed to be pretty good at it. That was, as long as there were clear instructions on which wire to connect where, because anything involving electronics had a tendency to short out if she had to come up with the wiring schematics on her own.

Caitlyn was blowing some solder smoke towards a cracked-open bedroom window when her cellphone rang.

"Caitlyn. It's Thomas."

"Hi, how are you?"

She wiped the remaining solder off on a piece of damp sponge, put the soldering iron in the holder, and switched it off.

"Fine, listen, I checked the 911 recording."

"Oh, how was it? I mean, did you get anything?"

"At first, I thought my buddy had sent me the wrong file, but then the paramedics described your car. At the end your name even popped up when they found your ID. So I know it's the right tape, but Caitlyn…"

"What??"

"It's not you calling. It's a man."

"A- what?"

"It's the right file, but it is a male voice. It's pretty short, though. The whole file is a little longer because they added the paramedics talking to the 911 operators at the end of it. It sounded like you were in pretty rough shape, I'm glad you're OK."

Thomas waited.

"Are you still there?"

Caitlyn's mouth had gone dry and she cleared her throat.

"Yes. I'm here."

"This man who called, he could have been an innocent passerby who didn't want to get involved, but chances are he's our perp. No strange accent or other distinguishing characteristics that I could tell, but again, the call itself was pretty short. He only said there had been an accident, to send an ambulance, and he gave your location. I think you were looking for a time too? This was at 19:04." Thomas said it as nineteen-o-four, military time.

"Hang on, I'm writing this down." Caitlyn reached for a nearby random scrap of paper with some blank space left to write on, still trying to process it all.

"Thank you, for doing this."

"No problem. Let me know what you want to do next."

Thomas hung up and for a long time Caitlyn just sat there, staring at what she had scribbled down.

So, there was a man, probably the man who hit her. And he had called for help. At least he had tried to make sure someone would find her. He hadn't left her to die alone. Somehow she found this thought a little comforting.

But why had he left at all?

She wondered what his voice sounded like. Maybe she should listen to the recording herself? But immediately Thomas' words echoed in her head. *It sounded like you were in pretty rough shape.* She shuddered. Better not.

Jessica and her boyfriend Ian came over for family dinner on Saturday. Which was only family dinner on those Saturdays everybody happened to all be home, and not as much a set routine. Ian did something in finance, maybe it was investment banking? Caitlyn wasn't exactly sure, because she tended to tune out whenever Ian talked about his job.

At first glance Jessica and Ian seemed like an odd pair, the pretty outdoorsy girl who trained horses for a living and the slightly balding six foot tall young man in the thousand-dollar suit. But Ian had grown up on a cattle farm in a small town and could ride with the best of them, and Jessica had always been the type of girl that could go from couch potato in her jammies to full on glam with false eyelashes and a cocktail dress, in one hour flat. And, Caitlyn thought, they were really good together. It wouldn't surprise her if he was the one her sister settled down with.

It had taken Martin, who wasn't a fan of bankers in general, a long time to warm up to him, but by now Ian Thumbstone was practically family. Ian was telling a story about an ongoing mini war between two of his coworkers. "In my office there are about twenty-five people in total, and we have a big fridge where we can store our lunches. One of my colleagues, he's an older guy named Jerome. His wife always packs a really nice lunch for him. And then there's

Vince. None of us really like Vince, but he is pretty good at his job, so there's no chance of him getting fired. Really too bad. The problem is that when he forgets his lunch and doesn't feel like buying his own, he just steals someone else's. And he often goes for Jerome's because he knows it will be good.

Jerome is getting very annoyed. HR got involved, and Vince got written up, but now he just does it in secret. We all know it's him, but it is really hard to catch him in the act, and we are not allowed to hang up security cameras. So we all thought about it, and we came up with this idea to put laxatives in his food.

But some of the other guys in the office are law school dropouts, and they all say doing that would be very illegal, something about intentionally poisoning someone. So, that would be problematic. But there is this little loophole in that, if you can prove you always put that same thing in your own food, and it's plausible, and then someone else just happens to grab it, then it's OK. Like someone with a shellfish allergy can't sue you if the food they stole from you contains shrimp.

Obviously laxatives are out. So now we came up with... Do you know those really hot peppers? What do you call them? You know, on YouTube, it was one of those stupid challenges where people would eat a whole one as a dare and video themselves. And they end up puking and barely being able to breathe and chugging down half a gallon of milk?"

"Ghost peppers." Jessica said.

"Exactly. So one of us will regularly put some ghost peppers in their lunch. You can buy them as a dried powder online. And then we only have to wait for Vince take a good bite, and then when HR calls us in we can all testify that we knew that person liked his food real spicy, and he can demonstrate if he has to. And that will hopefully be the end of Vince stealing our lunches. So now we've got this little secret office pool going, where we're predicting stock values. At the end of the month the loser whose predictions were off by the most has to do it. He has to build up to ghost pepper spiciness in secret until we're ready to execute our plan of forcing Vince to steal that lunch. I'm the youngest guy in the office, so I was really fearing they'd just appoint me, tell me to do it for the greater good. But I'm doing really well in the pool."

Martin pushed a stack of newspapers to the side of the table so he could put the table cloth on, and Anne served a hearty Dutch kale-with-sausage-and-mashed-potato dish.

Everyone dug in. Martin, in between bites, turned to Caitlyn. "Hey, I looked at those prepper guys you mentioned. There's plenty of 'em on YouTube. Those guys are amazing! They've got all this stuff and –"

Anne interrupted him. "Stuff, what? No more stuff! Caitlyn, what did you do?"

"There's this group of people all over the country, preparing for the end of the world, the zombie apocalypse," Martin explained.

"Or just a natural disaster," Caitlyn said quickly. "I saw an show about it on TV. It made me think of dad."

"Yes, disasters, that too." Martin continued. "They've got tons of food stored away, and very cool underground shelters. Anne my love, would you mind if I dug around in the garden a bit and buried one there? Maybe somewhere near the peach trees?"

"Caitlyn, wat is dit?!"

As usual her mom switched to Dutch when she got angry, she said it was the language she thought in.

"Meisje, je weet hoe je vader is, je moet dit soort dingen niet tegen hem zeggen! Straks spit hij me de halve tuin om!"

"Mom, slow down, slow down, I can't understand you in Dutch when you talk this fast. I doubt dad can."

"That's the point." Anne took a calming breath. "Martin, I love you, but please, don't go digging up my garden."

"I could even use this in class to demonstrate. Did you know that for every three inches of earth you go down, radiation lessens by fifty percent?"

"So show them a drawing. Or, you know, you could put everything inside your shed?"

"Nah, there's not enough room in there." Martin smiled and quickly checked that Anne was looking at her garden and not at him. He gave the rest of the table an obvious wink. "How about tornadoes? We'd have our own storm shelter."

"In Oregon? Unlikely," Anne said sternly.

Ian chimed in too, and Jess backed him up. "Earthquakes are definitely possible though. Dad's got a point."

When the laughter, encouragement, and warnings simmered down, Martin promised Anne there would be no underground shelter.

Caitlyn waited a few minutes, then spoke up.

"So, uh, I've got some news too," she said. "I'm looking into who hit my car."

The clinking of cutlery scraping over plates turned into a sudden silence, and everyone stared at her.

"Really sis, wow…!" Jessica was the first to break the silence.

"Yeah. Officer Dean, Thomas Dean, from… that thing at Monroe High? He is helping me." She looked at her mom. "For free. He says thank you for the Christmas cards."

"Oh, how wonderful", her mom replied on almost automatic pilot. Then she collected her thoughts and added.

"Are you sure about this, Caitlyn?"

"Yes mom, I'm sure. Thomas listened to the 911 recording for me. It… was a man who called it in."

Everybody started talking and asking Caitlyn a lot of questions, most of which she had to answer with "I don't know."

"What kind of serial killer do you think he is?" Jessica's mind always jumped straight to scenes from a horror movie.

"Jessica Nell!" Anne snapped, "don't say things like that!"

"What, why?"

"It's bad enough the crash almost killed your sister, and now you have to add a whole other scenario for me to worry about." Jessica shrugged in self-defense. "For all you know I could be right!" But after looking at her mother almost tearing up, she quickly added:

"But, I'm probably wrong. Sorry momsie. Much more likely to just be some random guy. Anyway, sis, what are you planning to do? You're not very mobile at the moment."

Caitlyn had written out a rough to do list over the past hour and was glad she could finally answer something.

"I'm going to start by retracing my route online to see if there are any cameras along the way that could have recorded the accident, or my car, or the car that hit me. Thomas told me that the call was made at a little past seven p.m. so that should give me a decent starting point. Maybe I will call some stores along the route, to see if they have security cameras. And then I guess I'll just go pick those up, if someone can drive me?"

"Sorry sis, busy couple of weeks coming up," Jessica said. "I've got a client who picked up three of those expensive Frisians from that breeder down the road, wants me to get them all broken in and ready for some serious dressage work."

Ian too shook his head, and frowned. "I think you may be overly optimistic about how long they keep those recordings. What has it been, two months now?"

"Two and a half," Caitlyn replied. "And I know. It's a long shot, but I hope I can find something useful. And I hope that whatever I find will make the insurance company pay out."

"Fine," Anne said, "Just be careful. You don't know what type of person it is that hit you. But I don't think anyone who leaves another person at the side of the road is the good kind."

That evening Caitlyn sat behind her computer. She had Google Earth open, and was recreating her route, and marking several roads that led up to, and away from, where the crash happened. In other browser tabs she had websites open that showed locations for red light cameras, traffic light cameras, and she had even found a website with a map of all known weather cameras in the area. One by one she added them to her customized Google map. She also added markers for all shops, as well as any visible cameras that she could see on StreetView. When she was done, she collected all the addresses and contact information of the places she had added. Finally, she saved her work and made sure the map worked on her cellphone.

She had initially planned to call all the stores and homes she wanted to visit in advance, but then decided against it. Asking in person would probably be better. It would take a lot longer, but she knew people usually found it harder to say no face to face. And being on crutches might help too, get some sympathy votes.

She sent Thomas a quick email with a summary of her plan, grabbed an envelope out of her desk drawer and put it in her pocket, then she went downstairs.

"Mom?"

"I'm here." Anne replied from the kitchen.

Caitlyn crutched over. "I'm going over to Michelle's for a while."

"OK. And honey?"

"Yeah?"

"Please be careful. Your dad and I always thought it was your sister we had to worry about most, with all her crazy horses, but Jessica was right. Well, probably not about the serial killer. Hopefully. But this could be dangerous."

Caitlyn leaned in against her mom's shoulder. "I'll be careful mom, I promise."

Michelle opened the door and Caitlyn followed her in. She loved visiting Michelle's small studio. Even in winter there was a bright but somehow soft light coming from large north-facing windows in an angled part of the roof.

There were low-pile tapestry rugs on the floor, and the room was filled with four large easels that always held paintings in various stages of done-ness. There were sketches, drawings and reference photographs taped to one of the walls.

The other walls were occupied by finished paintings and paintings that were hung there to dry, until they could be given a final few layers of varnish.

Michelle had studied art at some famous academy in Italy where she was trained in the Classical Method. Caitlyn absolutely loved the resulting realistic paintings. Michelle mainly painted people and pets, sometimes landscapes in a slightly looser, more colorful style.

She tried to keep a balance between commissioned work, and her own work that a gallery in the city showed and sold for her.

She also liked to copy paintings of the Old Masters. She said it gave her a better understanding of their brushwork and use of color and light. Caitlyn's parents had a small copy after Vermeer in their bedroom.

Michelle was wearing an apron and had her hair tied back in a loose and messy bun, with several curly strands escaping. There was a large gray glass palette on a small table next to her that she used to mix her paints on.

She was currently working on a copy of "A little coaxing" by William Bouguereau, a French painter who lived at the end of the 19th century. It was a painting of two girls on the front steps of a house. Caitlyn assumed they were sisters, because the youngest girl was giving the older one a kiss on her cheek, as her big sister held her in a loose but protective embrace.

"I'm still working on the grisaille layer," Michelle said, gesturing at the painting which was done in different shades of black and white. "Bouguereau didn't actually use this method of painting, but it relaxes me."

"And why is that?" Caitlyn pointed at an orange that was painted, well, bright orange, next to a small piece of dress fabric that had a layer of purple on top.

"Got a bit too relaxed and couldn't resist adding some color glazes," Michelle grinned.

Close to the door, away from the ceiling banks of daylight temperature fluorescent lights, Michelle had put a table and a few chairs, for when the occasional visitors came by.

She liked to meet possible clients at the gallery, but sometimes they came to her home.

Caitlyn sat down and inhaled. She liked the faint citrus-like smell that Michelle said came from the solvent she used. She especially loved seeing all the paintings and drawings progress each time she visited.

"I wish I could do this", Caitlyn sighed.

"You could," Michelle replied, "You'd just have to put in the years of training and practice. Learn how to see, and put what you see down on paper. Add some color theory, and a little light and shadow, and you're painting."

"You keep saying that, but I still don't believe you, no way this is just practice. It is pure talent."

Michelle shrugged and wiped her brush on a paper towel.

Unlike some artists, Michelle didn't mind it when people watched her at work. As long as you didn't talk too much and didn't need feeding or watering, you were welcome. She was even happy to answer the occasional creative or technical question.

"Is Sophie home?" Caitlyn asked after watching her for a while.

"Yes, she's upstairs doing homework," Michelle checked the clock on her wall, "but you can call her down, she could do with a break."

Caitlyn crutched to the bottom of the stairs.

"Sophie? Are you there? I've got something for you."

A few seconds later a door flew open and Sophie came running down the stairs.

"Let's go sit down in the studio with your mom."

They sat down at the table and Caitlyn took the envelope out of her back pocket, smoothened out some of the wrinkles, and handed it to Sophie.

"It's a little bit like our postcard puzzles," she said, "but this time you have to work a little harder to find the solution. Go ahead, read it."

Sophie took the letter out of the envelope and read out loud.

"This looks like a normal letter, but it's not."

She looked up at Caitlyn. "It's not?"

"Keep reading."

"There's a hidden message. When you find it and solve it, you will win a prize." Sophie shot Caitlyn a wide smile, then turned the paper around and studied both sides carefully. Her smile faded. "I don't see any hidden message."

Caitlyn laughed. "It's hidden! I'll give you a hint though. Remember the Tom Riddle diary in Harry Potter, where Harry could only read what Tom Riddle wrote after he spilled his ink on it? It's a bit like that, but without all the scary parts."

If Caitlyn was home, she often drove Sophie around when

Michelle had to work. Caitlyn had one rule for music in her car though - no autotune - which ruled out most of the modern pop artists that Sophie liked. Caitlyn had found a perfect solution in audio books. They both thoroughly enjoyed Jim Dale's masterful narration and had listened to all seven Harry Potter books more than once. But her car was totaled now, she remembered with a flash of sadness. She had so many memories that were linked to that car.

"So I have to pour ink on the paper?" Sophie snapped her back to the present, already looking around for some. "Oh, no! No, don't do that!" Caitlyn hastily said. "This paper has to stay dry or it won't work. We'll have to use a little bit of a chemistry trick to be able to read the hidden message."

Sophie frowned. "Will you help me with it?"

"Of course I will! Let's see if we can get closer to the solution. Or, I should say, if we can get *warmer*. Like *really warm*."

"This is so cool!" Sophie was so excited that she could barely stay in her seat. She kept looking at the paper, turning it around.

"Let's go to the kitchen."

"Guys, I hate to interrupt", Michelle said, "but Sophie is having a sleepover birthday party at Elise's house tonight. I'm not sure how long your little puzzle letter is going to take, but we'll have to leave in about ten minutes."

"Nooo, moo-oom!" Sophie begged.

"You heard me." Michelle said a bit more sternly. She started cleaning and putting away her brushes and other painting supplies.

"Sorry Sophie," Caitlyn apologized, "I should have asked your mom if you had time for this tonight. I didn't know you had somewhere to go. I hope you have a lot of fun at the birthday party though, and I will help you solve this letter later, OK?"

Sophie still looked a little disappointed, but nodded.

"Go find a safe place to put it," Michelle said.

Just after dinner Caitlyn got a text from Thomas.

```
Got your email. Have to be in the city tomorrow.
```

Happy to drop you off and help ask around after my
appointment. If tomorrow works for you, can you be at
my house at 09:30? Thomas.

He had added his address.

Caitlyn looked it up, and asked her mom if she could drive her to Thomas the next day. Then she replied with a quick

Thank you. Perfect.
See you tomorrow at 9:30AM.

That night she shut her eyes and once again let the images take over. Car lights, snow, airbag.

Am I bleeding? What the hell happened? Did I crash?

I think I crashed...

The heater in her car was blowing hot air through the vents, she could feel it gently push against her face and her arm. It was drying some of the stickiness. The ringing in her ears was dying down. She could hear music playing now, and the sounds of the car's still running motor.

I should probably turn that off. Fire hazard.

She tried to bend forward and reach for the car key, but something kept her firmly in place.

I can't move!

Panic was beginning to set in and she felt around with her hands until she found the steering wheel and dashboard that were pinning her down. After a few seconds she also found the car key, and the world got a little quieter.

CHAPTER SEVEN

Anne plugged Thomas' address into the car's navigation system and forty minutes later they stopped in front of a ranch-style single level home. It was a white wooden house with some of the beams painted green, and a narrow slither of pavement in between the road and a tiny front garden.

Caitlyn got out and struggled for a few seconds, juggling her backpack and a big plastic bag that kept swinging against her good leg. It was still freezing cold outside, but she was thankful there at least was no ice. She made her way up the three small steps that led up to the front door. Off to the left she could see a sturdy wooden wheelchair ramp curving around the side of the house. The snow had been cleared off.

She waved goodbye to her mom and shot a smile at a gorgeous and very fit looking woman with wavy blond Farrah Fawcett hair who came rushing out of the front door. A small, yappy black and white dog had followed her out of the house and was rapidly approaching Caitlyn. Caitlyn hesitated.

"Teddy, good job, but calm down, I can see her, it's good people," the woman said. She pointed to a spot behind her.

"Teddy, down."

The dog immediately stopped barking, trotted over to the spot and laid down, panting.

"Thanks!", Caitlyn said. "I wasn't sure…"

"Oh, he's completely harmless. You should see what Bradley sometimes tries when we're not looking. All bark, zero bite. Makes for a good alarm system. Here, let me take that from you. It's good to see you! Hi, I'm Ellen."

Ellen took the plastic bag from her and held out her other hand, but almost immediately retracted it. "Sorry, crutches, stupid. Come in, come in!"

Caitlyn followed her into a wide hallway with light hardwood floors, then into the living room. The furniture was spaced out to leave plenty of room for a wheelchair to pass and turn, and there wasn't a threshold in sight.

Part of the living room floor was littered with Lego blocks, and Thomas and a little boy Caitlyn recognized from the picture as Bradley were sitting on the floor. They were building something together.

"Ah, you're here!" Thomas said. He pulled his chair close and pushed himself up from the ground into the seat, then followed Ellen and Caitlyn to a wooden table in the kitchen.

Ellen pointed Teddy to his place again and put the plastic bag on the table. Bradley joined them and clung to his mother's leg, half hiding behind it and not making eye contact. Ellen smiled and put a gentle hand on the top of his head. "This is Bradley."

Normally Caitlyn would have knelt down to his eye level to introduce herself, and she felt a little awkward towering over him as she said hello.

"Please, sit down", Thomas said. "Coffee, tea? Do you need something under that leg?"

"Yes, thanks, if you don't mind. Tea please, if you have it ready. Otherwise water's fine."

Caitlyn put the crutches down, unzipped her coat, and put her leg up on the chair that Ellen pushed in front of her. The car ride had made her leg ache.

Bradley, who had now found safety on his dad's lap, watched her wearily.

"I brought some cinnamon rolls."

Caitlyn took a large Tupperware box out of the plastic bag and pushed it towards Thomas.

He opened the lid. "Brad, do you want to share one with me?"

Bradley was still hesitant, but nodded, his full attention now on what was inside the box. He clearly could smell the rolls.

Thomas pushed himself back from the table and got some plates from a low kitchen cabinet that he gave to Bradley to hold.

"My handy little third and fourth hand!", he joked. "Smart move using food to bribe him with. He'll warm up to you in no time. He's a little hesitant at first when it comes to strangers. We always let him go at his own pace."

Thomas took a big bite. "Mmmm, these are really good! Did you make these?"

Caitlyn nodded, but – like Ellen – declined one herself.

"I just had breakfast, thank you. I like to bake when I'm home, and I've got more than enough time now. It's usually just bread, but sometimes I go for something sweeter. You know, waffles, muffins, cinnamon rolls. I'm not very good with pies and cakes though, they always collapse in the center. I'm not really sure why."

She realized she was rambling, slightly nervous herself, and stopped talking. Teddy had come up to her again and was sniffing Caitlyn's leg.

"Relax, he really doesn't bite, ever," Ellen reassured her when she saw Caitlyn tense up a little.

"Sorry, I'm more of a cat person," Caitlyn confessed. She lowered her hand and let Teddy come close to sniff it. "What kind of dog is he?"

"Some kind of terrier mix," Thomas said. "Not really sure, we got him from a cop friend of mine two years ago. He found him wandering the streets and didn't want to take him to a shelter."

Caitlyn carefully stroked the dog's head, and Teddy wagged his tail, then collapsed on the floor and showed her his belly.

"See?" Thomas laughed. "Instant friends. Good boy, Teddy."

Caitlyn obligingly scratched the dog for a while, until he jumped up and started licking her hand and arm. Ellen called Teddy over. Caitlyn wiped her hand on her jeans, then looked out of the large glass sliding doors behind Thomas, into the backyard.

There was a tall, old looking tree in the center of the back yard, with a tire swing tied to one of its big branches, and a sandbox dug into the grass next to that. The two doors led to a deck from which a wooden ramp spiraled down into the garden in an elegant curve. It split at the left corner and went off to the side, presumably to join the ramp at the front of the house.

"That's really nice how you integrated the ramps into the design," Caitlyn said.

As an explanation she added. "My mom's really into gardening and all that design stuff. She used to be a landscape architect and she is always pointing out things like this. I guess some of it has rubbed off. She was pretty happy to have to drop me off here actually. She went to visit some guy who manages a botanical garden inside a large greenhouse nearby?"

"Small world!" Ellen said, "I bet that's Jasper. He is a friend of ours, he helped us with our garden design, actually."

Caitlyn looked at the backyard again and tried to hide her confusion.

Ellen laughed. "I think he would have liked to add a lot more plants, but that big oak tree and those few shrubby things over there were plenty for us. I'm pretty good at keeping people alive, but neither of us have much of a green thumb."

"Definitely not," Thomas confirmed. "My hands get dirty enough without pushing through mud."

After Bradley had taken a few more bites, he seemed to have made up his mind that Caitlyn was OK. He slid off his dad's lap and walked over to her, putting sticky cinnamon frosted fingers all over the table before Ellen swooped in with a damp cloth that she also offered to Caitlyn to wipe the Teddy slobber off.

"Do you want to see my Superman toys?"Bradley asked. "He's my best superhero. The real one was in a wheelchair, just like my dad!"

Thomas smiled and shook his head. "That's quite the peace offering Brad, but we have to leave soon. You can show her next time."

Bradley got back on his dad's lap and observed Caitlyn as he ate the rest of his cinnamon roll.

Caitlyn smiled at him and turned to Ellen. "You said you were good at keeping people alive? What do you do for work?"

Ellen smiled. "I'm a nurse in the ER."

"Wow, nice!"

"Does it surprise you?"

"Yes, well, no. I just... You look so strong and fit, I thought you maybe were a firefighter, or a cop like Thomas?"

Ellen laughed. "No, but thanks for the compliment!"

"Ellen is one of those gym junkies," Thomas explained, "you know, lifting heavy weights, jumping on stuff, flipping large tires. She tried to get me into it as well, claiming it was pretty accessible, but all that was a different lifetime for me. Been there, done that when I was in the Marines. I prefer to stick to basketball and martial arts these days. Not nearly as many confusing acronyms." He shot a teasing glance at Ellen, who purposely ignored him.

"Did you meet in the ER, when...?", Caitlyn asked.

"No, we were already together when he had his accident," Ellen said. "We met through a mutual friend, oh, about eight years ago now, at his housewarming party. It was love at first sight. Thomas was such a gentleman, and he completely swept me off my feet."

"I was still in the military then," Thomas added, "I switched to being a cop when my contract ended, so I could stay closer to home, and closer to her. I was ready to settle down, and I didn't want to have my future wife go through all those months of me being deployed. It was time for a change, and with my background it was relatively easy to get a job as a police officer."

"It all worked out exactly as he planned," Ellen added. "Of course, I didn't learn there was a plan until much later."

They talked until Thomas and Bradley had finished eating, then Ellen took Bradley back to his Legos in the living room. Thomas turned to Caitlyn. "I read the police report you emailed me this morning. There's not much in there that you didn't already tell me. There was some paint that was left behind on your car, transfer. The car that hit you is a black one. Most cars have several layers of paint on top of each other, specific colors in a specific order. So if some of the layers get transferred it's relatively easy to identify the make and model. They've sent it to the lab, but they always had a really long backlog. It will probably take at least another month before you'll get the results."

Caitlyn nodded. "I got the email right before we left home,

so I didn't have enough time to read it. I only glanced through everything briefly before I forwarded it to you. It's good to know we're looking for a black car though, right? They didn't even tell me that. At least that narrows it down. I will try to read the report again when I'm back home. It looked pretty complicated at first glance – way too many check boxes for one! – but I think I saw a drawing and a short summary?"

She hesitated, not sure if she wanted to know the answer to her next question.

"Do you think I caused this?"

Thomas looked at her, surprised. "Oh, it's pretty obvious you were not at fault. Did you think you were to blame for the accident yourself?"

"I don't remember any of it. It... was an option," Caitlyn said. "I'm not a very good driver."

"No way this could have been anything other than the other vehicle being at fault."

Caitlyn half grinned. "You still sound a bit like a cop."

Thomas grimaced. "10-4. And I've tried so hard to reintegrate into civilian society! You're right though, not all the jargon's gone yet."

"You're really sure it wasn't me?"

"Positive!"

Caitlyn smiled and relaxed, feeling very relieved.

Thomas continued. "That's the good news. The bad news is that I don't think there is anything else in the report that we could use."

Caitlyn nodded. "I expected as much. There were no witnesses, and there are no traffic cameras there either. I'm so glad I didn't cause this myself though!"

Caitlyn showed him the route she had created in Google Maps. A one-hour's-drive radius around the crash site, with the homes and stores she wanted to visit.

They briefly discussed their plan, then Thomas looked at his watch and pushed his chair back from the table.

"Right. I think we'd better go."

CHAPTER EIGHT

Thomas kissed Ellen and Bradley goodbye, and Caitlyn followed him outside through the garage where she watched while Thomas put on a pair of heavy wool-lined winter boots and zipped them up.

"I can't feel my feet, but they don't like being cold," he said when he saw Caitlyn look.

They used the ramp that indeed curved around the side of the house to the driveway. Caitlyn stopped next to the passenger side door of Thomas' black Mazda. Thomas was already in the driver's seat and disassembling his wheelchair. Caitlyn was surprised at how fast the whole process was, within a minute the wheels were off and on the floor behind the passenger seat.

As Thomas lifted the cushion and the rest of his chair next to Bradley's car seat in the back, Caitlyn opened the car door.

"Uh... how exactly are we doing this?"

Thomas put everything down again and looked at her, not understanding.

"I can't bend this leg. Can we push the passenger seat further back without squashing your wheels?

"Oh, damn, I didn't think of that."

Thomas thought briefly.

"I think it will work if we can push everything to the other side as far as it will go." He pulled his chair a little closer to the middle but couldn't get the wheels behind him. "My body doesn't twist this way, and I'm not getting out again. Can you just shove them out of the way with your crutches or something?"

Caitlyn opened the back door. She let the crutches dangle from her elbows, held on to the grab handle, and carefully moved a wheel so it would be on the floor behind Thomas' seat.

"I don't want to break anything."

"Shove gently."

Caitlyn paused.

"Just kidding, they're not that fragile, go for it," Thomas said.

Caitlyn suppressed a giggle at his comment, and at how silly this all must look.

When everything was relocated, Thomas pulled the lever that let the passenger side seat slide back. Caitlyn threw the crutches on top of everything else on the back seats, hopped to the front, and got in.

"Leg OK?"

"Yes, thanks."

Caitlyn looked at the Sponge Bob visors on both back windows.

"Isn't it a little out of season for these sunshine shades?"

"It is. But it prevents curious people from looking into my car when I'm doing surveillance. And that's what I've mainly been doing lately. Solid black ones would be much better, but you make do with what you have."

Thomas started the car and hot air blasted out of the vents.

"Remind me to take Brad's car seat out next time."

They first stopped at houses on several corners of the main road past the crash site. Caitlyn hoped that whoever hit her had continued in the same direction. But if he had turned at any point, a corner camera would have caught him. Thomas waited in the car while Caitlyn rang the doorbells.

"Any luck?" Thomas asked when she got back into the car. The first two homes had been unsuccessful.

"Yes, finally. The man said he had a break-in a while ago and put up cameras. He was happy to help me out. He'll email me the footage. That's three down," Caitlyn checked her map and counted the dots with her finger, "at least twenty-five more to go. It's a good thing I've got the type of face where people trust me with their stuff. Wouldn't be the first time a random stranger asked me to watch their money, or their kids."

There were a few traffic cameras along the way, but from what Caitlyn had learned from Axl3 on IRC, a lot of those were there to monitor traffic density. Most of them didn't record anything. And even if they did, they often automatically deleted any saved footage after at most thirty days.

Still, she had her laptop open on her lap. Both to watch the route she planned, and to keep an eye on the other screen to see if there were any cameras that were fitted with wireless connectivity. If she found one, she could try to access the server the footage was stored on when she was back home.

The war-driving tool she was using logged everything and came with a central database where all SSIDs and passwords the tool had ever come across were stored. But so far, she only got home Wi-Fi networks.

Axl3 had told her that if she got lucky, she would come across a HALO camera. HALO stood for High Activity Location Observation. These cameras were usually put in high crime or high-traffic areas, and they definitely recorded and stored video, often for at least a few months. When they were stopped at a red light, Caitlyn checked with Thomas that the HALO information she had gotten was correct, and asked what else he knew.

"I think it changes per region who owns them. Sometimes it is the DMV, sometimes the Department of Transportation. It can also be the local Police Department. I know we had access to a few of those. But," he added, "you need an FOIA request if you want to see any footage, and that will take a long time with only a slim change that, by the time it's granted, they still have what you want. We're already past the sixty days they would normally keep it. It's much faster to try to figure this out on our own first."

Caitlyn nodded. She grew more and more quiet.

Thomas understood. "Are we getting close?"

Caitlyn nodded.

"Are you OK driving past the crash site?"

"I don't know. I haven't been back here since."

Thomas gave her some space and slowed down a little.

Caitlyn looked out the window. There was no trace, not even a small piece of remaining evidence that anything bad had ever happened there, apart from the brand new utility pole. But what to anyone else was just a normal stretch of road, still gave her shivers, and she had to fight to keep her breathing calm.

"If it helps, and I know this sounds a little weird, but a lot of people I know broke their back or neck in a car crash. They say it gets easier driving past, that they even go back on purpose sometimes. Most of them actually celebrate their crash date each year."

"Celebrate?" Caitlyn was shocked and a little confused.

Who the hell would celebrate an accident?

"It's the day they could have died but didn't." Thomas clarified.

Caitlyn was silent for a while.

"I'm not sure if I'm ready to make it a party, but... I like the idea of reclaiming it, of knowing I lived. Do you celebrate yours?"

"No," Thomas said firmly. "I don't."

Caitlyn looked at him, curious.

"It's complicated."

She could tell from his tone and the expression on his face that he didn't want to talk about it.

Caitlyn checked the map on her phone again. There were fourteen locations along this one-mile stretch of road, but even if there were no visible cameras on the outside, she wanted to check some of the stores, homes and traffic lights anyway. Just to make sure.

They stopped at a gas station.

An attendant filled up Thomas' car and Caitlyn went inside to pay and ask for any security tapes. The owner allowed Caitlyn to transfer a copy of their footage to the external SSD she had thrown into her backpack that morning.

A few minutes later, Thomas dropped her off at the west end of a long road with various establishments on both sides. It was as if someone had planned to build a mall, but had only had enough funds to put in the stores one at a time, in a nice long neat row, with regular homes in between at random intervals.

Caitlyn shrugged herself a little deeper into her winter coat, thankful that at least the wind had died down. She decided to start where she was at and zigzag her way from one place to the next, occasionally entering some of the side streets.

Thomas left for his appointment in the city and said he would text or call her to meet up when he was done. She waved a quick goodbye as he drove off, then entered Prospero Gemstones. The jeweler's store had very visible security cameras both outside and inside. Caitlyn struggled with the heavy door and let out a small grunt at the final push to get it to open. Inside she was met by bright lights, and a lot of shiny objects in locked glass display cases. There were no other customers in the store, and the woman behind the counter quickly put the book she was reading down, and stood up.

"Good morning, can I help you find something or are you just looking around?"

Caitlyn shot a curious glance at the book's cover but couldn't make out the title.

"Good morning. Uh, I am looking for something, but I'm sorry to say it's not jewelry."

The woman's smile faded a little.

"A little over two months ago I was involved in a car crash. I saw your security cameras outside, and I was hoping that you would have some footage I could look at?"

Caitlyn quickly tried to wipe the fog off her glasses.

The woman looked her up and down and frowned. "I'm not sure I can give you access to that, isn't this more a case for the police?"

"It is," Caitlyn agreed, "but they closed the case, and I'm not sure they had the resources available to do what I'm doing now.

Do you know if they came by to ask for footage?"

Some of the woman's hesitation disappeared. "About two months ago you said? I don't think so, not for an accident anyway. It's usually for robberies in the area, so if they had, I think I would have remembered."

She looked at Caitlyn again, then decided. "Come on then, I'll show you. We got a new security system last year, and it's working really well. We haven't been robbed since." She seemed almost proud now to get a chance to show it off. "What date would you like to take a look at?"

"December twenty-first, from about six p.m. to eight p.m. would be great." Caitlyn replied as she followed the woman's clacking heels.

The one mile from the crash site to here would be about ten minutes by car at most, even in bad weather, but she wanted to keep things simple and had planned to just ask everyone for footage during the one-hour window both ways. This would also help her in case the person who hit her had been driving around the area for a while, or had come back to check on her later.

The woman stopped walking so abruptly that Caitlyn almost bumped into her.

"We only keep our recordings until we run out of storage space, December twenty first is a while ago, I'm not sure..."

She took Caitlyn into a backroom, moved the computer mouse to get rid of the screen saver – no password protection, Caitlyn noted – and browsed to a folder.

"This is all of December. Oh good, it looks like the twenty-first is still here." She double clicked the file, and the video started playing.

"Here you can see the time," the woman pointed.

"Could you fast forward to around a quarter to seven p.m.?" Caitlyn asked. "We are looking for my silver Toyota, or a black car that hit mine." She wasn't yet sure of the time of the accident, it all depended on how quickly after the crash the man had called, but Caitlyn figured it would have been close to four after seven. Also, if she saw her own undamaged car driving around, the accident happened after that timestamp.

A few minutes passed while they watched random cars drive by on the screen.

"Would it be possible to copy your files so I can review them at home?" Caitlyn opened her backpack and took out the external hard drive. She shot the woman a friendly and hopefully trustworthy smile. She knew any good security policy would strictly forbid anyone from plugging in unknown USB devices into store computers. She also knew most people ignored that.

"That way I won't take up so much of your time. I can imagine you probably don't like to leave your store unsupervised for this long either." *And this way I'll also have a better chance of visiting all the other stores I still have to check, before nightfall,* she added in her mind.

Caitlyn left the jewelry store feeling very optimistic. Three out of five, this was going much better than expected!

Almost fifteen minutes later she regretted that thought.

The high-end clothing store, the outlet clothing store and the fast-food restaurant she visited next, either didn't have any cameras or only stored their footage for thirty days or less. And by the time she walked out of the fast-food restaurant she was getting tired of having to explain why she was on crutches, and getting really cranky about her glasses fogging up every time she walked into a warm building from the cold.

She entered a bank through two sets of sliding glass doors and pulled a number. Caitlyn stood in line and studied the signs on the wall that showed current mortgage rates. She slowly crutched up to the teller and was relieved to see it was a grandmotherly looking woman.

Her white hair was neatly put up in an intricate bun, and she had an ornate gold brooch pinned to her blouse. But when Caitlyn requested video footage, the woman sternly replied. "Young lady, I cannot give you any of that without a court order." And no matter what Caitlyn said, she wouldn't budge. Caitlyn grumpily left the bank. Even a half-fake, half-real wince at pain in her leg hadn't turned the woman more sympathetic.

Instead she had seen right through Caitlyn and had pursed her lips. *No one better mess with her!* Caitlyn thought. But she really didn't like her lack of success here. She had no doubt the bank would have had some excellent high definition footage.

Next up was Firni, a tiny International Market place that was crammed in between two houses. But she quickly ran into communication problems with the man behind the counter who explained, in somewhat broken English, that his son was not there, and kept asking her what she wanted to order.

The burger place she went to next was pretty busy. Caitlyn had to wait in line for a while, and then wait for the teenager behind the counter to call his manager, only for the manager to tell her they didn't keep any video footage for longer than fourteen days.

She awkwardly swerved around the people carrying trays of food and drinks and walked outside again.

It was lunch time and clearly rush hour. Caitlyn was getting hungry too and decided to skip all the other busy restaurants for now, instead hopping into August's Bakery. She deeply inhaled the familiar smell of freshly baked bread and sugary frostings, with a heavy hint of vanilla and chocolate.

She looked at the tall glass cases to see what was on offer. She was tempted by the blueberry muffins, and the slices of cake and pie, but ended up with green tea and two big fluffy glazed donuts. She sat down at one of the tiny tables. She had to keep an eye on her leg so other customers wouldn't bump into her and put the crutches next to it as a small protective barrier.

When she was done, she threw her napkins in the bin and went back up to the counter to ask if there was anyone to talk to about security footage. The quick rise in blood sugar helped counter her disappointment when they, too, apologized and told her they didn't store footage for that long. She was starting to sense a theme here. She was also starting to really regret her decision to not call or email ahead to ask for footage. The lunch break had briefly helped lessen the increasing pain in her leg and the fatigue in her arms and shoulders, but now that she was on her way again, both were steadily ramping back up.

At Cinema 17 she got lucky, but had to wait for half an hour while the manager burned the footage to a DVD for her. She had completely forgotten to bring empty ones herself.

"So, what's currently running?" Caitlyn asked to break the silence.

The man pointed at a board behind them. "The Greatest Showman, A Quiet Place, The Rider", the man summed up. "Black Panther is still going strong too. If you have kids, there's some animated thing. I wouldn't recommend it."

"I watch more TV than movies myself," Caitlyn confessed. "But I think my sister saw The Rider last week. How's The Greatest Showman?"

She left with two tickets for The Greatest Showman in her pocket and texted Jess to ask if she was free next Saturday.

She decided to skip the lawyer and had just entered a hair salon when she got a text from Thomas saying his meeting was over and he was on his way.

The hairdresser was a bubbly young woman with very bright purple hair.

"I'm sorry, we don't have any cameras here." She studied Caitlyn. "But you know, if you want, I could give you some free advice on haircuts and colors that would maybe better suit your face and complexion?"

"Uh, thanks, maybe next time." Caitlyn smiled. "I'm in a bit of a hurry today."

The woman handed her a business card, and Caitlyn politely pocketed it.

Finally, at the corner, came Hart Middle School.

Lucky number thirteen, Caitlyn thought, *here we go.*

She crossed the playground and was quickly intercepted by a security guard who led her through the hall, past a long row of dented and scraped up blue lockers, to the main office. How come all schools smell the same? Caitlyn wondered as he guided her inside. It was a strangely familiar mix of bleach, body sprays, chewing gum, hormones and gym socks.

The inside of the office was toasty warm and smelled of stale coffee. The vice principal looked up at her over the top of her reading glasses.

"You don't go here?" She sounded like she wasn't completely sure.

"No, I don't. I was hoping you could help me?"

The woman took one glance at her crutches.

"Please, have a seat."

Caitlyn thanked her and told her story.

"I'm so sorry that happened to you. Let me see. Security tapes. Who do we call for that?"

She dialed a number and Caitlyn listened to her side of the conversation.

The vice principal hung up. "Most of our cameras are hanging inside the school, monitoring the hallways. But we do record the playground, and it does show part of the street. Would that help you?"

It took a long time, but finally a flustered looking man popped his head around the door and handed Caitlyn a VHS cassette.

"You'd better wait a few minutes," the vice principal said after a glance at the clock and another nod at Caitlyn's leg, "there'll be about a hundred students who will later swear up and down that they were not running through that hallway."

CHAPTER NINE

When Caitlyn exited the school, after all the talking, laughter and the squeaking of shoes on the hallway floor had quieted down, her phone buzzed again. She sat down on one of the benches outside, and checked her text messages. It was Thomas.

```
Getting close, where are you?
```

She texted him back.

```
Hart Middle school on SW.
I'll wait here?
```

His reply came instantly.

```
OK
```

Thomas rolled up a few minutes later and waved at her.
"You look tired," he said. "Any luck?"
"Five so far," Caitlyn replied as she got in the car and showed him her map.
"Jeweler - copied one file, didn't buy anything. I started off so good! And I also found out it's much better to get a copy than to watch everything in the store, man that took a long time!"
She scrolled the map a little and pointed.
"I tried here, but there was a bit of a language barrier. Nothing there, success here – I bought two movie tickets – nothing here,

nothing there either. Oh, the lawyer. I skipped that one, I thought he might respond better to you? Fellow law enforcing person. And the bank would not release any footage, maybe you could try them too? Don't ask the old lady though, I even tried to get a sympathy vote from her but that was a complete fail, she seemed like the type that reads the company rule book before bedtime."

Thomas grinned, then asked. "What language?"

"Huh?"

Thomas pointed at the dot on the map.

"Oh, I don't know. Foreign. Not Dutch. Didn't sound like Spanish at all. After those, I'm out."

"You know Dutch?"

"Uh-huh, my mom's from the Netherlands."

"Cool, I never knew. I'll try that one again too, I'm not at all fluent, but I did pick up bits and pieces of a few different languages when I was deployed."

Caitlyn went into a few of the places she had skipped at lunch time, when they were too busy. She met up with Thomas again after.

"I got nowhere at that bank either, the Firni guy is Afghan and although my Farsi is not very good at all, I did end up with a DVD." He waved a hand in the direction of the bag that was attached to the back of his chair.

"And the lawyer was very happy to email you a copy of whatever he can find tonight, I gave him your email address. He mentioned something called a drop box?" Thomas frowned.

Caitlyn nodded. "Dropbox, that's great. I have an account."

They got in the car again, and Thomas drove them to the next stretch of road. Caitlyn was happy to give her leg and arms a break and get some blood flowing again in her freezing fingers.

Thomas hung the blue parking permit from his rear-view mirror and put his chair back together while Caitlyn grabbed her crutches from the backseat and checked her map and the street in front of her.

"I'll get the bookstore and that lingerie shop on the corner."

Thomas leaned in a little closer so he could see the screen.

"OK, I'll go check that coffee shop and The Joint," Thomas said gesturing at a small place with a marijuana leaf on the storefront sign. "I know the owner."

"Hah, let me guess, you arrested him once, or twice, on possession?" Caitlyn asked.

"No. I'm a customer. Medical card. It's... one of the reasons I can't be a cop anymore."

"Oh..."

"I don't smoke, I'm not getting high. It really helps me with neuropathic pain and spasm issues. It allows me to sleep. "

Caitlyn almost physically moved back a little, from the force with which he said it.

"Sorry," Thomas said. "After all these years of being a cop, catching people with weed before they legalized it, I always feel the need to defend myself. This whole war on drugs isn't helping either. I could use opioids, my physician will prescribe them no problem, but it's such a hassle and I really don't want to risk losing access to something I depend on, in case laws change once again. I don't often tell people actually, it took a long time before I was ready to consider weed as an option, but I wish I had tried it sooner. It has been a real lifesaver."

Caitlyn angled her head and looked Thomas up and down.

"I've never used any drugs, I'm not even much of a drinker. But I know being in pain sucks, so I'm glad you've found something that works for you. And," she added, "I don't see any reason why weed should not be legalized in the first place. In my experience opioids are great, and definitely have a place in medicine, but they also have a lot of unpleasant side effects." She smiled. "In case you were wondering where I stand on this issue."

Caitlyn checked her map. Cornwall Books. An old-fashioned tinkling bell rang as she stepped inside. A middle-aged man with round glasses greeted her, as the silence inside the store enveloped her. It reminded her of a library, one with comfy reading nooks, central heating and dim lighting. She once again wiped the condensation off her glasses and put them back on so she could see.

"Oh dear, what happened to you?" The man had a British accent.

"Car crash," Caitlyn replied. Since he seemed to expect a little more of the story than that, she added. "On December twenty-first someone hit my car and fled the scene of the accident.'

"Oh dear, oh dear, how awful!"

"I broke my leg and spent some time in the hospital." Caitlyn gestured at her leg brace. "I've been asking all the shops on this street for help. I'd like to have a look at your security footage if that is possible, see if my car or the one that hit me is on one of your tapes. Maybe I could get a copy?"

"Of course. Please, wait here," the man said. "It's up the stairs."

He disappeared behind a narrow curtain in the back, and Caitlyn browsed through the rack of mystery bestsellers.

When she was done and he hadn't come back yet, she also looked at the Young Adult section, and - throwing all her plans to not buy anything else to the wind - tucked a heavily discounted box set audio version of the Tomorrow series under her arm.

I remember reading these when I was fifteen! These will be great to listen to with Sophie in the car in a few years.

A few other customers came inside the store, they were softly talking to each other and flipped through a few picture books.

The British man came back and put a big stack of about twelve mini-DV tapes on his counter. Caitlyn stared at them.

"Um, are these copies?"

"Oh no, that would take hours, love," the man laughed, "you can take these with you. Although I would appreciate it if you could return them at some point. We need quite a few for our camera system, and they are somewhat expensive to replace."

"Thank you, really. And of course I will."

She added, more to herself. "I just hope I can play these."

"Oh, no, don't tell me you're one of those modern types? I bet you have an e-reader too."

Caitlyn smiled sheepishly.

"I do buy some of my books in paper format, but yes, the majority of the books I read are in digital format. Or," she held up the CD's, "in audio format."

She paid, and put everything in her backpack. With the bell tinkling once again, she left the store.

The people at the lingerie store, while very sympathetic, had no footage to give her.

The sporting goods store clerk took one good look at her crutches before deciding to ignore her completely, and denied having cameras even after Caitlyn pointed them out to him. *Jerk,* she thought, and made a mental note of this.

She met up with Thomas outside, he had to take a small detour to get to a curb cut.

"Nothing from the coffee shop, but Adam from The Joint said his camera broke a while ago and he hasn't replaced it yet. That is good news for us, because all his files from December are still there," Thomas said. "You brought a hard disk, you said?"

Caitlyn followed Thomas in and blinked when she was met by the strong skunk-like scent. The burning incense in the corner did very little to mask it, and she left the store a little later with a few extra gigabytes on her hard disk, and what felt like a very slight contact high.

They grabbed a quick bite to eat and went into the next place together. The girl behind the counter looked up at them with bleary, watery eyes.

"Good afternoon, how can I help you?"

Both Thomas and Caitlyn stopped dead in their tracks and hesitated.

The girl noticed and added. "Sorry, there's a bit of a nasty stomach flu going around. But, when you have to work, you have to work. Soldier on, you know."

They were relieved when she said the store didn't have any working security cameras, and quickly left.

"Not the best combination on crutches," Caitlyn said. "When you can't quickly run to the bathroom."

"Same," Thomas replied.

"Got some of that hand sanitizer?"

"Always."

Thomas handed it to her, then used some himself.

"I never understood people who come to work that sick," Caitlyn said. "Almost like it's a badge of honor. While the reality is that you infect at least half the office in the process. Or in this case, everyone who goes to buy makeup today."

Next in line was a small Italian restaurant. Caitlyn held the door open with the tip of one of her crutches so Thomas could easily enter. The place was mostly empty, with only two people finishing a late lunch and a larger group of men talking in a booth nearby.

A waitress immediately greeted them with a warm smile. "Can I show you to a table?"

"No thank you, we're not here for food today, although I'm sure it's excellent. We're looking for someone who could talk to us about your security footage." Thomas shot her a charming smile.

"The boss is upstairs." She looked at Caitlyn's crutches, then at Thomas' wheelchair. "I'll go ask someone to get him for you."

She briefly spoke to another waiter, who walked off.

Caitlyn slumped down against the booth divider to give her leg and arms a bit of a break, and listened in on the conversation behind her while Thomas studied the chalkboard with the specials.

".. Thursday's shipment?"

"I don't know, Roy always arranges transport for the orders."

"Don't you worry about that."

"And what does Mr. Marino want us to do with it?"

"No idea, but we're getting snow."

The waitress came back and, somewhat loudly, said: "He'll be coming down in a second, please wait here."

The group of men abruptly stopped talking and looked at the

waitress who nodded her head almost unnoticeably at Caitlyn and Thomas, who were both hidden from sight by the divider. The men shuffled out of their booth and went up the same stairs the waiter had gone up a few minutes earlier.

Thomas looked at them, then turned to the waitress. "How long have you worked here?"

"Almost a month."

Not long enough to know anything about footage of the crash, Caitlyn thought.

Thomas kept chatting with her, making smalltalk. Caitlyn heard the waitress ask if he was injured in the same accident as Caitlyn.

The waiter returned, followed by a man in a tailored gray suit who – despite a well-groomed classy veneer of friendliness – instantly gave Caitlyn the creeps. It was as if a lava field of evil was bubbling underneath a paper-thin perfect surface. She almost hesitated to accept his outstretched hand, but after fumbling with her crutches, briefly shook it. The man turned to Thomas and a brief flash of darkness crossed his face as he took him in. Thomas didn't seem to notice and firmly accepted his handshake.

"Welcome to Basilico, I'm Roy Rubino. Eduard tells me you're looking for security footage?"

"Yes, I got in a car crash at the end of December last year, and I'm hoping you have footage that may show either my own car, or the car that hit me?" Caitlyn tried a smile. "It was a black one."

The man ignored her and turned to Thomas. "And who are you?"

"I'm a PI," Thomas replied. He gave the man one of his business cards. "I've been hired by her insurance company to track him down, apparently he's loaded but ducking all insurance calls. Once we track him down, he should be able to pay whatever fines there are pretty easily."

Another brief dark flash shot across Rubino's face before he corrected himself and gave them both a sympathetic friendly smile. Even his very white teeth gave Caitlyn mild shivers.

He looked at Thomas' card before he pocketed it. "I'm very sorry, but we don't have any security cameras, I can't help you."

They thanked him for his time and left after Thomas briefly talked to the waitress again and gave her a business card as well.

When they were outside, Caitlyn looked at Thomas.

"Why did you tell him you work for my insurance company?"

Thomas smiled with half a shrug and stopped to let a few people pass. "Pretext. Thought he'd be more likely to help out with that story than with the truth. It's part of my business to judge people." He grinned and his eyes twinkled. "I told that lawyer a completely different story."

He wheeled down a curb cut.

"Hey, did you happen to hear what those men were talking about?"

"Yeah, something about a restaurant supplies order and the weather, why?"

"Didn't like the look of them," Thomas said.

Thomas went to check in on a pharmacy and a walk-in clinic, and Caitlyn entered the Spies-R-Us. The guy behind the counter was around her age, in a very unflattering black and white striped sweater with a nameplate that read JOSHUA."

Caitlyn once again explained why she was there but paused mid-sentence. "Wait, are you Josh??"

The guy nodded.

"Do you process all the online orders for this store?"

Josh nodded again, looking slightly puzzled.

"I know you! We've emailed! I buy stuff from here all the time, I didn't know you were this close to me!"

Caitlyn told him who she was, mentioned a few issues they exchanged emails about and Josh started nodding and smiling.

"I remember that! Welcome to the store in person, and I can definitely help you with that footage, if you don't tell anyone."

He motioned for her to follow him into the back room and pushed a few sheets of paper and a soldering iron out of his way. There was only one chair and he started to sit down, then paused, looking at Caitlyn's leg and her crutches.

"One second."

He left.

Caitlyn glanced at the schematics he had pushed to the side and smiled as she recognized the logo of an underground group that released Arduino schematics for some *fun but not always intended for legal use* DIY projects.

Josh came back with another chair and saw her grin and look of recognition.

"Not mine." He deadpanned. "No idea how that got there."

Caitlyn had already taken the hard disk out of her bag and he was transferring the data.

"4K quality," he beamed at her.

Caitlyn checked the progress bar on the screen. It was slowly creeping up from six percent. 4K meant huge files. She rummaged through her bag and fished out her phone, then pressed her index finger briefly against the back to unlock it.

"Do you have free Wi-Fi?"

"Not free, but here." He took her phone, scrolled through the screens until he found the app he was looking for, and held the phone's camera up to a QR code sticker that was stuck to the wall. "It's the office one."

Caitlyn looked at her screen and laughed out loud.

"WinternetIsComing?"

Josh grinned sheepishly. "Big a Game of Thrones fan."

Caitlyn checked her email, sent her parents a text message saying she was about half way done, and waited for the transfer to finish while chatting with Josh.

She was about to leave the store when she changed her mind. This day was already very expensive, might as well add to it. She asked Josh if he had a Wi-Fi adapter with a certain chipset for sale. Josh looked at her with a very wide grin, knowing there was only one reason she'd request that specific one. "Not yours?"

Caitlyn nodded with a sly grin. "Exactly."

She paid, thanked him again for his help and made a mental note to add a kind message to her next order.

Outside she sat down on the edge of a big concrete planter. She didn't see Thomas yet, so she took out her laptop, plugged in the new Wi-Fi adapter and – using the Spy store's Wi-Fi again – downloaded the drivers.

Caitlyn disconnected and crutched to a bench close to the Sporting goods store so she could catch their signal. By now she knew where all the street cameras were and she double checked that she was out of sight. Caitlyn hoped things wouldn't take too long, because she was rapidly getting chilled to the bone.

About five minutes later she had forced a device to disconnect so she could catch the password when it automatically reconnected, and she was in. Happily digging through the Sporting Goods' network folders, and trying to figure out where they kept their camera footage.

When she had downloaded everything from December 21st, she tried to connect to two other nearby cameras. One wouldn't let her in, but she lucked out with the second one that was using default login credentials.

Caitlyn saw Thomas come out of the pharmacy. She waved, indicating she'd come to him, and he waved back, holding up 2 fingers. She closed the laptop and shrugged the backpack back on. It was getting pretty heavy.

They had to walk past a row of houses to get to the next store. A woman was checking her mailbox, and stopped them.

"What happened to you?"

"Car crash." Caitlyn answered automatically, for the fiftieth time that day, before realizing the woman wasn't talking to her.

Thomas' face turned very serious.

"Do you remember that story on the news a few years ago, about that horrible incident at the Olympics, with the spear throwing?"

The woman frowned. "I think I do, yes."

"That was me."

The woman looked absolutely horrified, and Caitlyn had trouble keeping a straight face.

"Oh God, how terrible! You poor man. I will pray for you tonight. May the good Lord bless you, so you will wake up tomorrow and walk again."

"Thank you," Thomas said curtly.

When they were out of earshot, a suppressed giggle escaped, and Caitlyn asked him. "Do you always make up stories like that?"

"Only when it's complete strangers and the first thing that comes out of their mouth is that question," Thomas replied grimly. "It's none of their business."

They entered the next store.

It sold comics and computer games and was appropriately called "Nerd Haven". After hearing Caitlyn's story, the store owner led Thomas and Caitlyn straight to a large backroom with rows and rows of shelving units. Most of the space was taken up by what looked to be excess inventory, dating all the way back to at least the 1980's.

Caitlyn wondered what types of goldmines were hidden in between the stacks of junk.

One shelving unit held what to Caitlyn looked like a brick wall made of VHS tapes.

"I once got into a lot of trouble that could have been prevented if the footage had not been overwritten. So I freed up some storage space, we've got plenty anyways, and now we have at least a full six months' worth of tapes at all times." The man explained.

"Wow." Caitlyn replied, lost for words.

"I know," the owner proudly told her, "and these VHS tapes are dirt cheap now too. I can pick them up by the dozen at yard sales, they're practically giving them away. It's a real shame though, sometimes I have to tape over family home movies... But, like I said, I've got the space, and we won't run into any issues ever again. Plus now I've even got something to give you! You needed December...?"

"Twenty first," Caitlyn replied.

She wrote down the man's address on a piece of paper and slid that into the VHS cover with the promise to send the tape back to him when she was done.

Thomas handed the man his business card.

On her way out, Caitlyn noticed a discount bin and had a quick look.

"Oh man! You've got MYST and Riven in here? I loved playing these games! Can you still play this?"

"Not too well on new computers, they've got an anniversary remake that fixes the issues...You could try these in a virtual machine though, that's –"

"I know, I know, great idea. I'm *so* getting these for Sophie," Caitlyn said. "Do you also have Commander Keen?"

The man checked his computer. "No, those came out on floppies. Too old."

"Did you play any computer games growing up?" Caitlyn asked Thomas when they were back outside.

"No. We didn't have a computer at home. I played some Half Life and Call of Duty when I was in the army, but nothing after I got out." He smiled at the memory. "Too busy with work and family, and too old for games in general, probably. But I might play something with Brad when he's a little older."

Caitlyn nodded. "Sounds like fun, playing with your kid. Hey, I forgot to ask before, why do you give everyone your business card?"

"Free promotion," Thomas replied. "I've been dropping them off at every place I've visited today. You never know where your next client or case will come from."

Caitlyn pointed to a place called Bits 'n Bytes. "Cybercafé. It's got stairs, I'll take that one."

"Thanks, I'll get that bicycle store. Although, just so you know, with handrails like that I could make it up and down those stairs if I had to."

"Huh! Really?"

Thomas nodded and jokingly showed his biceps in a mock pose that completely got lost underneath his winter coat.

"Just hold on to the railings on both sides and pull myself up backwards."

Caitlyn entered the Cybercafé and once again felt right at home. The rows of monitors, the atmosphere, the clicking of keyboards and mice. She connected to their free Wi-Fi and patiently waited in line. The girl behind the counter was happy to copy their footage to Caitlyn's SSD for her.

Quick and easy. One more place to check! Caitlyn thought, feeling relieved. Her leg was hurting, and her pace had slowed down considerably. Her shoulders were killing her, and she was starting to get blisters on top of blisters on her hands.

She walked into Pho Saigon, but came out again a few minutes later. No cameras.

Caitlyn looked around and decided to go into the bicycle shop, where it would be warm.

She quickly found Thomas, sitting on a regular chair at a table while one of the shop employees was following his instructions on how to disassemble his wheelchair.

Caitlyn raised her eyebrows and sat down opposite him.

"They're copying tapes for us," Thomas explained, "and while I'm waiting, he's lubricating some parts on my chair. I like it when it's as quiet as possible. I also bought a really good hand pump." He pointed at a plastic bag on the floor. Thomas then turned to the employee, a young man in his early twenties with his hair in a high man bun. "Hey, do you guys have any bearings? Could you replace the front caster ones?"

"Sure, no problem."

They watched the man work for a while.

"Are all wheelchair parts interchangeable with bicycle parts?" Caitlyn asked Thomas.

"Depends on what brand you have. Mine are. It makes for much easier repairs and replacements. Also, these bike people can fix pretty much everything."

The man looked up. "A wheel is a wheel, man. They all work pretty much the same. It's just old school mechanics."

Caitlyn showed him the blisters on her hands and joked.

"Got anything to fix this?"

The man paused for a few seconds, then nodded. "I think foam handlebar grips might work. Give me a few minutes and I'll find you a free sample."

Ten minutes later they left the store.

"Smooth, nice!" Thomas commented. "No squeaks. No rattling. Perfectly stealth again! I love it!"

Caitlyn was testing the black foam grips the man had put around the handles of her crutches. They lessened the friction and already her hands felt a lot better.

"Definitely an improvement, I'm glad I came to get you!"

They backtracked to Pho Saigon for some takeout, then walked back to the car. Caitlyn dumped all the contents of her backpack into her lap, and started sorting them.

Thomas put the bag with takeout on the central console armrest and handed her the tapes from his backpack too. "What's our total count?" he asked.

Caitlyn did a quick tally.

"We have... 8 DVDs, 3 mini-DV tapes, 3 VHS tapes, and however many files and formats were transferred to my hard disk today. I lost count."

She tried to get her leg into a more comfortable position and stretched her shoulders. "Who the hell still uses VHS anyway?"

"You were there when he explained that," Thomas replied, somewhat distracted. "Duck, please".

Caitlyn squished herself against the side of the car and Thomas lifted both wheels and his chair past her.

"I don't think I can even play any of them at home, they're that old."

"Really? I still use them. And I have one of those players that can play both VHS and DVDs, you can borrow that for a few days."

She gave him an apologetic glance.

"Thanks, that would be great." Caitlyn let the whole stack slide back into her backpack.

"Don't get your hopes up. In case you hadn't noticed yet, I'm still bad with any and all technology. I was supposed to convert all our VHS tapes to DVD, that's why I bought the device. I haven't started on that yet, maybe soon."

Thomas closed his door, threw the blue tag in the glove compartment and they ate most of their takeout with the engine running idle. Warming up, and getting some energy back, before Thomas turned onto the highway.

Caitlyn grew quiet and leaned her head back, mindlessly rubbing her shoulders and leg.

"Too much walking?" Thomas asked with a brief glance in her direction.

"Hmm. Yes."

"We'll drive by my place to get the player, and then I'll drop you off at home."

It was close to four when they got there. Martin, in full-on bee gear, was in the driveway. He ducked into his shed and handed Thomas a jar through the open car window, while taking off the suit.

"Thanks for helping my daughter out. Here, take some honey. Do you want to come in for coffee or anything?"

Thomas glanced at the clock. "Oh no, I couldn't. And, no problem, it's my pleasure."

Martin pushed his hood back and leaned in closer, then paused and frowned as he noticed the wheels and chair on the backseat.

Thomas turned to Caitlyn and laughed out loud. "You didn't tell him??"

Caitlyn grinned sheepishly, "I think I only told my parents you got shot."

"Yeah," her dad cleared his throat, "I thought in the arm or leg or something. You know, flesh wound. I'm really sorry."

Thomas waived a hand. "Don't worry about it. Thank you for the honey."

He was still laughing when he drove off.

After dinner Caitlyn got started on sorting through the video footage. With the digital footage it was a quick and easy process to cut out only the part of the video she was interested in, but it still took her a few hours to edit everything. When she was done she had nineteen files, each two hours long, from six to eight pm.

Too bad I can't automate any of this, she thought.

She rubbed her leg absentmindedly. It felt good to not have it restricted in the knee brace, but also very stiff and a bit fragile, like one wrong move could re-break everything that wasn't still broken.

She began watching footage at two times normal speed after the first half hour, pausing when she thought she saw her own car, or a dark one, rewinding when she thought she missed something. But it didn't speed things up by much.

By the time she had gone through the first folder, and a whole bag of chips, she was ready to call it quits and go to bed. She had seen her own car twice. As expected she had also seen plenty of dark cars, but on grainy footage in snowy conditions in the dark, it was really hard to tell if a car was black or dark blue, or some other dark color. She got a few sheets of printer paper and wrote down a list of cars, timestamps and locations, and whatever she could make of any visible parts of the license plates. She decided to give up for now and went to soak her sore muscles in the tub before she hopped into bed. And soon found out that, once again, she couldn't sleep.

Her leg and knee were sending loud and clear reminders that she shouldn't have walked as much. That where before she had no trouble running ten to fifteen miles, walking for hours on crutches had been a very bad idea.

Do not repeat.

The icepack she used got melted before it had eased the throbbing in her leg, and the painkiller she got after, only took the most annoying edges away. She considered taking another one, but that meant having to get up again. And she also didn't like how loopy and out of it a double dose made her feel. Her shoulders were aching, and no matter which way she turned, she couldn't find a comfortable position.

Eventually she fell asleep, only to wake up two hours later, with her heart rate through the roof, pounding a solid drumbeat into her ears as she tried to deliberately slow her breathing.

She had dreamed about the crash again. About being trapped, about the pain, and the blood, and the airbag. But this time something was different. Something was new.

She remembered a pair of dark black eyes glaring at her through the car window.

He didn't just call 911.

He stopped to check on me.

I saw him.

CHAPTER TEN

Caitlyn's alarm woke her at eight thirty. After digging through the Big Box of All Cables in the garage she had found a way to connect both a DV camera and Thomas' VHS player to her PC. Caitlyn sat down with a bowl of frosted flakes and put her leg on an extra chair. She was capturing all the camera footage she was interested in the built-in Windows screen recorder. It was going to take a lot of time to fast forward to the correct date and time, then record the two hours of footage she wanted to look at, then switch to the next tape.

She hadn't been able to completely shake off the nightmare; those eyes staring at her through the window, like soulless dark holes in a white face.

She decided to call Jess.

"Hey sis."

"Hey, are you busy?"

"Nah, what's up?"

"Bad night, need some distraction while I'm watching and recording all these security tapes."

"Sorry to hear, you know you can always call me when that happens, right? I don't mind, even if it wakes me up."

"I know, thanks Jess, but I mind."

Jess said something she couldn't understand.

"Jess, your phone is cutting out."

"Sorry, this better?"

"Yes." Caitlyn moved the phone to her other shoulder so she could use the mouse with her right hand. "I think... I think I remember someone being there that night, looking at me through the car window."

"Are you serious?!" Jess' sound changed and Caitlyn could hear her talk in the background.

"Whoa boy, easy, you're OK, I wasn't yelling at you."

"Are you on a horse?!"

"Yes. Really, sis, someone was there? Did you see him? Did you see his face?"

"No, I only remember his eyes. Dark, almost black. Dark eyebrows, too. And Jess, do you remember the last time we talked about this?! The horse thing? One broken child at a time is enough for mom and dad I'd think. I don't want to be responsible for you falling off! I'll call you back later."

"Oh, geez sis, you're starting to sound like mom. Don't worry so much, I'm indoors in the arena, I'm wearing a helmet *and* a body protector. Because, like you say, there should only be one injured Harrison at a time, max. I'm just cooling down on a long rein. And this horse is almost totally fine now anyway, I've got him to where he thinks for a moment when he panics instead of making a stupid blind run for it. Doesn't really buck or rear anymore either. Much better. He's still a little jumpy, but he'll get there. I think he'll make someone a good barrel racer when I'm done with him. He's got the speed and agility, don't you boy?"

Caitlyn knew she had lost Jess to a horse now, but she didn't want to refocus on the nightmare anyway. "So, anything else going on on your end?"

"That website you set up for me is really helping! I'm getting a lot of emails and calls from potential clients. It's how the lady with the Frisians found me, too. She told me yesterday."

Jessica was working for a small local Quarter Horse breeder who had given her permission to bring in her own clients to take on in her spare time. She gave him a small cut of her profits, and in return could use all his facilities. Caitlyn had gifted Jessica a website for her birthday last September, with a nice advertising budget that should see her through at least a whole year. With maybe a little extra help from a small script Caitlyn had written to monitor local horse groups and social media, it was steadily bringing in more clients.

"I just had a white mare dropped off for evaluation, they're interested in buying her if I can fix her. She does perfectly fine on the ground, but every time they ride her and ask her to collect she doesn't move well. We'll see how she does when I ride her. It's either them interfering, or something pain related. If I can adjust it, I'll have to get a vet to look at her."

"Do they want to compete with her?"

"Yes, pleasure horse. So, let's hope for both the horse and the owner that it's not something serious. She's got great papers though."

Caitlyn paused the fast forwarding and was a little annoyed with herself when she noticed the video's time stamp had gone past six p.m. She rewound and set her computer to record the next two hours. She put the cereal bowl to her mouth and drank the last slightly too sugary bit of milk, then copied some of the digital files to her laptop to watch later. Caitlyn leaned back in her chair and listened to Jess.

"Oh, and there's a really fat chestnut Arab that came in last week. I don't think I told you yet. He's a bit risky to be around at the moment, he's tried to eat me twice so far. I'm giving him some time to settle in. Do some groundwork, teach him some manners. By the looks of it he's just spoiled and over-fed and jumping out of his skin. I think I've got my work cut out for me with this one. I really hope he calms down some after a few days of the correct amount of calories and exercise."

"Be careful little sis, he sounds like fun."

"Actually, I think he will be. The problem is convincing the owner to keep feeding him less and ride him more after I'm done."

"Hah, so it's once again more a people problem than a horse problem. Good luck with that!"

"Thanks. Not looking forward to that talk. Hey, how's your rehab going? Any chance we'll be riding again this summer?"

"I really hope so!" Caitlyn said.

Jessica had always taken her riding during summer break, a tradition they had kept over the years. She teasingly called Caitlyn her 'good weather riding buddy'. But at the same time, she always made sure to put her sister on a calm and level-headed horse.

Caitlyn was a good enough rider to not fall off too easily, but she was not the excellent rider Jessica was and preferred a horse who was a tad lazy. One who wouldn't buck or run off with her.

Jessica had this instant connection and trust, a true two-way communication with almost any horse she handled. She could feel the slightest resistance and knew how to figure out the cause, and often how to fix it. She also had a lot more guts than Caitlyn.

Caitlyn gently pushed Newton aside, he had heard her talk on the phone and was now trying to get her to pet him by parading around in front of her monitors. His big fluffy tail was completely blocking her view. She picked up the cat with one hand, turned him around mid-air, and draped him over her shoulders. He immediately relaxed, laid down and pressed his head against the side of her head into the frame of her glasses, loudly purring into her ear - and the phone.

"Awwww. Is that Newt?" Jess asked.

"Yup."

"He's still doing that with you, eh?"

"Yes. He was 'helping' me, it was getting a bit annoying. Ugh, I'm not even really sure why I'm watching all this footage, it's taking ages. And the cops couldn't find him, what makes me think that I can?"

"The cops didn't collect any tapes, right?"

"Well, no, I don't think so."

"It's pretty cool actually, you turning into some kind of sleuth. Or maybe you've just been watching too much Person of Interest."

"What do you mean?"

"You know, limping computer wizard, solving crimes."

Jess had expected laughter but heard nothing. She looked at her phone. "Caitlyn, are you still there?"

"Yes, sorry. Good one. Hey, I think I found something. I'll call you back later."

Caitlyn hung up and pressed the rewind button so she could

watch the video again at a slower speed. This was NE Prue Street, which led up to the location of the crash. The time stamp read 18:54. And there was definitely a very dark car.

Martin was preparing dinner in the kitchen, and Caitlyn peeked into the pan before she sat down. She opened her laptop and was soon intently watching video footage again. Some of the tapes had been taped over so many times that ghost images of older footage showed through, and she really had to pay attention in order to not miss anything important.

Sophie knocked on the kitchen door and walked in without waiting for a reply.

"My mom said I could eat dinner here?"

Martin looked up. "Hi Sophie. Yes, she called me earlier. I hope you're hungry, we're having pasta with zucchini and red sauce."

"Ooh yummy!"

Sophie sat down next to Caitlyn and pushed a piece of paper in her direction.

"I brought the letter with the puzzle."

When Caitlyn didn't respond, Martin put a lid on the pan, turned down the gas, and sat down next to Sophie.

"A puzzle? Let me see that!"

He held it to the light, then smelled the paper. Sophie wrinkled her nose, but Martin smiled.

"Mmm, citrus-y I think, right?" He elbowed Caitlyn. "Was this what you needed the lemon for?"

Caitlyn briefly looked up. "Huh? Yes, lemon. Give me a few more minutes, OK?"

Martin looked at Sophie, then at his daughter.

"I think she's really busy, but I'm the one who taught her this. Want me to teach you too?"

He let Sophie smell the letter, then motioned for her to join him at the kitchen stove. He got a cast iron pan from a shelf, and waited for it to heat up.

"Kid, I'm gonna show you some real magic, can you see this?"

Sophie was standing on her tippy-toes. "Yes, Mr. Martin."

Martin put his hand above the surface of the pan to check the temperature and put the paper on top. It took a while, but then words began to appear in shades of brown, rapidly darkening in between the lines of blue ink.

Caitlyn reluctantly closed her laptop, she wanted to keep looking for the black car, but Sophie deserved her full attention. The footage would have to wait. She scooted her chair over.

"See, when you write with lemon juice, it dries invisible. But then when you heat it, it turns brown."

"This is so cool!", Sophie gasped as her eyes widened.

Martin took the paper out and flapped it around to cool it down a little before handing it to Sophie.

Sophie started reading then stopped. "This is not English."

"Go get a pen and paper," Caitlyn said. "It's a cipher. A secret code."

Martin unclipped a ballpoint from his shirt pocket and grabbed a random envelope from the mail stack on the table, and pushed it towards her.

"OK," Caitlyn said as she wrote on the back of it.

"This is the whole alphabet"

A B C D E F G H I J K L M N O P Q R S T U V W X Y Z

"If you write down ABCLPS, what happens if you add 3 letters to each of these?

She showed Sophie how to count up.

"DEFOSV!"

"Exactly. What about PLMEFB?"

"S-O-P. Sophie!"

"OK. Now you write down all the brown letters"

She waited for Sophie to carefully copy them onto the envelope.


```
LXWPAJCDUJCRXWB. HXD QJEN MRBLXENANM BNLANC RWT. HXD
LJW WXF LUJRV HXDA YARIN!
```


"So now we add three letters?"

"Nope. That would be too easy. This kind of code, where you add letters, it's called a Caesar cipher, and you can add any number you choose. What do you think would be a good number?"

Sophie thought for only a second. "I don't know?"

"How old are you Soph?"

"Nine."

"Correct, so I added nine letters."

Caitlyn walked Sophie through the logic of solving the cipher by subtracting nine from the cipher text, showing her how you went from A to Z to Y, and Sophie went to work.

"Congratulations!", she read, "You have discovered secret ink. You can now claim your prize."

Sophie looked at Caitlyn, practically bouncing in her seat.

"If you go upstairs into my room, there is a small package inside my desk, in the drawer on the left. It's wrapped in red wrapping paper."

Sophie ran off, and came back with the gift a little later, slightly out of breath.

"You know, a long time ago when people wanted to write each other secret messages, they had to come up with a good way so their enemy wouldn't be able to read it. The Romans used a Caesar cipher on parchment just like this, but there were also people who shaved the head of their slaves – back when they didn't know slaves were a bad thing I guess – and then tattooed the secret message on their head. Then they waited for the hair to grow back so no one would see it. The slave traveled and had his head shaved again so the recipient could read the message."

"That's so crazy!" Sophie said.

"I know! Much better to do it on paper, don't you agree? You can use lemon juice or milk. There are small carbon bits in there, and they break apart when you heat them up. When the carbon escapes, and it touches the air, it turns brown. It's just like how iron turns brown and rusts when it touches air. They used to use a candle for this, but I think they ended up accidentally burning a few too many important letters."

"Quit torturing her with the lecture," Martin interrupted. "Let her unwrap this prize already!"

"Fine, fine, sorry. Go ahead Soph."

Sophie carefully took the red paper off. The small box contained a clear fountain pen, a bottle of clear ink with a slight yellow hue, and a mini blacklight.

"What you won is the modern-day version of lemon juice ink."

Caitlyn showed her how to put the ink in the pen and told Sophie to draw or write something. Sophie started drawing on the envelope. "It's not doing anything?"

"It is, you just can't see it yet".

When Sophie was done, Caitlyn showed her how the ink would light up a bright fluorescent blue under UV light.

"See? It's even better in the dark, when it's glowing more. You can also use the flashlight when you're writing or drawing, so you can see what you're doing."

"Woah!" Sophie was impressed, then stood up and tightly hugged Caitlyn.

"Good gift?", Caitlyn asked.

"Awesome gift!" Sophie said. "I'm gonna draw something for my mom!"

After Michelle picked up Sophie, and admired the drawing under blacklight, Caitlyn finally called Jessica back.

She had gotten multiple texts along the lines of "Sis, don't keep me waiting, what did you find??" and Jess picked up with an impatient: "Tell me!"

Caitlyn laughed.

"I'm so sorry, I should have called you back sooner. We just had dinner, Sophie was here. I think I may have found the car that hit me in the footage, it's a black one, and I've seen it twice now."

"Excellent, good work sis, but call me back next time, would you?"

"I will, I promise. Good night Jess."

Minutes later the phone rang again.
"Jess?"
"Um, hi, no, it's Meagan."

"Oh! Uh, hi."

This was awkward

"How are you?"

"OK. Well, actually not so good. Broken leg and all."

"Right. So, um, are you coming back?"

"Not any time soon."

"Right. So... I emailed you, but you never replied."

It only now occurred to Caitlyn that she had not set her school email to forward to her gmail address. *I never checked it!*

Meagan kept talking. "Is there any chance you could come pick up your stuff? I mean, I'm fine with it being here, but you could stop paying rent and there's already someone else who's willing to move in and..."

Caitlyn swallowed. *So,* she thought, *this was the real reason Meagan called.*

Caitlyn knew that saying yes to moving out would mean a definite end of medical school for her, at least for a while.

She could hear someone whispering on the other end. "What is she saying?"

"Who's that?" Caitlyn asked.

Meagan was silent for a second, then completely broke down.

"I'm so sorry. The new roommate is going to be Todd. I mean, nothing happened between us when you two were dating, but after... I'm really sorry, I didn't mean for you to find out this way. And I know the timing sucks. Please don't be mad at me."

Caitlyn was too stunned and hurt to say anything.

"Cait? I'm really sorry. I–"

Caitlyn cut her off.

"Just overnight everything, pack it up, I'll pay you back for the shipping."

Caitlyn hung up.

That's half the decision to quit made then. Or, if I go back, I'll just have to get a new dorm assigned.

She texted Jess.

Meagan just called if I could come get my stuff,

Todd is moving in with her.

Jess texted back a few minutes later.

Are you serious?! No way!

She said everything happened after Todd broke up
with me. But it still hurts.

It's betrayal sis.
We already knew he was an asshole, now we know
she is too. They don't deserve you and I hate them
both! *hug!* See you Saturday!

Caitlyn smiled through her tears, her sister could always make her feel better.

CHAPTER ELEVEN

On Tuesday morning a big box arrived. Martin lifted it up the stairs and put it in Caitlyn's bedroom. All her clothes, her medical textbooks, everything was in there. Meagan had even wrapped the small ficus they had bought together in bubble plastic.

She might have kind of stolen my ex-boyfriend, but she is making sure she isn't stealing anything else, Caitlyn thought wryly.

She sat down. Her whole student life in one big box, indefinitely on hold. She wondered when she would ever use any of these things again. She wondered if she would ever use any of these things again.

Caitlyn sighed and started unpacking. She refolded her clothes and put them in her closet, shoving her white lab coat in the far back of it. She flipped through her Anatomy and Histology textbooks, then put all her school books on a shelf.

Biochemistry. Yikes, I'm definitely not going to miss this one!

When she was done, she folded the box and gave it a few good whacks with a crutch to keep it flattened. Her dad poked his head around the door.

"Sorry, dad."

"I'm heading off to work. Are you OK? Mom told me about Todd and Meagan."

Caitlyn nodded.

"Yeah, I'll be fine, thanks. It could be worse. And I'm done crying over him, it's time to move on, I'll be OK. Have a good day at school."

She checked the shipping costs and reimbursed Meagan via PayPal, then figured that while she was getting things in order, it was time to get all the other school stuff figured out too.

She took a mini KitKat bar from the bag Meagan had returned

and took a big bite off it.

When in doubt, chocolate or productivity. It's often one of those, or both, that will make you feel better.

She checked her school email and found her inbox full of get well soon messages from classmates and even a few TA's and professors. Her mood instantly lifted. She replied to them, and archived all Meagan's and Todd's emails without reading any.

Caitlyn spent some time browsing her school's website and filled out the form to request a medical leave of absence. She emailed Student Health services and the Dean of Students Office, and for good measure sent a mass email to all her professors and TA's to let them know what was going on as well, apologizing for the delay. Finally, she emailed student housing.

I should have done this a lot sooner, she thought, and felt a little guilty, but at the same time very much like a real adult, and also a lot calmer now that everything was all sorted.

She collected all the tapes and disks she had borrowed, ate another KitKat, and spent some time writing thank you notes and addressing the return envelopes.

Caitlyn briefly checked IRC, got herself something to drink, and sat down again to continue watching more video footage.

First, she opened the notebook that had been in the box Meagan sent, and gathered all the random scraps of paper she had scribbled something on. Now that she wouldn't be using the notebook as a school planner, she might as well put it to good use and collect all the information she had so far in one place. She loved technology, but always could think much better when she was putting actual ink on paper.

She ran some whiteout tape over all the future lecture and test dates that she had already filled in and turned to the first blank page.

Crash: December 21. 19:04
Man called 911.
Black car hit me.

She had gone through almost half of the roughly fifty hours of total footage so far. She had a list of her own car, as well as a long list of every single dark car she had seen, at several times and locations.

But when she was done writing, she still had no clear idea of how she could recreate her route.

There has to be a better way to organize all this!

Caitlyn thought for a while, then her eye fell on the PhonePhinder icon on her desktop. She could make a map just like that program did!

Soon she was so busy that she forgot all about Meagan and Todd.

She opened VS Code, and typed out the list of timestamps, cars and location, then added some code that would animate everything and put it on a map.

When Caitlyn was done, she pressed play and leaned back.

Much better!

Her own car was moving across the map as a blue dot, following the route she had taken. It was very clear now that the accident must have happened somewhere between 18:50 p.m. and 19:04 p.m., when the call was made. The man who hit her had very likely called immediately after it happened.

A lot of other colored dots on her map either moved or popped up and disappeared at certain times.

Now that she had a visual representation in front of her, she could eliminate a few cars that were driving in the wrong direction, and she commented out their code. The problem was that it was still really hard to tell if that one dot she removed was the same car as another dot that was still on the map.

She went back to the video fragments she had saved of each dark car, exported a series of still frames, and tried to manipulate the images in Photoshop to get a better view of the license plates or the drivers. She tried adjusting the levels, the brightness, the contrast, and even tried sharpening and enlarging the images, which – as expected – only made things even harder to see. In the end she could only match a few of the many dots to the same car, but at least it was better than nothing.

She copied the list of remaining partial plates over to her notebook and blew on the ink to help it dry before she closed it. At least she now had a good idea of the location and time of where her car, and hopefully the car that hit her, had been.

Thomas called her after dinner.

"Hey, how is it going?"

"I made an animated map of the route I took, and every dark car I saw in the footage. It took ages but it's making everything a lot clearer. I can see who was where, at exactly what time."

"Wow, that must have been a lot of work. I can think of a few cases I worked on where that would have helped tremendously. My department didn't have the budget or tech for things like this."

Thomas cleared his throat.

"Any chance you are done with all the VHS tapes? I wouldn't ask, and if you still need the player, please take your time. I was just checking up on you to see how things were coming along. Bradley likes to watch these old videos of when he was a baby, and of his mom and me before he was born. And you know how it goes, they've got a toy they never play with, until it gets lost. Then it's a disaster and their absolute favorite of all time and they need it right now. He has been bugging me for the past couple of days."

Caitlyn laughed. "Don't worry, I've got everything on my computer. Let me see..."

She checked her phone. "I've got PT tomorrow morning at 10:30 a.m., Michelle is taking me. Your house is sort of on the way. Could I drop it off around 10:00 a.m. ish?"

"That would be great, thank you. I'll be home."

Caitlyn hung up and decided she was done for the day.

She uploaded the map files to her server, turned on the TV and stretched out on the couch.

Thoughts of Meagan and Todd crept back in.

To hell with both of them.

But she immediately felt a little bit guilty. Sure, it hurt. But if what Meagan said was true, they had only hooked up well after Todd had broken up with her. It was nothing a friend would do, at least not without asking first, but it also maybe just a little bit was none of her business anymore.

Caitlyn made herself some tea and called over Volta so she could snuggle up with her while she re-watched a Season One episode of Person of Interest. The cat was purring, her leg was no longer bothering her as much, and the blisters on her hands had finally healed.

And she was making progress, getting closer to finding out who hit her.

It was a good ending to a weird couple of days.

CHAPTER TWELVE

"Hey Soph? Come on, we have to go! It's super foggy so I can't drive very fast, and we have to go by Caitlyn's friend too. Hurry up, you don't want to be late."

"Did you see my new boots, Caitlyn?" Sophie stuck her leg out.

"Ooh, pink, they're nice Sophie!"

Sophie nodded. "Can I sit in front?"

Michelle looked at Caitlyn. "Is that OK with your leg?"

Caitlyn quickly judged the room in the back of Michelle's metallic blue VW Beetle.

"Fine with me, I can stretch out on the backseat. It's how I got home from the hospital too, although I slept through most of that trip."

Michelle and Sophie talked about the upcoming school day, Sophie's friends, and the play date she had after school. Caitlyn listened to them as she leaned her back against the door and looked out the opposite window at the gray desaturated world. She had to wake up much earlier than she had gotten used to, and she wasn't fully awake yet. Michelle turned her head slightly towards her. "Where do I drop you off again?"

"Oh, right, I forgot your car doesn't have a navigation system. Hang on."

Caitlyn took her phone out of her pocket, entered Thomas address and gave Michelle directions. She felt a bit queasy from having to read in the back of a car, but the nausea quickly faded once she got out and the cold air hit her face.

Thomas opened the door.

"Hi." He looked at the car. "Don't they want to come in?"

"No thanks, that's Michelle and Sophie by the way. But we can't stay or Sophie will be late for school. Where do you want this?"

Thomas raised a hand at Michelle and Sophie and turned his wheelchair around.

Teddy let out a few half barks and got up to check Caitlyn out, but lost interest after briefly sniffing her pant leg.

"See, I told you, he likes you! If we don't stop him, he usually barks a lot longer. You should have heard him last night, barking his little head off at the squirrels in the dark."

Caitlyn laughed but hesitated before bending down and briefly petting Teddy's head.

She was still a little bit distrustful, but Teddy relaxed under her touch, and after a few seconds walked away again and deposited himself on his doggie bed next to the couch.

"Thanks again for letting me borrow this." Caitlyn handed the VHS player back.

Thomas put it down on the floor in front of the TV, put the brakes on his chair and tried to reach behind the TV for a couple of dangling cables. He couldn't quite reach them.

"Do you want me to plug it in again?" Caitlyn asked.

"No thanks, I'll get it later." Thomas sounded slightly annoyed.

"So, how do you like getting a taste of the PI life?" Thomas asked as he straightened up.

Caitlyn smiled. "It's a lot more fun than I expected! It's almost... exciting. I didn't expect it to be like this."

"It is a lot of fun." Thomas agreed. But then he looked a little apprehensive. "You know, it's not always worth it, knowing."

"What do you mean?"

Thomas shook his head. "Forget I said that, doesn't matter. Also, you'd better go," he nodded at Michelle and Sophie. "Get that little girl to school. Where does she go?"

"Davis Middle School."

"Bradly is Pre-K, he'll go to Hopkins next year. Anyway, thanks.

Brad will be glad you stopped by. I'll have to mentally prepare myself to hear that spider song over and over again for the next couple of days."

Thomas bumped off the small steps in front of his house, and followed her to the street. "It looks like this fog might finally clear up a little. Drive safe. "

Caitlyn installed herself on the backseats again and waved to Thomas as they drove off.

Sophie looked at her in the rear-view mirror. After a while she asked: "Caitlyn, are you playing a new game?"

"What do you mean?"

"Well, sometimes you hold your breath. And at first I didn't know why, but then I thought maybe you were playing a game, like you're pretending you're under water?"

Caitlyn half laughed and half gasped, she hadn't even realized she was tensing up every time they passed a side street where oncoming traffic suddenly popped into view from out of the mist. She was annoyed that the fear of getting hit was still very much there, but had to laugh too, because it was just typical Sophie. Whenever Sophie didn't understand something, her mind often jumped through a series of very logical hoops only to end up at a very plausible yet very incorrect conclusion.

"I, uh, think it's the cars," she said.

Michelle now also figured it out and glanced at her, a little worried. "You OK, Cait?"

Caitlyn nodded.

"It's not a game, Sophie," Michelle said. "You know how, when something suddenly scares you, you often stop breathing for a little while? I think Caitlyn is still a little scared from the accident. And when she sees a car suddenly coming from the side, she holds her breath."

"Really, I'm fine." Caitlyn reassured them. "Tell you what Sophie, I think playing a game is actually a great idea. I spy, with my little eye, something... green."

Caitlyn hoped she could will her mind to snap out of it, force her body to relax, to breathe. She hoped it would help if she let

Sophie distract her.

Sophie looked in the direction Caitlyn had been looking in.

"That's easy. It's that sticker on the window, it's the only green thing here."

"Yeah, it's been a while since I played this. Your turn."

Sophie took a few seconds, then said, "I spy... something dark blue."

"Is it my bag?"

"No."

"Your mom's jeans?"

"No."

"My own jeans?"

"No!"

"I need a hint."

"It's outside. It's that car behind us." Sophie pointed at the station wagon tailgating them.

"OK. Let me try another one. I spy... something pink."

"Caitlyn! You have to make it harder, it's my boots!"

"Fine, fine. I spy something... yellow."

Michelle parked in the drop-off zone and gave her daughter a kiss.

"Have a nice day, Sophie!" Caitlyn said.

Sophie ran off to join her friends, forgetting all about Michelle and Caitlyn the moment she vanished into the mist.

Caitlyn hopped out and took Sophie's place in the front seat. She turned to Michelle.

"I didn't even realize I was doing that. Holding my breath I mean. And it's not true fear, really, more like... an annoying reflex. I don't even remember the accident, at least not the moment the other car hit me. But I've been getting these nightmares, at first it was just fragments, but the longer they get, the more I seem to remember. The man who hit me - he didn't leave right away. He checked on me. I remember his eyes, very dark, looking at me through the window."

"Wow, that's ... creepy. But, why didn't he stay?"

"I don't know." Caitlyn made a face. "I just hate how paranoid, and jumpy this has made me. I've got to get rid of this, this fear, the nightmares."

"I guess maybe subconsciously you remember? Like you said, your body reacts as if you do." Michelle put a hand on her shoulder. "I wish I could help."

"This is helping," Caitlyn said. "And I've almost finished watching all the security footage I collected. I know I'm getting closer, I can feel it. Maybe finding him will help too."

CHAPTER THIRTEEN

Jessica was sitting on the couch eating something very sticky while watching a video of a horse on TV. She had a huge sweet tooth, with a miraculously fast metabolism to counter its effects.

"Morning sis!" Jessica raised an eyebrow. "Is that what you're wearing today?"

Caitlyn looked down. Bunny slippers, dark jeans, gray knit warm winter sweater.

"What do you mean?"

"It's a bit ... dull, boring. You know." Jess gestured with her hand, waving at everything.

"Yeah, well, nothing goes with a clunky knee brace anyway." Caitlyn said a little annoyed, "It's cold. This keeps me warm."

Jessica shrugged and started on her second jelly-filled glazed donut.

Caitlyn made herself a salami sandwich and held it in her mouth as she crutched to the living room. She sat down next to Jessica and asked with her mouth still full. "What are you watching?"

"Woah, sis, garlic breath! It's a video from a fellow trainer. Started playing it and my phone connected to that Chromecast thing you put in the TV." Jessica restarted the video. "Pretty handy. See how he tenses his neck and tosses his head there?"

"U-huh."

"Guy asked me to take a look at it. I have to ask if they checked his teeth. Could also be the bit or headstall they're using don't fit him well and something is pinching. He's a pretty good trainer though, see how he's giving some rein there?"

"Not really. But hey, it's better than watching fifty hours of cars driving past in the dark."

"Hah, right, how's that going?"

"It's going. I've finally finished watching and re-watching them all. I've got a pretty good timeline now. I've collected a list of dark cars. but I still need to narrow it down."

"What do you mean?"

"Can't really tell if some of them are the same car. It was snowing, and not all cameras have the best recording quality to begin with. Honestly, for some of them you wonder why they bothered putting them up in the first place."

Jessica nodded.

"Did you fall of that jittery barrel racer yet?" Caitlyn asked.

"Almost," Jess grinned and paused the video. She took another big bite of donut and continued while chewing: "but he's doing well, we made a lot of progress with the groundwork. I've got control over speed and direction in all three gaits, and he's getting close to having an excellent brake on him. I need to get him to relax a bit more, get him a bit more flexible and a lot more responsive. Then see if he likes barrel racing, or if he'd be better on trails." She paused to swallow. "I'm sure he'll be fast, but I don't want all that speed and pressure turning him back into a ball of nervous energy. He needs to be able to keep a cool head. We'll see. The owner wants to sell him when I'm done, so thankfully he's got options. It's really good when I don't have to make a horse fit into any goals the owner has, but let a horse do what he's naturally good at."

Caitlyn didn't mind talking horses with her sister, even though she lacked the knowledge to truly understand most of what Jessica was talking about.

From a very young age Jessica had known exactly what she wanted to do in life. At first her parents had tried to persuade her to go to college, have a backup plan, but it had always been horses for their youngest daughter. And, as Jessica kept reminding them, training horses is something you can only learn well through hands-on experience. Jessica had quickly built a name for herself as someone who could handle and fix problem horses. When she was seventeen, she had gotten a job at the Quarter Horse stud farm, and had moved into a small prefab house on the premises. Jessica loved her job. She did everything from handling the foals and monitoring pregnant mares, to starting the three-year-olds and teaching lessons. In summer Caitlyn sometimes helped with the evening feed, riding along on the back of a rickety faded red tractor that pulled the hay cart and smelled strongly of diesel fumes.

"Hey, gimpy, almost ready?" Martin was getting impatient.

"Oh, yes, sorry dad, I know I'm late, Jess and I only just got back from the Greatest Showman, it was amazing! And then I kind of forgot I had PT at that new place today, which is a longer drive. Ugh!" Caitlyn tossed the crutches on the backseat with an annoyed grunt.

"Not looking forward to physical therapy?"

"No. I'm not even sure if it's helping much lately. I still can't straighten my leg, I still can't walk. It's just all going so slow!"

"You'll get there. Just be patient."

"Patience, hrumpf. For all I know I'm doing this for nothing, since no one can actually tell me if this leg will get back to normal."

"Yeah, your mom told me the doctor was not as optimistic as we had hoped."

Caitlyn grunted something noncommittal, and her dad changed the subject.

"You know that prepper thing you mentioned? Now, don't let your mother hear this, but I'm reconsidering the bunker. Those guys are awesome! They've got their own store and everything. There's one somewhat nearby that I'd like to check out. I'll try to make it back in time, but I might be a little late picking you back up, is that OK?"

"Sure, dad. At least one of us is going to have some fun." They circled around the parking lot a few times, but the only parking spots available were all the way in the back.

"This day is just getting better and better. It's freezing, and the whole workout starts before I've even gone through the door." Caitlyn grumbled as she got out.

"Maybe that's a good thing, you're getting a bit chubby with all the sitting down you're doing."

Caitlyn glared at her father, then burst out laughing. He normally would never comment on her weight like this, but the way he'd said it made her realize just how grumpy she had been during the ride there.

"Nice one, dad!"

He smiled back and slowly followed her across the parking lot for a few seconds with the passenger-side window rolled down.

"Go, go, go! Faster! You can do it kid, I'm proud of you!"

"People need to stop bringing me chocolate!" Caitlyn shouted back over her shoulder as she hurried into the warmth of the lobby.

She wasn't sure where to go and looked around. There were several large support pillars in the entrance area, with large bright yellow planter boxes that held huge and very healthy looking spathiphyllum plants and a whole bunch of ferns. Someone obviously took care of these plants regularly. She spotted a front desk with two busy looking people, and almost went over to ask for directions when she noticed the signs hanging from the ceiling.

Physical therapy. Third floor.

An elevator icon pointed her to her right.

Well over an hour later Caitlyn crutched out of the building. The first PT session with the new therapist had gone well. She had liked him, and how he made her work hard but within her limits. Although her mood had improved, she was now tired and her leg ached, and she longed for a long, hot bath. She scanned the parking lot but didn't see her dad yet. She texted him and his reply was almost instant.

10 mins out.

Caitlyn crutched back inside. She leaned her shoulders against one of the big pillars and watched the people walking past. Most of them didn't notice her, with the pillar and the plants mostly blocking her from view, and she felt a little sneaky. Caitlyn played a mental game of 'guess what's wrong with them'. With some people it was obvious, but with others she had to look closely at the way they moved. Sometimes there was a slight limp, or one arm that was held closer to their body. Some people seemed perfectly fine but moved slowly.

A middle-aged woman was pushing a young boy in a brightly colored wheelchair, Caitlyn smiled at him when he waved at her then switched her attention to two men. One of them was talking on his phone and they were looking around, at the front desk and the signage on the ceiling.

They both seem perfectly healthy, Caitlyn thought as she listened to the one-sided phone conversation.

"Yes, I'm sure she's here."

"No, I don't know why she went back in, that's what I'm saying!
"

Caitlyn leaned back and hid a little further behind the plants, as the men walked past and stopped near the elevators in front of the notice board.

"Jesus Ed, are you listening? Do you have any idea how many people are on crutches here?"

Caitlyn frowned, *someone on crutches who went back inside?* She felt her heart rate increase a little and was suddenly fully alert.

Three more men came into the lobby and joined the other two. The first man put his phone away and all five all huddled together. Caitlyn could no longer hear what was being said, but the rhythm and speed made it seem like they were arguing.

She silently crutched around the side of the pillar and tried to get a closer look through the lush fern leaves. The man that had been on the phone seemed to be the one in charge, the others were all listening to him. One of the others reached under his jacket, and adjusted something that was tucked into the back of his waistband.

Does that guy have a weapon?!

Caitlyn felt a strong urge to get away from there as quickly as possible.

Where the hell was her dad!?

She almost jumped out of her skin when her phone vibrated, then felt a wave of relief pass through her as she read her dad's message.

```
I'm here
```

She scanned the parking lot and saw his car close to the entrance, running idle. Caitlyn watched as the five men walked up the stairs and quickly crutched to the exit. When she was outside, she glanced back over her shoulder. She couldn't see the men anymore.

"What were you doing behind that plant?" her dad asked as she got in.

"Nothing, just some men... I thought ..." She realized how silly she would sound. "Never mind. I was waiting for you. People watching."

Caitlyn put on her seatbelt. She took a deep breath, and forced herself to think.

Calm down, who says they really were looking for me?

I have to stop being so paranoid!

"How was the prepper store?" she asked her dad.

Martin started talking about all the amazing and useful things he'd seen. And, judging by the long receipt on the dashboard, he had bought at least half of them.

Caitlyn joined Newton on the couch and he slightly moved one of his ears. Caitlyn threw an ice pack on her knee and considered taking a nap as she wrapped a soft blanket around her. The broken nights were catching up with her, and the adrenaline rush after PT hadn't helped.

"Miss Anne, can you check this?"

Anne was sitting at the kitchen table, doing paperwork for OCD and helping Sophie with her homework. Volta was trying to decide whose stack of papers to lay down on top of, and occasionally attacked a moving pen or pencil, which made Sophie giggle and Anne grumble a reprimand.

Caitlyn listened to them talk for a while, to the somewhat comforting sounds of people writing and working. She took out her phone and texted Thomas.

When Sophie was finished with her homework and started to look bored, Caitlyn shortened her crutches and let Sophie play with them for a while.

"Soph, do you want to watch a movie with me until your mom comes to pick you up?"

"Yes!"

"You pick one." Caitlyn pointed at the row of DVDs under the TV. A small collection of Jessica and Caitlyn's favorite childhood animated movies.

Sophie knelt down and flipped through the stack. She held one up. "The Sword in the Stone?"

"Ooh, I love that one! Merlin, Wart and Archimedes, good choice!"

Caitlyn took the half-melted ice pack off her leg and lifted the corner of the blanket so Sophie could join her.

"Did you get a good gift for your mom's birthday tomorrow?"
Sophie nodded. "And breakfast in bed."

When Caitlyn went to sleep and checked her phone one last time, she saw she had missed a reply from Thomas.

I remember that, seeing possible danger everywhere.
Hang in there, it will get better.

Caitlyn smiled and turned off the lights.

CHAPTER FOURTEEN

Michelle turned thirty-two and celebrated with a small party that Sunday evening. Caitlyn had ordered a couple of hand-made paint brushes online. She was humming a tune from the Greatest Showman as she crutched over to Michelle's house.

Caitlyn spent most of the night talking with Gabrio Meza, one of Michelle's painter friends. He was a tall guy in his late twenties with a shaved head and a long dark beard who had immigrated from Cuba. Caitlyn, used to her dad's wild Viking looks, was not at all intimidated by his appearance. They talked about art, music, and Cuban street food, and the evening went by fast. She climbed into bed, feeling slightly fuzzy after a fun, relaxing evening with a little too much wine.

Caitlyn's car came to a sudden, crashing stop. The first thing she noticed was the darkness, the inability to move, and the pressure of warped metal on her lower body.

The car radio was playing songs from her phone's playlist, Hugh Jackman, but with a lot of Cuban salsa drums setting the beat.

And then the pain hit her like a freight train.

Like several freight trains, passing one after the other in a never-ending row of fully loaded train carts. It came in sharp, nauseating waves that took her breath away and turned her into a sweaty, panicky ball of nerve endings.

She heard someone scream and for a second felt relief, thinking help was close, only to realize that she was the one who was screaming.

Caitlyn shot up in bed, her hand went to her leg in a half-reflex. Her heart was beating so hard and fast it felt like it was trying to hammer its way out through her ribs. She moved her arms and legs, relieved at the liberated feeling it gave her, and tried to slow her breathing.

Man, I am so done with this same old stupid nightmare!

She shook her head, trying to force out the intrusive fragments. Her heart rate slowly settled down to where she could no longer feel every beat. She pressed some random buttons on her watch until she found the one that made the face glow in a soft shade of neon green.

Five twenty a.m. She set her alarm for two hours later.

When she woke up again, she felt a little better. She leaned to the side to grab her laptop from underneath the bedside table and scrolled through the last IRC log to catch up.

She searched for *panicked_kernel* to see if anyone had tried to

contact her, with a wry smile at how fitting her chosen nickname
was, then read the whole thing.

Axl3 was moving to Washington State.

WatchDog5 said he had found an exploit for…

Yada, yada, yada.

At a little before eight a.m. her phone buzzed. It was a text
from Thomas.

She immediately dialed back.

"Hi, Harry, are you home?"

"It's eight a.m., yes I'm home. Is everything OK?"

"It's nine a.m., daylight savings."

"Oh, right."

"Listen. About those men you saw yesterday. Tell me what
happened?"

Caitlyn laughed.

"Just a group of guys who walked past. They were looking for
someone on crutches at PT, and I thought one of them had a knife
or a gun stuck into the back of his jeans. It's so silly! I never was
this paranoid before. He was probably just tucking in his shirt."

Thomas was silent for a while.

"I don't think it's paranoia."

"What do you mean?"

"They're following me too."

" - What??"

"There are men in a dark blue Ford station wagon parked
outside my house, I think it's five of them."

Thomas sounded angry.

"They followed me. And at least one of them is definitely
armed. There's a way people walk when they are carrying. I was
leaving Haweville last night and thought I noticed a car trailing
me. I drove around for a while to make sure, and then I ditched
them. And I am *very* sure I ditched them. But now they are parked

right in front of my house. Go have a look out your window, do you see any cars you don't know?"

Caitlyn pushed the covers off and shivered at a sudden chill that did not only come from the cold. She quickly put on her robe and hopped to a window.

"I don't see anyone here. Hang on. Let me check the other side... No, no cars here, I think."

"Good."

Thomas thought.

"Did you recognize any of them yesterday?"

"No, but I was hiding behind a plant, and I only saw their backs, mostly."

"Well they're definitely amateurs, very easy to spot. And, wait, looks like they are growing tired of sitting around. Some of them are getting out of the car to smoke. Hold on, I'm gonna put you down for a minute, I'll be right back."

Caitlyn heard sounds she couldn't place.

After a long while Thomas came back on the line.

"Alright, I got a clear view and I think I recognize one of them, from when we were in the city, at that Italian restaurant."

"Wait, that slick guy that gave me the creeps?"

"The waiter who went to get him. I'm sending pictures. What do you think?"

Caitlyn checked her phone.

"I don't know, it could be him I guess...? So, what do we do now? Should we call the police?"

"I am the police. Or, I was," Thomas corrected himself. "And no, not yet anyway. We don't want the men to know that we know they're watching. Not if we can help it. First, we have to figure out who they are, what they want, and why they're following us."

"Did you say it's a dark blue car? Could it be the car that hit me?"

"No, that was a black one, remember, the paint? I thought you said you were awake?"

"Sorry, didn't sleep well."

"To be fair, it's five people. This might not be their only car.

One of them could drive a black one."

"So... One of them hit me? And now they are following me, us. Do you think they want to prevent us from finding out what happened? Or find out how much we know? Or maybe their boss wants to protect his reputation? Because I'm pretty sure one of your employees almost killing someone isn't great for business if you own a restaurant." Caitlyn's mind was spinning fast now.

"Could be any one of those things," Thomas said.

"Or maybe they just want to talk?"

"I don't think so. There are much easier ways to exchange insurance information."

"Oh, yeah, right, sorry. Man, this is not going to help with my nightmares at all! How do they even know where we live? Do you think they followed us all the way back from the restaurant? But we went to all those other places first, before we went home."

"I don't know, but I don't think so. And I'm not sure they know where you live. Wait until you see them to confirm. We have to get to the bottom of this." Thomas was starting to sound a little grim. "This is not something I'm OK with, I can't have these guys here, with Brad and El. They're way too close."

"I'm really sorry I got you involved."

"No - no, don't worry, I didn't mean it like that, it's fine."

Thomas thought and then muttered.

"They think they can just show up at my house, I'll show up at theirs."

"What do you mean?"

"Like I said, we should play this safe, but I think it can't hurt to turn the tables on them. I've got plenty of time today. I'll follow them right back to the hole they crept out of. Let's see where they're going and who they report to, if it's not their boss at the restaurant. I will call you back when I know more."

Thomas hung up without saying goodbye.

Caitlyn gently pushed Volta off the bed and took a quick shower, then went downstairs to join her parents for breakfast.

"You know," her dad said, "I didn't really miss that loud singing voice of yours so early in the morning."

"It's not early anymore, apparently," Caitlyn said with a yawn.

"I don't understand why Daylight Savings can't be a global thing. You know, where everyone puts the clock one hour ahead on the same date," Anne complained. "It's the second Sunday in March here, but the last Sunday in March in the Netherlands, and it's messing me up!"

"Or we can just cancel the whole thing?" Caitlyn said. "I could have slept an hour longer."

"We're partnering with a Dutch organization." Anne continued. "It really helps that I speak the language, but I made a horrible first impression by calling at the wrong time. They have been working on a few projects in Kenya with the local Maasai. It's been going on for a few years now and they've had great success. Although, I think they had some minor issues convincing them to not immediately graze everything to death again, but now they're flourishing, literally. They just started a seed bank for native grasses. The women sow them, then later harvest and sell the seeds. It's beautiful, it's self-maintaining, and expanding."

"That's great mom! Will you go?"

"To Kenya? Maybe. I'll go to the Netherlands first though, it's always good to talk in person, and I can visit oma, it's been too long."

Caitlyn kept checking her phone during the day and quickly picked up, barely registering it was an unknown number.

"Uh, hello?"

"It's Thomas."

"Oh. It said caller ID withheld. So, what happened?"

"I'm calling from the landline, it's cheaper."

"Ah."

Thomas continued.

"They're definitely from the restaurant. They went straight back there this afternoon. I saw them talking to their boss. I followed two of them to a gym. I'm not sure where the others went, but I had to make a choice. They almost spotted me, but I ducked into an elevator just in time, I think. I stand out, it can't be helped. They all ran upstairs to try to relocate me. Like I said, definitely amateurs. And not the sharpest tools in the shed."

"I asked a former colleague about their boss, Roy Rubino." Thomas continued. "He warned me to be careful. Word is Rubino has connections, friends in low places. Not Italian Mafia, although he fits the mold, but a small player. I am going to take the warning very seriously, considering my source. We should keep a safe distance. I'm sure he has already made me as a cop - or, well, former cop - when we went there. Harry, are you listening?"

"Yes, sorry. Possible danger, tread lightly. Makes sense to me. I mean, he was polite and all, but that guy just really made my skin crawl." Caitlyn gave an involuntary shudder.

"Always trust that first gut reaction," Thomas said, "It has saved my life countless times. Most of Rubino's staff have a criminal record, it's like it's a requirement in order to work there. But, that means good news for us. I'm supposed to get some names and pictures from another buddy who has access to their rep sheets. I'll see if I can match them to our five new friends."

Caitlyn heard Thomas press a few computer keys.

"Damn all technology to hell and back!"

"Uh, is everything OK?"

"My computer is frozen. Again. I swear this thing knows when I want something to happen quickly, and then does the exact opposite."

Caitlyn couldn't help but laugh out loud.

"I'll forward all relevant information to you when I can get these pictures to show up, so you know who to look out for."

"Thanks. I still haven't seen them here by the way, I've been checking the street. Do you think I'm missing them?"

"No, I don't think so. They are very obvious. If they're there, you'll spot them. Let's see what I can find out tomorrow." Thomas briefly paused, then added: "Do you want to come along? Surveillance 101?"

CHAPTER FIFTEEN

Thomas pushed up the small incline of the Harrison's driveway and rang the doorbell. Anne opened the door.

"Hi, Officer Dean. It's good to see you again. She is almost ready." Anne shivered, "Gosh it's chilly today! Please, come inside."

"Hi Mrs. Harrison. Thanks. Please call me Thomas."

"And Anne will do for me."

Thomas tried to hop over the doorstep, but it was a little too high and he didn't have enough momentum to make it in one go.

Anne's smile faded, and she worriedly stepped even closer so she could help him out.

Thomas stopped her with a short smile and a raised hand.

"I've got it, thank you."

He pulled himself over, using the door frame, and followed Anne into the living room.

"Caitlyn!" Anne yelled upstairs.

"Please have a seat."

"I could, but I think we have to get going soon, so if you don't mind I'll keep this one," Thomas replied.

"Oh! I'm sorry I..." Anne looked horrified.

"I was really sorry to hear about your accident."

"Thank you," Thomas said. "Oh, it's so nice and warm in here!"

He blew his hands and moved closer to the burning logs in the fireplace.

Caitlyn came hopping down the stairs.

"Sorry, I was checking my messages, I have some friends online who are helping me out."

"No problem. I love this wood-burning fireplace! It reminds me of going camping. Take your time, I'm good warming up right here. Might have to talk to Ellen about getting one of these, it's a really nice kind of heat." Thomas checked the raised letters of the brand name on the cast iron.

"It's great, right?" Caitlyn was tying her shoelaces.

"Excellent for those days when it's so cold that you lose all feeling in your fingers and toes." Anne turned a deep shade of crimson as soon as she'd said it, and glanced uncomfortably at Thomas.

"Nice one, mom," Caitlyn said with a wide grin, then she laughed out loud at a sudden memory. "Hey, do you remember when I was a kid? Me and Jess always stood in front of the fire to warm up, too. I ruined my favorite snowsuit once. I'm not sure anymore what happened now, maybe a spark landed on it when the door was open, or I stood too close and the heat melted it?"

"I remember," Anne nodded. "You two always fought over who would get the best spot."

Thomas looked suddenly worried and backed up his chair a little and felt his lower legs with his hands. "Wouldn't be the first time I burnt myself and didn't notice," he muttered.

"Right. So, do you want something to drink, or do you just want to get going?" Caitlyn asked.

"I'm good, thanks, if you're ready?"

Caitlyn got up.

Thomas followed her back into the hallway, with Anne trailing behind them.

"Any idea when you will be home again, Cait? Do you have your keys? Your dad is at school until four and I'm not sure if I'll be home all afternoon. I'm going hiking with Ginny."

"Thanks mom, I've got keys," Caitlyn said while checking her pocket. "Don't think I'll be too late though."

She looked at Thomas who nodded.

"Few hours tops."

Caitlyn crutched out and stepped to the side so Thomas could pass. "Mom, what the hell are you doing?"

"I, uh, wasn't sure if I needed to help him over the doorstep."

Anne turned to Thomas. "I mean, I would help you, but you don't have any..." She motioned with her hands and looked at Caitlyn. "Handvaten?"

"Handles." Caitlyn translated.

"That is intentional," Thomas said almost apologetically, "It's almost always unexpected when people decide to help me. It can be risky when someone starts pushing me around out of the blue. My balance is... not optimal. So I removed the handles."

Anne paused and blushed again.

"I sort of almost did that, didn't I?"

"Little bit. Thank you for the offer to help though, I do appreciate the intention. Just let me ask for it. I promise I will, when I need to."

Anne nodded. "Got it."

Thomas popped a controlled wheelie and bumped off the doorstep, and Anne closed the door behind them.

"Sorry about my mom," Caitlyn said. "As we found out during my first week of rehab, she's a bit awkward around disabled people. No idea why, she's fine with me. Maybe it's different when it's not temporary."

Thomas shrugged and took a good look around in all directions.

"You still haven't seen them here?"

"No, nothing."

"They were at my place this morning, all five of them. They followed me when I left. I lost them after about a mile, which wasn't too hard. I wanted to see if they could make it here on their own. The fact that they didn't, leads me to believe that they don't know where you live. You don't see any other cars that don't belong?"

Caitlyn looked down the street.

"I don't think so."

"Is there anywhere they could park out of sight and still see us?"

Caitlyn shook her head. "No. Our street ends there." She

pointed to the end of the cul-de-sac. "And all the neighbors would complain if there was a group of strangers parked in their driveway. We would have heard about it. I know all the cars I can see." Caitlyn pointed. "That's Michelle's, Mr. And Mrs. Highland, Ms. Adams... Do you think I should put up cameras or something, to watch the street?"

Thomas hesitated, then shook his head. "No. I don't think that's necessary."

Caitlyn waited for Thomas to get in and threw her backpack and then herself into the car.

She noticed Thomas had taken Bradley's car seat out.

"If the heat's blasting too hot for you let me know, I'm having a hard time staying warm today."

"No problem. I'm what my mom calls a koukleum too."

"A what?"

"Koukleum." Caitlyn pronounced it *cow-klumm*. "It's Dutch for someone who's always cold or gets cold really easily."

"How can you even pronounce that second part?"

"Hah!" Caitlyn laughed, "don't get me started, that's not even one of the difficult ones!"

Thomas started driving.

"OK, so here's a quick PI lesson on surveillance. Step one: find the people you want to follow." He paused to think. "Let's backtrack to my place and hope they went back there when I shook them off. I forgot my gloves, so even if they're not there, at least I can get those. Push rims get freezing cold in winter."

A few streets before his own, Thomas slowed down.

"I'll give them a chance to hide when they see me drive up. It's what they've been trying to do every time, while I pretend I'm too busy with the chair to notice them. Don't stare at them too much, please."

Thomas took the turn and cruised on slowly while two men scrambled to get into the dark blue station wagon. The stationwagon quickly backed into a nearby driveway.

"Did you get the pictures and names I forwarded this morning?"

Caitlyn nodded. She had studied their faces, their names. Had tried to memorize them.

"Eduard Timms, Joseph Garritano, Jesus Lira, Oscar Laurent, and Vincent 'Vinny' Ferra. They're too far for me to tell who's who though."

"Black over black next to the car, that's Eduard." Thomas nodded.

"Black over what?"

"Sorry, black jeans, black sweater."

Caitlyn tried to watch the men without being too obvious about it.

Thomas picked up his phone. "El, are you still home? I forgot my gloves."

"They're on the table I think."

A moment later Ellen opened the car door and handed a pair of gloves to Thomas.

"Thanks, babe." Thomas gave her a quick kiss.

When Ellen was back inside, Thomas drove off.

"We will let them follow us for a while. Drive to the city, pretend we're going somewhere."

Caitlyn flipped down the visor, re-did her ponytail, and looked at the car tailgating them in the mirror.

"Seriously. These guys don't have a clue what they're doing," Thomas muttered, checking his side-view mirror. "Lesson two: always keep two or three cars between you and your target."

"I think it's Eduard who's driving? He's the waiter that went to get the boss, right?" Caitlyn asked.

"Yes," Thomas said. "And Vincent is sitting next to him. The other three are in the back, I can't see who's who either."

Thomas barely made the green light, and the blue station wagon had to stop for red.

"Perfect. This is where we lose them," Thomas said with a smile. He took a right turn, took the first left, then right again and pointed ahead. "That's where we're going."

He checked his mirror.

"Good, they're still there. They're trying to catch up."

Thomas turned into a very large, very busy parking lot. He drove to the other side and turned onto the road again, then quickly reversed into a random driveway and stopped. He turned off his lights but left the motor running.

"We'll wait here for a while. They probably think we stopped in the parking lot and got out, so they're checking all the rows. We can see both exits from here, so it doesn't matter which one they take, once they realize we're not there. When they leave, we'll follow. Let's hope the owner of this driveway doesn't come to check us out before that happens. But if he does, let me do the talking. I don't think we'll be here for more than a few minutes though. They're stressed and when they can't find us, they'll act without thinking. They'll make mistakes."

Caitlyn nodded.

It wasn't long before the blue station wagon turned onto the road and drove in their direction.

"There!!" Caitlyn said excitedly.

"Duck down a bit more, just in case," Thomas said, "and never point like that again. They probably won't even look this way since they're searching the roads, but it's best not to risk it."

Caitlyn slid down in her seat, and Thomas bent forward as if he was adjusting the radio, holding on to the steering wheel, hiding his face from sight.

"And there you go." The car drove straight past them. Thomas waited for a few other cars to pass, then followed. "It's OK if at the start you have five or even six cars between you, as long as you can still see the car you're following. It makes it less obvious that you are on their tail. We can always try to get closer when we need to."

CHAPTER SIXTEEN

They drove through random streets for a while, following the dark blue car while blending in with other traffic. The men in the station wagon were still obviously looking for them, gestures flying as they argued with each other about which way to go. But they never thought to look behind them.

"A lot of people don't," Thomas explained. "And if they do, it's mainly to check how close the car behind them is, they don't look at who's inside it. It makes surveillance on untrained people a lot easier."

He had overtaken a few cars to avoid losing the station wagon at stoplights, and there now was only one car between them.

"It's a little inconvenient that they know what we both look like," Thomas said, "or I would have shown you the best way to tail someone when you're right on top of them. We'll save that for another day."

After a while the men seemed to give up and headed for the freeway.

Thomas followed.

"I like to stay in the same lane as the car I'm following. See how each lane is moving at a different speed? If I would move to the left lane now, we would be going too fast to stay behind them."

Caitlyn was starting to feel like she should be taking notes.

"I never expected there would be any kind of science to this. It's a lot more than just the excitement of following someone and hoping you don't get spotted!"

For the next few miles they drove in silence. No radio, no talking. Only the rhythmic sound of the engine and the road. From the highway they turned on to the off ramp, and finally into the city.

"There you have it," Thomas said, "people are creatures of habit."

They had stopped at Basilico, the Italian restaurant. The station wagon had parked in the parking lot, in a spot marked "reserved". Thomas found an empty space on the opposite side of the street, in between two other parked cars, where they could keep an eye on the front and the side of the restaurant.

The men got out.

"That is Eduard and Vinny. The guy with the narrow face in the light jeans is Joseph, the tall bald one is Oscar. The guy that's slightly shorter than him, with shoulder length curly hair, must be Jesus. Must have grown his beard after his mugshot was taken."

Caitlyn noticed all men wore the same black shirt with Basilico's logo on it.

"They're all dressed for work. I've seen that logo somewhere before though, that green basil leaf?"

"You mean inside the restaurant? It's probably all over the place."

"No, it's not that. Somewhere else." Caitlyn frowned.

Thomas checked his watch. "I think this could be the start of their shift."

They expected the men to all walk into the restaurant, but Eduard and Oscar went right past the front door. They walked along the side of the restaurant and vanished around the corner.

"Might be a back entrance. Let's double check," Thomas said. "Normally when you watch someone close up, where they can see you, you try not to stand out. Like with a wheelchair, or crutches. But we'll have to make do. We have the advantage that they don't expect us here at all, and they're definitely not trained in counter surveillance. So as long as we can keep out of sight, we should be fine."

He motioned with his hand at the side street. "I think the alley behind the restaurants stretches all the way up to the end there."

Caitlyn wrapped her dark gray knit scarf around her neck, put on her gloves and zipped up her coat. She waited for Thomas to lock up the car, then followed him.

Thomas had been right. There was a long and narrow back alley. It was lined with dumpsters and torn pieces of cardboard boxes that were once soaked and now frozen solid.

"You're gonna need a lot of hand sanitizer after this." Caitlyn grinned nervously, her voice a little lowered.

The alley dipped down in the center so rainwater could drain into the grids that were placed every few feet. Most of this center part was iced over, and Caitlyn almost lost her balance when her crutch hit a patch she didn't see.

"Careful!" Thomas grabbed her elbow. "You OK?"

Caitlyn nodded.

Occasionally wire fencing separated the shops from the alley. In some places the fence was boarded up with wooden slats, all adorned with graffiti, but mostly the wire was left bare. Over the years people had cut or kicked holes in it that never got repaired.

They could see three men in the distance, Eduard, Oscar, and their boss Roy Rubino. Eduard and Oscar were unloading heavy looking cardboard boxes from the back of another parked black restaurant van. It had a green basil leaf logo on the side.

Caitlyn felt like a real-life Sydney Bristow, half ducking down behind a large dumpster, next to Thomas. They watched as one by one the boxes were carried into the restaurant through the back door. Some of the boxes had brand names or logos on them, others were plain brown. Rubino was looking on, talking to his men without helping them.

"Do you have one of those parabolic microphones you can point at them?" Caitlyn whispered.

"No," Thomas whispered back.

"Do you think there's food in those boxes and they're carrying it to the kitchen?"

"I don't know. Just try to listen."

They were a little too far away to clearly hear everything that was being said, but they caught some fragments of the conversation.

"Boss... lost them."

"How... could... happen!?"

Rubino was visibly agitated and Eduard held up both his hands in an apologetic and defensive gesture.

"... all over..."

"No, take that box in the back... shelf."

Oscar put the box he was holding down, picked up the one Rubino was pointing at and disappeared through the open door.

Rubino turned to Eduard again.

"Did they see you? Is that..."

"No... careful!"

"...".

They argued for a while, then Eduard took another box into the restaurant. Rubino picked up his phone and slowly walked around to the front of the van. Thomas and Caitlyn could hear him a little better now.

"Mr. Marino please."

"Yes, we're following the girl and the cop."

Caitlyn not very gently poked Thomas' shoulder with her elbow.

Rubino turned his back towards them. He headed towards the restaurant, then turned back again.

Caitlyn strained her ears.

"....... hit her car...... money!"

"No, not yet."

Rubino paused briefly.

"Understood. We'll try, but that cop..."

Then he hung up and walked inside.

Caitlyn looked at Thomas. "Did you hear that!" she said excitedly. "They are talking about you, and me, and my car! See I told you that guy was creepy! He must be the one who hit me, and now he has his employees follow us. Did you hear?"

Thomas shushed her but nodded.

"Let's wait a few minutes, see if they come back out."

Nothing happened until a small group of four people entered the alley from the other side.

Caitlyn thought they looked pretty shifty.

Thomas saw them too and changed his mind.

"Let's get out of here before they spot us and start asking questions. Best not to have anyone know we were here. And don't look back at them when you walk away, it raises suspicion."

Caitlyn followed him back to the car, resisting the natural urge to look over her shoulder.

"That was interesting," Thomas said with a glove clenched between his teeth.

"I knew it!" Caitlyn said with a mix of anger and excitement. "I knew that guy was evil! Did you hear him talk about money? Do you think Rubino will try to pay me off so I won't sue him once he knows we can prove it was him? That sounds like something he would do, right? Only pay me when he has to. Or maybe he's not insured? Did you hear the rest of that sentence?"

Thomas shook his head with an apologetic smirk. "I think your ears are a lot better than mine. You're younger, and I've shot a lot of guns."

"So, what do we do now?"

Thomas thought briefly. "We can't do anything yet with the information as we have it. We have to find concrete proof. And we have to be very careful. He just confirmed he knows I'm a former cop. That means he has been asking around about me, just like I've been asking around about him. And while his crew looks like the *'hit before you ask questions'* type, he seems like the type who hits to kill, not to hurt. And he might have more backup than just these five if he's part of a bigger organization. I still don't think that is the case, but we can't risk it. We don't want to accidentally end up swimming with the fishies, if you know what I mean."

Caitlyn looked at him a little scared.

"Do you really think he would kill me, kill us, over a hit and run, over insurance money?"

"Depends on how much he wants to avoid the bill, or the jail time. Or on how much money he doesn't want to lose. Felony hit and run is two to fifteen years in prison, with about a five thousand dollar fine. People have killed for less."

"But," Thomas added, "I don't think he would kill us if he didn't have to. They probably wouldn't be following us if that was the case. Much easier to kill someone right away. And there is more good news. It is the same team of five every time. Six if you count Rubino. I don't think there are any more of them.

We know what they all look like, and they are easy to spot. They're definitely not trained in surveillance or counter surveillance, which makes everything we do a lot easier and safer. Also, it doesn't look like Rubino is doing any of the legwork himself. As long as we avoid this restaurant and don't do anything else that lets them know we're on to them, we should be just fine."

They went back to their parking spot and watched the front and side of the restaurant from inside the car for a while. Thomas said it would be too obvious to leave the motor running and the cold was slowly creeping into their bones. Caitlyn opened her backpack and took out a few containers filled with thick sandwiches and a thermos with hot tea. She offered Thomas a container and one of the extra cups she brought.

"Here, I brought lunch and tea, if you want some?"

"Thanks, I could do with something warm. Any nuts in here?"

"No. It's mayo, lettuce, tomato, and a fried egg. Are you allergic?"

"El is, so I never eat them. Not worth the risk. Thanks for this! I usually go for takeout or a quick burger, but this is much healthier."

Thomas took a bite.

"Mmm, and much better! Did you bake this bread?"

"Yesterday." Caitlyn replied. She took a big gulp of her tea.

"Better not drink too much." Thomas warned. "There are no bathroom breaks on surveillance."

"You've got tea and about half a gallon of orange juice there!" Caitlyn nodded at the bottle he had gotten out of his bag.

Thomas grinned at her. "At the risk of giving way too much

information, there occasionally are small advantages to being paralyzed. If I know I'm going to do surveillance, I can plan for it. Also, I'm a guy. It's a lot easier for us in general."

They sat there for a good thirty minutes longer. Eating, drinking and watching the restaurant. Not much was happening. When more and more customers arrived for lunch, Thomas turned to Caitlyn.

"Looks like they'll be busy here for a while. I've got a meeting with a potential client later and it's getting way too cold in here. Let's head back home, I'll drop you off."

Caitlyn yawned, stretched her good leg and arms, and tried to rub the tension out of her right shoulder.

Thomas stretched his arms above his head and turned to grab his seatbelt. Then all color drained from his face and he tensed up.

"Jesus, are you OK?" Caitlyn said, unsure of what to do.

Thomas nodded and held up a hand, but it took a few seconds before he could speak.

"I'm OK," he said, letting out a slow long breath. "This is normal. My body doesn't like it when I move in certain ways. Shouldn't have done that."

Caitlyn grimaced. "Can't you take something?"

Thomas laughed wryly and carefully shifted in his seat, then relaxed a little more. "Who says I don't?"

"Well, that there just sort of did."

"Neuropathic pain. It's pretty common after a spinal cord injury. Pain in body parts that otherwise lack sensation. If I twist a certain way it really sets it off." He gently stretched his back. "Before I tried the weed, it was a lot worse. Exercise helps too, but with the cold in winter..." He half waved a hand. "This sometimes happens. It hurts but it thankfully doesn't last that long."

"Man, that's horrible!"

"It is what it is." Thomas shrugged.

"Huh." Caitlyn grinned in an attempt to lighten the mood, "I'd better stop complaining about my leg now."

"I don't know about that," Thomas said seriously. "Complaining can help too, sometimes. And it's not like this is a competition. So please don't stop on my account. You seem to be moving better though?"

"Yes! I got the results from my x-ray and my femur is healing, finally! PT OK'd me for partial weight bearing starting this Friday, as much as my knee allows."

"That's excellent news!" Thomas smiled. "Here's to progress and recovery!"

Back home Caitlyn collapsed on the sofa with her Kindle, but she couldn't focus on what she was reading and kept having to turn back a page.

How can we find proof that Roy Rubino hit me that night?

Suddenly something clicked in her brain. The leaf! The basil leaf logo! She remembered where she had seen it before!

She rushed upstairs, as fast as her leg and crutches would let her, got the notebook out of her desk drawer, and waited impatiently for the fifteen seconds it took for her computer to boot.

Caitlyn flipped to the notebook page with the list of all the dark cars she had seen on the footage.

Right in the middle of the list it read:

Black delivery van at South Cincinnati and East 15th @ 18:30
Black delivery van (same) at Seymour and Stanley @ 18:52

She quickly found the image files she had saved to her hard disk. There it was. A black van, with a large green basil leaf on the side panel.

Proof!

But when Caitlyn opened her animated map she quickly saw that this van couldn't be the one that had hit her. She checked, and checked again, but Seymour and Stanley at 18:52 p.m. was at least twenty minutes from where the crash happened. There was no way that black delivery van could have made it to the crash site in time. Especially not in bad weather.

She ran some calculations and deleted a few of the other dots for cars that were too far away, but still felt defeated.

With heavy strokes she crossed the van off her list.

Caitlyn pushed the notebook away from her and peered at the grainy video still picture, but the face of the driver was a tiny blob of pixels. It was impossible to tell if it was Rubino or not.

But it is a restaurant van, maybe they traveled in packs?

Maybe there was another one that was close to the crash site?

Or it could simply have been out for delivery?

No. It has to be Rubino! I just need to prove it.

CHAPTER SEVENTEEN

The next morning Caitlyn took a long hot shower. She had tried to think of ways to prove Rubino owned one of the other black cars on her list and wondered if the old DMV backdoor was still in place. That would be the fastest and easiest way to narrow down the long list of partial license plate numbers she had written down as well, figure out the full plate and eliminate all cars that were not black.

She got dressed, put two shoes on, and logged on to IRC while blow-drying her hair.

She thought for a while about the best way to phrase her question. Even with all their precautions, you never knew who was reading along.

```
[08:46] <panicked_kernel> @all - Anyone here knows if
I can still go to the DMV for license plate info?
```

Instantly a few people replied.

```
[08:46] <DonnyR> Still good, went last week, helpful
people. Unusually short waiting time :)
```

She typed in the command to start a private chat with DonnyR. He confirmed the backdoor still sworked and gave her a quick recap of how to get access to the system. He also reminded her which log files she had to alter after she was done to erase any proof of her poking around.

Caitlyn thanked him and logged off. No matter how often she accessed a system she shouldn't have access to, she still got nervous every time. It was as if she should be looking over her shoulder. As if, as soon as she typed in that password, someone would walk in and catch her red-handed.

I guess I have a bit of a history when it comes to scary situations making me paranoid forever.

She double-checked to make sure her VPN was on and took a quick peek at what she had access to. She shouldn't really do this from home, ever, but she also knew the DMV sysadmins never thoroughly checked their logs. The backdoor had been in place for years, and as far as she knew no one had ever been caught using it.

She hit enter and was greeted by a handy graphical interface, with a form that accepted wildcards for a license plate search.

She typed in Roy Rubino's name, and a long list of black vans showed up, as well as the dark blue station wagon. But none of the plates matched, and he owned no other black cars.

Maybe the title wasn't in his name?

It only took her a few more minutes to run all the partials she had written down in her notebook. She exported the results to an Excel file and checked the list. All the license plates, complete with the car's color, make, model and the name and address of the registered owner. She opened a command line window to erase her tracks, logged out of the DMV system and closed the VPN.

Caitlyn sorted the Excel file and, on the animated map, deleted all the cars that weren't black. She decided to remove all out-of-state cars, then went to Google and compared images of car models on her list to the screenshots she had saved. She could match most of them by the shape of their headlights. The more cars she crossed off, the more excited she became.

In the end there was only one car left.

25A Q32, a black 2015 Nissan Versa, owned by a car rental company.

She googled the company name and found they had an office in Haweville, close to the airport.

She googled some more, but could find nothing that linked the car rental company to Rubino.

Why would Rubino rent a car and not drive his own, or one of his many restaurant vans? Did someone else rent it for him?

Did he fly in and use it to get home?

Caitlyn wrote the address of the car rental place in her notebook.

She also added the names of the five men that had been following them.

- Oscar Laurent: tall slim guy. shaved/bald head.
- Eduard Timms: short. pale. hair slicked back. sides shaved
- Jesus Lira: curly hair to shoulders. beard. medium height. broad built.
- Joseph Garritano: narrow face. very short dark curls. tall and skinny.
- Vinny Ferra: hair very short at sides. longer on top. square face.

Caitlyn turned off her computer and went downstairs to distract herself with an older episode of House on Netflix . She needed to figure out what to do next.

Fellow limping doctor, please lend me some of your powers of deduction!

Thomas called her from his car half an hour later.

"I followed three of them to a warehouse this afternoon, close to the steel mills in the city. I have no clue what they were doing there, I couldn't get any closer. There was a long stretch of asphalt that led up to and around the building, and me rolling up would have been too obvious."

Caitlyn made a sympathetic sound.

"They must have had a staff meeting or something, the place was crawling with those black restaurant vans. I waited for a while, and followed Rubino to his house. I watched him for an hour or so. Nothing happened. He's got a wife and two kids. Boys, teenagers. I had to leave to meet with a new client. I could get busy in the coming days, so you might be on your own for a while."

"No problem, thank you. Good news here, too. I'm pretty sure

I've found the car that hit me. It's a black 2015 Nissan Versa. It's not registered to Roy Rubino though, but to a rental car company."

"Do I want to know how you got this?"

"Uh... No?"

"You know I have legal access to these types of databases, right?"

"Oh... I hadn't thought of that." Caitlyn felt a bit stupid.

"Well, now you know. Listen, I have to go. I'm turning into my driveway. Looks like our friends are back here too, in a red car this time. As if I hadn't already noticed them... Little beat up Ford, they barely fit in. I'll send you a picture, keep an eye out." Thomas hung up.

It was a quiet rest of the afternoon. Caitlyn paused House when Jessica texted to ask if she had time to update her website. She grabbed her laptop and called her back.

"I'm ready, what do you want changed?"

"Could you add something about a waiting list? I think that would help. I've spent the last hour answering emails."

"Sure little sis, hang on."

Caitlyn typed something and uploaded the file to the server.

"Check it now?"

"Perfect sis, don't know what I would do without you!"

"How's your fat Arab doing?"

"Better. Thank god. The reduction in calories seems to be kicking in, he's a bit more mellow, and better at keeping a respectful distance. How's your search going?"

"Found out that the car is a black Nissan. I'm getting closer."

After dinner Caitlyn and Michelle sat on the front porch, both with a warm blanket wrapped around them.

"Funny how it's always in the wind and the air that you can first notice the seasons changing," Michelle said. "It's softer and warmer somehow."

Caitlyn nodded. "It was this afternoon, but I think that might have been temporary. It's freezing again now. I'm ready for proper spring! It's not quite porch sitting weather yet." She wrapped the blanket a little tighter around her. "Sophie's having fun though."

Michelle looked at her daughter who was running around the backyard with a piece of string that had a ball of crumpled-up paper tied to the end. Newton's inner lion had surfaced, and he was trying to hide behind a scraggly looking bush, wiggling his butt, getting ready for an attack.

"I'll have to brush half the backyard out of his fur later," Caitlyn half complained.

"Be happy we don't have to check both of them for ticks yet," Michelle said.

Caitlyn couldn't suppress an involuntary shudder, she was fine with spiders, but she hated ticks. It was something about the way their tiny legs stuck out of them where their black triangular head met their bodies. That, and all the diseases they could carry.

Michelle hesitated. "I went for a run yesterday; the ground is getting softer too."

Caitlyn sighed. "I can't wait to go running with you again, I'm getting restless. And fat."

Michelle stood up.

"Nonsense. I'm getting more wine; do you want some? Red or white?"

Caitlyn thought. "Better not. I took a painkiller earlier, I'm not supposed to mix them with alcohol. I'll take some tea if you want to make it?"

"Sure. Is your leg OK?"

"Yeah, it's fine. I'm finally allowed to put some weight on it. It's not real walking yet, but it's a good thing. It's just throwing a bit of an annoying hissy-fit, I'm using muscles that haven't seen any action in months."

Michelle drank her red wine, and Caitlyn took a tiny sip of the still-slightly-too-hot-to-drink green tea Michelle had brought her, warming her hands on the large blue mug.

"How's the big investigation going?"

"From the 911 call we found out - Oh, wait, let me backup. Do you know how I met Thomas?"

Michelle shook her head.

"You know I got into a little trouble at school when I was sixteen, right?"

"Yes, your dad told me once."

"They brought in a cop to scare me straight, so to speak. He's no longer a cop, but a PI. Runs his own firm. He got injured, and he's in a wheelchair now. I met him at the hospital. He's helping me investigate."

"Wow, a wheelchair, that's so tragic!"

"Hmm, yeah. Anyway. The police report said they found traces of paint on my car, so we knew the car that hit me was black. Thomas got the 911 tape for me. I always thought I called for an ambulance myself, but it was a man in the recording. That was the first thing we found out."

"Really! Wow, I didn't know! Must have been weird to hear his voice."

"I... didn't listen to it myself. I'm reliving things enough as it is."

"Ah, right. Good point."

Caitlyn blew on her tea and took another careful sip. "Two weeks ago we went into Haweville and got surveillance footage from a lot of stores along the route. I spent most of the past weeks watching way too many videos of cars driving past."

"Look at you, you little sleuth!" Michelle studied her face. "You're having fun with this, aren't you?"

"Kind of, yes."

"It suits you. So, what's next? And I want all the details please, remember I paint for a living. I'm going to be living vicariously through you!"

"Well... a few men have been, uh, following Thomas."

"Wait, there's people following you?! Is this safe?"

"It's a little scary, but they're mainly following Thomas, and he used to be a cop. And they're not coming close. We think their boss is the one who hit me. They all work at his restaurant in Haweville. They use black delivery vans, do you know Basilico?"

"I think I've been there?" Michelle said, sounding unsure.

"I found out it was a black Nissan that hit me. The car is registered to a rental company. I can't link Roy Rubino, that's the boss, to the rented car yet. My mom will take me to the car rental company tomorrow. As soon as I have proof Rubino is involved, we can turn him in. "

CHAPTER EIGHTEEN

Caitlyn made her way across the parking lot through rows of cars. She was a little more stable now that she could put her other foot down too, but still needed to watch out for possible slippery parts.

"Good morning." The young man behind the counter looked up as she entered. His smile faded a little. "Ahhh, I don't think I'm allowed to rent to you while you're on crutches."

"Oh, I'm not here to rent a car, don't worry. I'm actually looking for someone who rented from you and I was wondering if you could help me?"

"I'm sorry, I'm not allowed to give you any information about our customers." His smile was completely gone now.

"It's the person who did this to me," Caitlyn leaned against the counter and held up a crutch, "he rented a black Nissan Versa from you. He hit my car with it on December 21st."

"I'm sorry, I'm not allo– Wait, did you say a black Nissan Versa?"

"Yes, 2015. I've got the plate too if that makes it easier for you to look up."

She hoped he wouldn't ask her how she got the plate, and would just assume she had seen the car that hit her.

He briefly pressed his lips together, then turned to his computer.

"One moment."

He started typing, occasionally clicking his mouse, and then took what felt like at least ten full minutes to read what was on his monitor. Caitlyn leaned forward a little, but the monitor was angled away from her and she couldn't see anything.

Meanwhile, the man's expression kept turning darker. Finally, he looked up.

"I'm not telling you this, privacy laws and all, but to hell with this guy."

Caitlyn gestured locking her lips and throwing away the key.

"That car was rented out alright, and it came back with a big fat dent." He paused abruptly. "Pardon me. I didn't mean to offend, it wasn't you that caused the dent?"

"No, he hit my car."

"OK, good, well, not good, but... Anyway. Turns out the driver gave us completely false information – I mean he was dressed really nicely. Armani suit, nice watch, great hair. And he paid in full up front. So I had no reason at all to think he wouldn't pay for the damage. They took it out of my paycheck. I'm not even sure if that is legal, come to think of it, I may have to contact my union about that. Anyway. He parked the car in front," he pointed to the parking lot, "right there, all busted up, and then he made a run for it! Can you believe that! I mean he wasn't actually running, because then I might have suspected something was wrong and I could have tried to chase him or something. But he just... casually walked off. Just like that! Didn't even come in. Left the key in the ignition, and, poof, vanished."

Caitlyn gave him a sympathetic smile, and hoped he'd soon get to the part of the story where he told her something she could use.

"I mean we kept his security deposit of course, but it wasn't nearly enough to cover all the repairs that were needed. The ID he gave us was a fake too, same with his address. We sent him the bill via certified mail, and it came back as undeliverable. And of course, we immediately called the police when it happened, but you know how that goes. So. To keep a long story short, he landed himself on our blacklist."

Caitlyn wondered how long his not-short stories usually were. "Blacklist?" she asked.

The man pointed to a row of pictures on the wall behind him. "We scan all the driver's licenses, saves a lot of paper clutter and it's much easier to look them up again later. Those who don't pay, or those who dump a dented car on your doorstep never to be seen or heard from again, get their photo printed out and pinned to the board there. The whole company does it. Those are all the people I put up, I like to think it's a deterrent. Clearly, in this case, it wasn't."

Caitlyn put both her elbows on the counter and leaned forward, trying to find Rubino in the row of faces. "You mean you have a picture?"

She could feel her net tightening around Rubino.

"I'm sorry. Strict privacy laws. But... if you happen to see his picture hanging on the wall behind me, that's not something I have any control over."

He checked his computer screen again, then walked over and quickly scanned the row of pictures. He ripped one off the wall, not bothering to take out the push pin first, and put it on the counter.

"This is him."

Caitlyn stared at it, victory turning into confusion.

He didn't look anything like Roy Rubino.

"Are you sure this is the right guy?"

The guy nodded. "Positive. Why?"

Caitlyn's mouth had gone a little dry, and she had to clear her throat. "He looks different... Could I get a copy? Or can you email it to me?"

He only briefly hesitated.

"Sure, I can do both, hang on. I'm Dan by the way."

"Caitlyn", she replied on auto-pilot.

Dan took the piece of paper back from her, put it back on his wall, and walked to his computer.

"What's your email address?"

"It's caitlyndharrison@gmail.com," she spelled her full name out for him.

"Aaand, it's sent."

"Thank you so much."

Caitlyn thought.

"What's the name on his license?"

"I'm really sorry, I can't give you his name. I can't lose my job."

"Is it Roy Rubino?" Caitlyn asked.

Dan checked his computer and shook his head. "Different name."

Caitlyn was still trying to wrap her head around the mismatch.

Maybe Rubino had a driver, or this man rented the car for him. But this man wasn't a restaurant employee, at least not one she knew of. Could it have been a random driver? But why would Rubino protect a random driver? And, no, a driver wouldn't use a rental car. It had to be someone Rubino knew. Maybe they had both been in the car? In the video footage she had only seen one driver, no passenger, but what if Rubino had been in the back? Or maybe it had been Rubino driving, but after the crash he had made this man take the car back for him, so he wouldn't be on the hook for the damages?

Caitlyn considered trying to get a better look at the screen, but didn't want Dan to regret he helped her. Besides, if she had to, she could find a different way in. The email he just sent her would give her his IP address.

She checked her phone and looked at the image Dan just emailed.

So, this is what he looks like. Nothing special really.

Dark hair, maybe somewhere in his mid forties.

This is the man who messed up my life.

She had somehow expected him to look meaner.

"Hey, if you find this guy, you will tell me, right?" Dan tapped her lightly on her arm.

"Oh, sorry! Yes, of course. I'll come by, or... I have your email now. Yes. I will let you know, for sure, promise."

"Just don't tell anyone you got it from me. And here, take a business card too," Dan handed her one. "For when you find him, or for when you need a rental car."

Caitlyn grinned. "I will, Dan. And really, thank you."

She hesitated.

"He did look like this picture, right?"

"Yes." Dan replied. "And I'm sure about that too, I always check and refuse to rent when the ID looks fake or doesn't match the owner."

Caitlyn nodded and turned to leave, saying her goodbyes to Dan and waving at her mom in the parking lot, but she turned back around to face Dan when he added. "You know, I think he might have been a local."

"What do you mean?"

"Do you know that building on Jefferson, with that ugly statue in the front of it?"

Caitlyn thought. "Near the courthouse?"

"Exactly. It's the Pittsfield building. But when that man asked me for directions he called it the Pitts. I've only heard locals call it that. And it's not exactly some place a tourist would visit? I mean, who would go to a courthouse on their holiday? Most tourists go to –" Caitlyn wanted to interrupt him but stopped herself. After all his help it would be much nicer to just let him talk.

"–the Museum of science, or the Zoo, or the Grotto." Dan pointed at the row of colorful flyers in a wire display near the window. "You know, all the default places."

Dan chatted away for quite a while, about tourist locations, his job, cars, and somehow finished with his favorite places to eat.

When Caitlyn finally got back in the car, she showed her mom the picture on her phone.

"It's not the man from the restaurant, but I think this could be the man who hit me."

Anne looked at it.

"Doesn't look as evil as I imagined him to look."

"I know, I thought the same."

Anne started the car and headed for the OCD office.

Halfway there, Caitlyn got another email from Dan. The Subject line read: Changed my mind. There was a scan of the driver's license attached.

She smiled and sent an *I owe you* back, then forwarded the picture to Thomas.

I have a copy of his driver's license. See attached.

It's not Roy Rubino!
It's someone called Sal DiNovo. License and address
are fake, but the picture is really him.

She took another good look at the picture herself.

Do the eyes match with what I remember?

They were dark, but because of the low resolution she couldn't be sure if she recognized the man.

Thomas called her back within fifteen minutes,

"Do I want to know how you got all this?"

"Uhhh, I promised I wouldn't tell."

"Right."

But Caitlyn could hear him smile.

"On the plus side I made a new friend who will be happy to rent us a car if we ever need one," Caitlyn said. "He remembered the guy because of the damage he did to the rental. Turns out he skipped there, too, and stuck them with the bill."

"Yeah, that'll do it, that'll make people not forget your face." Thomas paused. "So, it's not Rubino."

"No, it's Sal DiNovo. I think maybe he rented the car for Rubino?"

"Not to get your hopes up, but that name is very likely fake. In case you were planning on looking him up in the phone book later."

Caitlyn indeed had planned to do just that.

"Doesn't matter," Thomas continued, "it's still a lead.

Like you said, he could have rented the car for Rubino, or he could be our driver. Either way, we want to find him and see what he knows."

"Right. Oh, Dan – that's the guy who just, uh, helped me – he thought the man probably was a local because even though he asked for directions, he seemed to know the area well."

Thomas took the phone from his ear to take another good look at the picture.

"I don't recognize him," he said. "It's not someone who I've come in contact with when I was a cop I think, definitely not a regular."

"Hold on." Thomas was silent again while he zoomed in on several parts of the image, then he came back on the line. "It is a really good fake driver's license though."

"Well, good for him."

"And good for us. It means we have another lead."

"What do you mean?"

"There are not too many people who can make them this good. Usually these things can be bought as a package, you know, ID, license, passport. All under the same name. And it's definitely not some high school kid with his home printer, it's got the hologram and everything by the looks of it."

"I didn't think of that," Caitlyn admitted.

"That's why you have me. Maybe you can talk to that DMV friend of yours again? This fake ID business is not something I have easy access to. Not my area. Let me know when you get stuck though and I might know someone I can ask.

You said the rental guy thought he was probably a local? That means the forger probably is too - you don't go six states over to get a fake license for your home state. And these things are usually done in person anyway. You pay a percentage up front and wait a week or so for the guy to get the IDs ready with your name.

Then you go meet in person to take the picture and, from what I know, it only takes a few minutes for the forger to laminate everything. You pay the rest of the amount, end of transaction. And–"

Thomas stopped talking, and Caitlyn heard someone talking in the background.

"Sorry. I have to go, El is working tonight. Four days on, four days off. I've got to throw Brad in the tub and get him to Ellen's parents before my class starts. Let me know when you find out more."

He hung up before Caitlyn could say goodbye.

Caitlyn sat down in the OCD lobby, looking at Sal DiNovo's picture. She went over all the possible options in her mind again, why Sal DiNovo had rented the car, and how Rubino could be involved, but got no closer to any answers.

Caitlyn's mom had disappeared into her office, and Caitlyn knew it would at least be a full hour before she would come out again. She took her laptop out of her backpack, logged on to the Wi-Fi, and turned on her VPN. She prepared a file, generated a long random password and copied it into the field to let 7zip encrypt it. Caitlyn then logged on to IRC.

```
[14:26] $panicked_kernel logged on.
[14:26] $panicked_kernel joined channel.
```

Caitlyn created a temporary private room and waited for others to join.

```
[14:33] <FunkyYep> Hi PK.
[14:33] <Axl3>Any updates?
[14:33] <panicked_kernel> Plenty!
[14:34] <panicked_kernel> Got copy of image of
fake DL. Could be the driver, could be innocent - but
still would like to talk to him. Here's a link to the
zip with all the info I have so far bit.ly/2JGI2i1
pw 2eSCnf6AeS5S&73GAduSy@x2 Any info you can find is
welcome!
[14:34] <panicked_kernel> Does anyone know someone who
could help with image ID?
[14:35] <N0Sc0p3Str1k3r> No problem PK, friend of mine
is in a group that owns a bunch of bots. They borrowed
some facial rec algos from FB and G. Will forward, see
what they come up with. Dedicated Amazon instance.
[14:35] <panicked_kernel> Thank you!!
[14:37] <N0Sc0p3Str1k3r> Any date range? Other params?
[14:37] <panicked_kernel> Age looks to be 40s? Try
30-50 to be safe? No need to go back further than 2007
I think, at least not at first, to speed things up.
Would run my own script, but don't have one to reverse
search/match photo. Tried TinEye, Google etc, obv.
Nothing there.
[14:50] <N0Sc0p3Str1k3r> Sent. Will ping you when

we've got something.
[14:50] <panicked_kernel> Thanks, IOU.
```

[14:50] <N0Sc0p3Str1k3r> I'll remember ;=P
[14:50] <panicked_kernel> Also, does anyone know who
in OR/CA area would be able to make fake licenses like
this?
[14:51] <FunkyYep> I'll look into it, I know some
peoples, will let you know.

Caitlyn hoped the other group would be able to get her a match
and, more importantly, a name. Even though their search would
run much faster her own PC could, she knew it could take a very
long time – if they even were able to find anything.

She shut down her laptop, and slowly crutched up and down
OCD's hallway a few times, testing how much weight she could
tolerate on her leg while letting her mind wander. She looked at
the large wallpaper mural. It consisted of several photos stitched
and faded together to show a slowly transforming landscape.

At the start it was a barren desert, nothing but sand and bright
blue sky. As you walked further into the hallway, you could see
how shallow wells were dug into the soil and how those captured
the rainwater.

How, instead of the soil just eroding away during the rainy
season, the water now got a chance to pool and seep down,
waking up seeds that had been dormant for years.

A few steps ahead there were grasses sprouting inside
the shallow wells, with a cutout showing how the network
of grass roots stabilized the soil and helped it retain
moisture, and how the earthworms and insects returned.
Then the landscape turned even greener. There were grasses,
bushes and small shrubs now, with at the far end of the hallway a
lush green savanna landscape full of trees and wildlife. All fenced
off and now forming a sharp contrast with the bordering patch of
still barren desert.

It reminded Caitlyn that, even if something takes a long time,
it's often well worth the wait and effort.

CHAPTER NINETEEN

Caitlyn was walking through a forest; it was fall and sunlight was sparkling on the fallen leaves. With every step she took she could hear them softly crackle under her feet, the sound and her footsteps dampened by a layer of moss underneath.

Suddenly she was sinking, it felt like she was being sucked into molasses, and the more she moved, the more effort she put in, the stickier and thicker it got.

A man appeared, his dark eyes staring at her.

The scene changed and suddenly she was running through a dark alley, somewhere in the city. Basil leaf logos were graffitied onto the walls in a shade of green that almost chemically glowed in the light of the street lamps. The man was chasing her, the same man, the same eyes, and she wasn't fast enough. There was something wrong with her leg, with her knee. She couldn't run, she couldn't even walk anymore! No matter what she did, she could not escape. The man came closer and closer. She looked over her shoulder right as he lurched at her, got hold of her ankle and pulled her to the ground.

She tried to crawl, tried to kick him with her good leg. But he twisted her foot, her knee, slowly, until one by one all her bones snapped and her whole leg was facing the wrong way. She looked at it, and thought, this can't be good...

Caitlyn woke up and took a few seconds to calm down, half sitting up in bed, propped up on her elbows.

At least it's not the same old nightmare anymore!

Her right knee was throbbing and when she groggily pulled off the duvet, she could see it was swollen and a pocket of fluid had formed under her kneecap.

Well crap, I guess I overdid it yesterday.

Not the best start of the weekend.

She got dressed, checked her email and dragged herself to the kitchen to eat breakfast before she slowly made her way over to Michelle's studio.

"Good morning. Yikes, are you OK? What happened?"

Caitlyn carefully lowered herself on a chair and put her leg up on another. Michelle was working on a portrait of two dogs but stopped painting and was watching her.

"Day one of full weight bearing yesterday," Caitlyn explained.

"I thought you were supposed to take it slow?"

"Don't remind me. I thought I did. Don't worry, this is about all the walking I plan to do for today." Caitlyn looked at the painting. "Commission?"

"Yes, I have to hurry up and finish this, or it won't be dry enough to varnish and ship."

"I won't stay long then, just came by to fill you in. My mom took me to the DMV, and I got a picture of the guy who hit me. It's not who we thought he was."

She held her phone out to Michelle.

"Looks like... just a regular guy."

"I know."

"I've never seen him before."

"Didn't think so. I've got some friends who are looking for him online. The name and address on the license are fake so they're matching images. I'll let you know when there's more."

Caitlyn had never told Michelle about her hacking skills. All Michelle knew was that she was good with computers, and happy to help her fix hers when there was a problem.

Even though she completely trusted Michelle, the fewer people knew, the better. Caitlyn had learned her lesson.

She watched Michelle paint for a while, then crutched to the painting of the two girls. About half of the black and white layer was now covered in color. The whole dress was purple and there was a light-colored plaster wall behind the girls that was slightly crumbling in places. A potted plant with soft coral blossoms stood on the left side in a large dark green stone pot. The orange still stood out a little, and all the human flesh was still in gray tones. Michelle often saved the skin tones for last.

Caitlyn thought it made the girls look eerie and ghost-like. It reminded her of the nightmare, and she shuddered involuntarily.

Anne was singing a Dutch pop song while she was loading clothes into the washing machine. Caitlyn sighed as she waited for the machine's door to close so she could pass.

"Do you have to sing mom?!"

"Yes, my sweet little grumpy head, I do."

Caitlyn grumbled some more, the good mood she had been in after visiting Michelle had quickly evaporated when she crutched back and realized she was back to being pretty much immobile.

She went over to the living room and propped her leg up on a few pillows on the couch, but just as she was settling in her phone dinged. She took it out of the front pocket of her hoodie.

It was a private message from IRC, on the push notification screen only the first few words of the subject line were visible.

FOUND REAL NAME.

She quickly swiped through to the IRC app on her phone and started reading.

Her mood instantly lifted, and she started typing.

```
[11:06] <N0Sc0p3Str1k3r> FOUND REAL NAME.
@panicked_kernel you can download the file with info
here.
[11:06] <panicked_kernel> Thank you so much! You rock!
Superfast!
[11:06] <N0Sc0p3Str1k3r> I know, filter for radius,
OR/CA states only. added WA just in case. Limited date
range helped too. Will let you know if I get more.
[11:07] <panicked_kernel>thankyouthankyouthankyou!
[11:07] <N0Sc0p3Str1k3r>no prob.
```

Caitlyn hopped upstairs uttering a few mild curses under her breath at her protesting knee, and her phone for not being able to unzip encrypted files. A few minutes later her eyes were flying across the screen.

Leonardino - Dino - Augeri, age 42.
DiNovo. Dino. It hadn't been a completely fake name after all.
He was living in Haweville from October 2008 to at least March 2016, which was the date the matched photo had been taken. There was a list of addresses he lived at before 2008, the people he had lived with, and quite a few links to websites that mentioned his name in 2015 because of some award.
He was married to Donna. They had a daughter.

Caitlyn grabbed her notebook out of her desk drawer and copied everything, then opened a new browser tab and one of her software tools. She searched for both Leonardino Augeri and Dino Augeri and clicked through the results. She found a lot of links referencing the same newspaper article from 2015. Caitlyn clicked on a few of them until she found one with the full article and a picture.

Dino had been a chef at Cottura for 7 years until it closed down at the start of 2016. There was an image to go with the article that showed three smiling people in front of a restaurant door when they had won a food award.

She found a few social media accounts, but they were all related to his work, with only a handful of messages posted in total. *Useless.*

He had posted to a few Facebook Groups, selling and buying items, but didn't seem active on there either. Caitlyn grabbed her phone and flipped through her images to the one of the fake driver's license. She held it up next to the screen with the 2015 article. No doubt about it. This was definitely him.

She saved the picture from the article to her computer and went back to the search results. She tried a few more variations of his first and last name, and tried using his initials, but eventually gave up. She couldn't find anything other than what she had already found.

The newspaper article also mentioned the owner of Cottura, Stephen DeBartolo. A quick White pages search showed that he had moved to Boston and opened up a new restaurant there. She wrote all this down in her notebook as well.

She spent over half an hour modifying, and then debugging, one of her Python scripts so it would crawl non-indexed pages and search for variations on Dino's name, as well as the social media usernames she had found for him.

Caitlyn hit enter in the command line window and watched for a while as the script ran. Occasionally a new line of text appeared that let her know the script was still searching and working well, and that X amount of new lines had been added to a csv file on her hard disk that held all the script's findings.

She went back downstairs and put some flour, water, salt and yeast in a glass bowl. She mixed it up and set it to rise near the fireplace. No sourdough today, but something quick and easy.

That evening after dinner she copied and opened the text document with the first of the crawler's results. It had found one account for a local Buy and Sell ad on Craigslist where Dino had sold his motorcycle in 2014. It also found some pretty old information. Apparently somewhere in the late 90s Dino had lived in Tulsa and worked at a burger place.

He was starting to feel like a real person to her, not just some random man that hit her, but someone with a life.

The script continued to run, and she checked the results again the next morning, but it hadn't found anything of real use yet. The latest date it had logged was September 2017, when Dino had logged in to Facebook.

She checked the DMV, but it didn't show any current cars registered to his name. He had owned a silver BMW but had sold it on April 24th, 2017.

She called Thomas.

"Thomas, I've found his real name. It's Leonardino, Dino,

Augeri."

"Great work!" Thomas said.

"Last known address was in Haweville. And there were a lot of links to an article in the Gazette. He used to work as a chef at a restaurant called Cottura, won an award there. I couldn't find anything after September of last year, it's like he completely dropped off the map right before he hit me, although he wasn't very active online before that either."

"OK. I'll ask one of my former colleagues if he can find something. Can you spell his name for me?"

"I'll email you everything later."

"Good." Thomas changed his phone to his other ear. "I followed Rubino again today. He went back to that warehouse. Hang on, my battery is dying, let me call you back when I'm home."

It took almost twenty minutes.

"Sorry about that, where were we?" Thomas asked.

"You went back to the warehouse?"

"Right. There's something fishy going on there. Can't tell what yet. I saw one of my former colleagues walking around, off duty. I have no idea how he's involved. Had to get out. I didn't feel like explaining my presence to him if he saw me."

"Not a friend of yours?"

"No."

"Hey, did you get that new case?" Caitlyn asked. "You mentioned meeting a potential client? I don't want your real job to suffer because of me."

"Oh, yes. I took her on. It's keeping me busy, but don't worry, I've got time. It's a woman who's having me tail her husband. She says he keeps disappearing. She thinks he's having an affair, but before she files for divorce she wants to be sure.

It's a lot of following this guy to his work, the grocery store, and the gym so far. All I've got is a lot of boring pictures. I'm starting to think this guy is not cheating, he doesn't fit the profile, he doesn't act like it. I'll give it a few more days and then I'll either go confront him or tell her she doesn't have anything to worry about."

"Sounds like fun."

"It's paying, so I'm not complaining about a thing."

"Fair point."

"Hey, is our group of Rolling Stones parked somewhere near you?"

"Our what?"

"Rolling Stones. There were five of them."

"Oh, right. Uh, no, I still haven't seen them here, why?"

"They're not at my house either. I haven't seen them in a couple of days."

"That's a good thing, isn't it?"

"That depends on why they stopped following me. Keep an eye out for them, would you?"

CHAPTER TWENTY

Thomas called her back on Sunday. "My friend couldn't find anything else on Dino Augeri, but I did find something about that restaurant he worked at. Guess what?"

"What?"

"Cottura closed, but the space was rented out again and was renamed to Basilico at the end of 2016. The new tenant is Roy Rubino."

"Wow! So do you think they know each other? Maybe Dino stayed and worked for Roy Rubino. Do you think he was driving Rubino, or is covering for him, and they don't want us to find out?"

"Slow down, Harry. Yes, I think Dino Augeri used to work for Rubino, but he doesn't work there anymore. We can't go back to the restaurant to ask if they know where he went, for obvious reasons. I think you're making a good point, though, it's possible that Dino is protecting Rubino - or the other way around. It would explain why they are following us. They're waiting to see if we get too close, so they can stop us before we can link Dino or Rubino or his restaurant to the accident. We don't have enough yet to go to the police and let them handle it from here, so if we can get at least a confirmed location for Dino, or confirm he or Rubino were driving that night that would be good. Especially if it's coming from me I don't think the police will act unless we have a lot more more. And if it's coming from you, I think they are going to ask you questions you'd rather not answer."

"Oh, yeah. Good point," Caitlyn said. "Why wouldn't they listen to you though?"

"Long story. For another time."

Thomas paused and thought.

"Dino Augeri doesn't have a record. All of Rubino's employees have a long rap sheet. So he doesn't quite fit in. But he could be just as dangerous. It could mean he just never got caught. As for Rubino, he is squeaky clean. Suspiciously so. He was arrested a couple of times, but nothing stuck. It's likely Rubino has a lot of money, either himself, or available to him. Once we can prove he is involved, and he finds out, we become a problem. And he's the type of guy that will pay to get his problems fixed. We have to be extremely careful going forward."

"I know. And it's not like I can drop the crutches and run if something happens." Caitlyn shifted uncomfortably in her chair. "So, what's next? We go find Dino and try to confirm who was driving, and who's protecting who?"

"That would be my plan. Find Dino, get proof of who hit you, and hand everything over to the police."

Caitlyn hung up and opened a new tab in her browser. She typed in Cottura and looked at Google Images for a more zoomed out picture than the one she had seen before. She found one that was taken in summer, that showed a dozen small tables outside in front of the large window. The logo on the awning was simple, a white spoon, knife and fork in a black circle. By the looks of it, Rubino had painted everything, changed the logo and the curtains, but it was definitely the same small restaurant.

Caitlyn wrote everything down, then logged on to IRC.

```
[17:09] <Sayid> PK! I've been waiting for you.
[17:10] <Sayid> I have a list of ID makers for you who
can deliver good work. pastebin
[17:10] <panicked_kernel> Thank you! You should have
PM'd me!
[17:10] <Sayid> Welcome.
[17:11] <Axl3> Sayid, great work. PK I looked into the
name for you, couldn't find anything after September
2017 either. Your guy totally vanished.
[17:11] <grep>Do you think it's possible he's in
```

```
WITSEC?
[17:11] <Axl3> Serial killer in hiding, should we
nickname him Dexter?
[17:11] <Sayid>Went to travel the world?
Climb Cilo-Sat?
[17:12] <panicked_kernel> You guys are having way too
much fun with this
[17:12] <Axl3> It's like a digital treasure hunt!
[17:12] <panicked_kernel> Guys, remember. It's all fun
and games, but if I die, there's no respawning.
[17:13] <Axl3> Buzzkill. Be safe though.
One near-death experience is enough.
[17:13] <panicked_kernel> Thanks. Will do.
[17:15] <WatchDog5> joined
[17:15] <WatchDog5> Hey, does anyone have access to
the XBOX game database?
[17:15] <grep> Do you really think they keep that on a
networked system?
[17:16] <WatchDog5> Probably.
[17:16] <grep> Probably not. But let's see you get in.
Reward: 0.5 BTC
[17:16] <WatchDog5> You're on!
```

After dinner, Caitlyn called Fred MacLain.

"Hi Fred. Could you send me the set list for Friday?"

"Sure, no problem. I'll email it to you."

"Thanks!"

"Hey, did you hear about Ayana and Howard?".

"Are they dating?"

"So, you heard. Damn. I thought I had a scoop."

"Didn't hear, guessed it when you guys were at my place."

"Well, they're going steady, as Webber put it.
He caught them in the break room, kissing."

When Caitlyn checked the IRC log the next morning, more
information had come through.

[08:08] <Ax13> PK. Wife address confirmed. Pic here.
Facial rec match confirmed Donna Augeri. Now works at
Nail Salon called Paullished in Camellia, see Donna on
employee page here.

Caitlyn stared at the address. It was in Camellia, about three hours south of Haweville. She opened her notebook and flipped to the list of ID makers and the towns they operated in, that Sayid had given her. She got out a highlighter pen. There was one in Camellia, and one in Mayfield, a bit closer to Haweville. There was another one up north, that Sayid had marked as potentially low quality, which she also highlighted.

She copied the .onion addresses she had gotten for each of the ID guys and pasted them into Tor. She carefully considered what to write; she wanted the appointments to be as soon as possible.

"Want to meet for new papers. Need to get out of
state. Need speed, discretion and good quality results."

She contacted two of the ID makers via PM.

The third had left specific instructions for how to contact him through some complicated system involving a self-destructing email address. No logs, no trace. No second chances if you messed up.

She pinned the tab to leave it open, and spent the next 10 minutes repeatedly refreshing it, but she didn't get the instant reply she had hoped for.

Caitlyn opened her YNAB budgeting software and went over her numbers. She had pretty much ignored her finances over the last couple of months and felt a little guilty, but also good now that she was finally catching up.

She knew she would need quite a bit of money to pay all the ID makers, even if the down payment was only a percentage of the total. She had a few thousand dollars in a cryptocurrency portfolio that had been going up in value for the past years. *I'd rather not use that, but after using my savings account for the splurge when we collected video footage, I think it's time to cash out.*

Caitlyn hoped that, combined with her savings account and what was left of the last month of scholarship money, it would be enough to cover all her expenses for the next couple of months. At least until her leg had recovered to the point where she could start looking for a job.

She stared at the "Medical Debt - Pay Back Mom & Dad" category for a while, trying to suppress the uneasy depressing feeling it caused her. Her parents had always taught her debt was bad. That the only thing you went into debt for was a house, or your health. Maybe a car, if you could pay it back within three years.

She had overheard her mother argue with her dad last night.

"If this had happened in the Netherlands, the insurance company would have covered it, no questions asked. Premiums and deductibles are much lower there too. Should we start thinking about moving back? We're getting older too, you could still get a job there and OCD will let me work anywhere I want. With Jess on those horses all the time, who knows what's going to happen. At least in the Netherlands no one goes bankrupt over a hospital bill. We can't deal with another medical hit like this again."

To Caitlyn's surprise, her dad had agreed with her mom that moving to the Netherlands was a possibility they seriously had to consider. Maybe not now, but in a few years.

Caitlyn wasn't sure if she would move with them. She loved to visit, and she was sure that with a little practice her Dutch would become much better. She would love to see her oma, her mom's mother, much more often. But deep down she was American. And she knew Jess wouldn't want to leave her horses, or Ian, behind either. Caitlyn sighed. She needed to get better. She needed a job. Enough money to find a place of her own and get some independence back, and maybe pay for school.

After dinner she called Thomas.

"I've got an appointment set up with two of the ID makers. The third one is not responding, yet. Could you drive us to Camellia next Sunday? With a pit stop in Mayfield for the first one?"

"We have church on Sunday morning, but I can be home around 11:30 if we go to the early service. I can drive us then?"

"Oh, right, church, I forgot about that. Hang on..."

Caitlyn did some quick calculations.

"It's about two-and-a-half hours to the first guy in Mayfield, and from there another thirty minutes or so to Camellia. So..." she double checked her calendar, "could you maybe do Wednesday? Leave around 10:00 a.m., be home by 18:00 p.m.?"

Thomas checked with Ellen.

"Works for me, as long as I'm home before 19:00 p.m."

"Great, thank you, see you then."

"Hey, do you think you could take a look at my PC? It's been acting up for a while and it is getting very annoying."

"Of course, no problem! How about I come over to have a look at it tomorrow? Hold on."

Caitlyn put her hand over the phone and turned to her sister.

"Jess, are you driving Ian to Haweville tomorrow? Can you drop me off at Thomas'? It's kind of on the way."

Jess looked at Ian. "We came in his car."

"No problem," Ian said.

"Ugh, I hate not being able to drive!" Caitlyn muttered, then took her hand off the phone. "All right, I've got my family Uber dropping me off." She mouthed a 'thank you' to Ian.

Martin had been listening in. "What time are you leaving? They're warning for ice. The main roads will be cleared, but the smaller ones might be slippery if you leave too early. One car crash is enough for me for a lifetime."

"I'll be careful with your girls, Martin," Ian promised.

Caitlyn spent the rest of the evening preparing a happy little arsenal of useful tools and gadgets. She had a varied collection of them in a desk drawer, most of them courtesy of foxx78, and was happy to finally be able to put some of them to use in the real world.

She also packed a few USB flash drives that would help her analyze or troubleshoot Thomas' PC. At the last minute she added a small Bluetooth parabolic microphone that paired with an app on her phone.

Just in case we need to listen in on people talking again.

CHAPTER TWENTY-ONE

Ian and Jessica dropped her off in front of Thomas' house and Caitlyn somewhat carefully made her way to the front door, avoiding the patches of ice where snow had melted and then frozen to the street. Thankfully Thomas' ramp and driveway were clear.

Thomas let her in and asked over his shoulder. "How were the roads?"

"All good. And way better than the sidewalks. Why?"

"It was pretty slippery earlier this morning."

"I've got crutch tips."

Caitlyn held up a crutch to show Thomas the spiky metal underside of the rubber tip. "One of my physical therapists had a whole bucket full. Something about not wanting all her hard work ruined just because it was winter. As if she's the one doing most of it."

"Getting impatient?"

"Yeah." Caitlyn grinned and shrugged.

"But at least I'm kind of walking on two feet again. Hey, how do you deal with ice?"

"I usually switch to studded mountain bike tires."

Caitlyn laughed. "For real?"

"Yes. Wheelchair tires are really just bicycle tires with a push rim. Those mountain bike tires give a lot of traction, even in icy conditions, they're just a little hard on certain floors. And I mean, there are chains you can buy that fit around a regular wheel, or if you're on a real tight budget you can attach a lot of zip ties for extra traction. But it's quicker to just take the summer wheels off, and click the winter wheels on. It's snow that's the real problem."

Caitlyn followed Thomas into his home office. She sat down behind Thomas' desk and noticed a neat row of small, thin notebooks on a shelf next to her.

"Case notes?"

Thomas nodded.

Caitlyn turned on Thomas' computer and waited.

And waited.

"Uh... How long does this normally take?"

"Oh, a while. That is not the problem though, it keeps hanging on me."

"Does it always make this sound?" Caitlyn was already getting slightly annoyed at the loudly blowing fan.

"Yes."

Still nothing was happening

"Do you have a virus scanner?" Caitlyn asked.

"Do you think I have a virus?"

Caitlyn frowned and suppressed a laugh as a Windows logo appeared.

"Maybe... maybe not. How old is this computer?"

"I don't know, not that old, maybe 15 years or so? Why?"

"You know they officially ended support for Windows XP a few years ago, right?"

Thomas shrugged. "It's giving me pop-ups about that, but if I close them again everything keeps working."

When the computer finally chimed its ancient startup sound, Caitlyn scooted to the side and let Thomas show her the problem.

"See, if I turn on my email, and the internet, and then try to use this, everything will freeze. And this video editing software always hangs too."

Caitlyn opened Task Manager.

"Yes. I can see why." She pointed. "Look. Everything is maxed out."

She checked the PC properties and suppressed another laugh. "You know what? If it's OK with you, I will take this one home with me. Can you miss it for a few days?"

Thomas nodded. "If that will fix it. I've got my phone for emails."

"Good. I've got a parts bin. I'll see what I can upgrade, get you some extra RAM at the very least." She checked something else. "You definitely need a bigger hard disk too, this one is almost full. I'm guessing you keep all the surveillance pictures and videos you take on here?"

Thomas nodded.

"Thought so." Caitlyn paused then muttered, half to herself. "Actually, I'm not sure if I've still got parts that will fit this thing, it's pretty old."

"I could buy new parts, if you let me know what I need to get," Thomas offered.

Caitlyn shook her head. "Nah, not worth the money, I'll figure something out. I just have to back up everything first. Promise I won't look at anything confidential."

Caitlyn inserted a USB drive into Thomas' PC, also a drive to backup to, rebooted and ran through the Clonezilla wizard.

Thomas looked at the monitor.

When it turned into a blue screen with a progress bar, Caitlyn leaned back.

"This will take a while."

"It's all magic to me anyway." Thomas laughed and pointed to the phone on his desk.

"Any chance you're this good with phones too? The landline has been acting weird too."

"Weird how?"

"It's not all the time, but sometimes the sound is cutting out, and there is a weird echo."

Caitlyn looked worried.

"For how long? Any clicks on the line?"

Thomas laughed. "Not that long. A few days, I guess. Maybe a week? What, do you think it's bugged?"

Caitlyn nodded and took a small screwdriver set out of her backpack.

"Hey, I'm joking!" Thomas said, as she began taking apart his phone.

"Just making sure... "

"You'll put it back together again?"

"Of course!" Caitlyn said. "These old phones are easy."

There was nothing in the phone, nothing attached to the cable, and from what she could tell, the outlet hadn't been tampered with either.

"See, I told you. No way someone would have gotten into my house without me knowing. I've got a very good alarm system, and a camera at the front door."

Caitlyn still looked worried.

"What?"

"I wouldn't try entering your house either, with all the visible security. But how about the outside of the house?"

Thomas suddenly looked worried too.

"There's a box on that side where everything comes in, you don't think..?"

"Like you said, it's unlikely, but we'd better make sure, considering, you know, Rubino."

A few minutes later Caitlyn and Thomas had put on their coats and slowly went around the outside of the house over the frozen grass.

They stopped and stared at a bunch of wires sticking out haphazardly from a gray metal box.

"That's supposed to be closed," Thomas mumbled, half in shock.

Caitlyn started to pull some wires to the side, trying to get a closer look.

"Don't disconnect anything," Thomas quickly warned her.

"Why not?" Caitlyn asked, surprised. "It's a bug. On your landline. See this thing? That's a transmitter, with a SIM card over there. Here's its power source. Do you... want to keep it?"

"No. But we'd better leave everything just as we found it. Pretend we don't know it's there. This way we can at least control the information we feed to whoever is listening in, while we figure out who put it here. That way we also don't have to worry about someone placing a new bug where we can't find it."

"Do you think it was Rubino?"

"Not sure. It must be recent. That shiny scratch on the metal is definitely new." Thomas hesitated. "There is also a small chance it's local PD – there's an ongoing case regarding my accident. I never know what they'll pull next. But this," Thomas gestured at the jumble of wires. "This was not law enforcement, no way they would do something this big and obvious. So yes, my bet is on Rubino and his team, but we can't rule anything out yet. I didn't think he'd go this far..." He paused and made a face. "El is not going to be happy about this." He blew on his hands, trying to warm his fingers. "Let's go back into the kitchen, I'll make some coffee."

He noticed Caitlyn's face. "You're not a big coffee drinker, are you?"

"Not really, sorry. Tea or water mainly."

"We've got that too."

Ellen was sitting at the table with a mug of coffee and a newspaper that she put to the side when Thomas and Caitlyn came in.

Caitlyn sat down and put the crutches against the wall behind her.

"How's the leg?" asked Ellen, "feel free to put it on a chair or something."

"No need, doing better, thanks! I'm finally allowed to put some weight on it. Started out a bit too eager, but I've been walking more the past few days and my knee is holding up."

Thomas waited for the water in the stove-top kettle to come to a boil, grabbed a tea bag, and poured himself some coffee. He held his coffee mug in one hand and carefully rolled himself to the table with the other.

"El, I don't want to upset you, but the phone has been bugged. I'm working on it. It's likely related to our current case. There is no immediate danger. I just wanted to let you know in case you discuss something about work. I don't want to get you a HIPAA violation."

Ellen pursed her lips and looked as if she was about to say something, then she glanced at Caitlyn who started to apologize, and said. "I don't like this Thomas."

"I know, me neither."

He suddenly looked annoyed and started tugging at something near his side.

"I thought I fixed this, but it keeps coming loose!"

He pulled out the black plastic side guard and fiddled with it. He tried to put it back, then took it out again.

"Better try fixing that again, love." Ellen said, still a little tense, but visibly glad to change the topic. She paused, then laughed out loud. "Remember that time when you were in rehab?"

"Huh?" Thomas was still focusing on trying to get his side guard to stay in place.

Ellen turned to Caitlyn since Thomas was only listening with half an ear.

"When he was in rehab, there were these two Marines who both got injured around the same time, similar levels of injury, both quads - quadriplegics, broken neck, limited arm and hand function, no leg function. Quads have all 4 limbs affected. For paraplegics," she gestured at Thomas, "it's only their legs, two limbs."

Caitlyn nodded that she understood.

"Anyway, these guys were very competitive, and they kept egging each other on about who could do more reps. Or who could transfer faster. Pretty risky at times, but also a great way to motivate each other. So, this one guy claims he's faster, and the other guy disagrees and says he's cheating or, I don't know, something." Ellen waved her hand. "And they got into a fight. But, being new quads, their upper body strength and balance were absolutely terrible, so they took some half-hearted swings at each other, then went looking for objects they could pick up reasonably well. They ended up pulling their chairs apart, trying to whack each other with arm rests and side guards. The PT's had to break them up."

Thomas was now laughing too. "I remember that! They ended up the best of friends by the way."

Ellen looked at her watch and stood up. "I don't want to be rude, but I have to go, my shift starts in an hour."

"Not sure I could do shifts like that," Caitlyn said. "Thomas said you're doing four days on, four days off? I get super cranky when I don't get enough sleep."

"You'd better not choose Emergency Medicine as your specialty then." Ellen smiled. "I mean, I love my work, but the hours can be pretty crazy at times, you really need the four days off." She noticed Caitlyn's expression and quickly added. "You get used to it though. And to all the random people on the street walking up to you for medical advice when you're wearing scrubs."

"Not sure I'd like that either." Caitlyn half smiled back.

"You don't mind me asking about the computer?" Thomas asked, slightly worried.

"Oh, no! Not at all. Really, this is no problem. It's kind of fun actually, figuring out what's wrong. It's... different... I think, from actual work."

"I'm really glad you can help him," Ellen said with another gentle poke at Thomas, "I hope it will improve his mood a little, he gets grumpy each time he has to do something on that PC."

"I just don't like computers." Thomas shrugged. "It's not this particular one."

"Do you want to check if the backup is ready?" Caitlyn asked.

"Sure." Thomas turned his wheelchair.

Caitlyn got her crutches off the floor.

"Hey, have you guys heard about Blues night at Jimmy's?"

"Yes, why?" Ellen asked.

"I'm, uh, actually playing."

Caitlyn blushed, suddenly a little self-conscious. "If you're free this Friday, I can get you both in if you want."

"Do you think I can get in?" Thomas asked.

"Oh, I can always get a few extra people in, even if they're full."

"That's, nice, " Thomas clarified. "but I meant, is it wheelchair accessible?"

"Oh, right. I think so? There are no stairs and I've seen other people in wheelchairs there before. What exactly would make it accessible?"

"A door that's wide enough for me to fit through, no stairs outside or inside, enough room to get to where I need to go, and an accessible toilet. A few curb cuts and a ramp if I'm picky. But if other chair users were there before, it should be fine."

"I could call Darryl if you want, and double check? He owns Jimmy's now."

"I'll risk it. Or I'll call myself later. Didn't want to make a big deal out of it. I just need to be able to get in and out."

Ellen and Thomas looked at each other and shared a moment. She gently bumped a hip against his shoulder. "Hey. We've got connections now, honey. Blues Night."

"I guess we do, El."

"I'll call my parents," Ellen said. "If they can watch Brad on Friday, we're in."

"Great!" Caitlyn smiled.

"Hey," Ellen added, "the blue thing, they still do that?"

Caitlyn nodded.

"Just when we changed to purple scrubs last month.."

When the back up was ready, Caitlyn disconnected her hard disk and put everything back into her backpack.

"My dad will pick me up in.., " she checked her watch, "about fifteen minutes. I'll ask him to put your computer in the car. And I guess I'd better check our own landline for bugs when I get home."

"Good idea." Thomas nodded, then looked worried. "Do you think they got our cell phones too?"

Caitlyn shook her head. "I don't think so. Those are easy to track, but a lot harder to bug unless you clone them, and judging by that thing outside, they're using 90's tech. But here, give me your phone?"

Thomas handed her his cell and Caitlyn installed IncogniDial.

"Here you go. I've got the same app. If you use this to call, everything is encrypted. Can't be bugged, can't be traced. It can do video calls too, but only to other users who have the same app."

Thomas thanked her and put his phone away again.

"Can you remember what we talked about on the phone?"

Caitlyn thought. "How long do you think the bug has been there?"

Thomas frowned, then his eyes widened. "Teddy! He was barking like crazy! I thought there were squirrels. That was..," he counted on his fingers and his face grew darker, "almost two weeks ago."

Caitlyn went over their conversations in her mind.

"So, at the end of February. Yes, I remember we spoke on the phone right before I switched PT's. That must have been how they knew I was there!"

Thomas nodded.

"Then the day after, when you saw them outside of your house."

"That was from my cell," Thomas said. "But I called you that evening from the landline that my cop buddy had warned me about Rubino. So that means he knows we're watching him. Damn."

"You had me check my windows then, to see if they were watching my house as well." Caitlyn remembered. "And he must have heard I would be at your place the next day, and that we planned to follow them back. But why would he let us do that?"

"Maybe he hadn't listened yet? We left pretty early," Thomas said. "I called you from the car on my way back from following them to that warehouse the first time. Then from home... I'm pretty sure we were talking about Dino's fake driver's license. So we have to assume he knows we know about Dino, too. This is not good."

"At least we didn't know his real name yet then," Caitlyn said, "Or wait, did I call your cell or your landline?"

Thomas thought. "I think that first part was in the car, and then my battery died."

"Right, I remember. I think we didn't really say anything important after that though."

They were both silent for a while, thinking.

"I think that's it," Thomas said. "You still haven't noticed anyone following yo, right? No one near your house?"

Caitlyn shook her head. "No. But with everything we talked about they probably knew where I was half the time. I didn't see them anywhere, but I've only really been looking when I was at home."

Thomas nodded.

"At least they still don't know where you live."

CHAPTER TWENTY-TWO

"Oh, good you're here!" Fred, half disappearing inside a very heavy winter coat, popped up next to their car almost before Martin had shut off the engine. Caitlyn wondered how long he had been waiting for them outside.

"Hi Fred", she pushed her car door open and shoved her crutches in his hands. "Could you hold these while I put my coat on?"

"Sure, sure. Did you get the playlist?"

Caitlyn was relieved to find the parking lot completely free of ice. Her dad had to drive really slow at times on their way there. She balanced on almost two legs as she zipped up her coat and swung a backpack over one shoulder. She took the crutches from Fred again and wrestled with her own thick coat and the arm cuffs.

"Thanks. I can't wait to get rid of these things. And yes, I did. Don't worry Fred, I know I had a bit of a concussion, but I haven't forgotten how to play. I thought we were early?"

"Didn't mean to imply anything,Caitlyn, just --. There's a lady friend who might be coming tonight that I'm hoping to impress. And it won't be much of a show without a decent piano player. I'm happy you're here."

Caitlyn laughed.

They entered Jimmy's, and Caitlyn relaxed at the welcome warm embrace that always was. The music, the people. It always felt like coming home.

She looked around and spotted the others at one of the large tables. The fact that most of the people there wore some shade of blue always made it a little harder to find your friends.

"Hey, Lucy! Oh wow, you cut a lot off your hair!"

"Yes, much better." Lucy ran a hand through her hair.

Last time Caitlyn saw her it had reached halfway down her back. Now it was barely over her shoulders.

Caitlyn angled her head. "I like it. It suits you."

"Thanks. Oh, before I forget, my mom made dumplings. They're in the break room."

"Niiice!" Caitlyn smiled. "The beef ones?"

Lucy nodded.

Martin ordered appetizers, and Caitlyn kept an eye on the door in case Thomas and Ellen arrived.

Jimmy's had started out as a small bar and grill, but over the years – with it gaining in popularity – they had completely remodeled and expanded to where they now could seat about one hundred fifty people each night.

Guests could choose to sit at the stained oak bar, or one of the tables opposite it. There were fairy lights covering the ceiling, and the inside was pretty bright, yet warmly lit. There were large windows that looked out over the outdoor terrace, which although it was not in use at the moment, had wood burning in the fire baskets in each corner, to provide some warmth for any smokers. A small wooden fence that was covered in ivy partially closed off the deck and obscured half the parking lot from view.

To the left of the bar, in the corner, was the stage with a brown wooden baby grand, drums, guitar and violin stands, and a row of microphones. A door to the side led to the back, through a hallway past the kitchen, into a cozy break room for staff and musicians. It had lockers where they could store their belongings and some of the more portable instruments.

There was a dressing room area with a shower, and there were a few couches to relax on.

More and more people were trickling in. Darryl gave a short talk welcoming his guests and reminded them that a big portion of tonight's proceeds and tips would directly benefit the local Middle School. Caitlyn was very familiar with his standard welcome talk by now, and tuned out a little until he introduced the Blues Crew. Caitlyn trailed a little behind, moving a little slower than the rest of the crew, and crutched up the few steps that led up to the stage. She had been walking much better this past week, but stairs were still tricky with a knee that didn't bend all the way. She sat down behind the piano and quickly checked that the microphone was at a comfortable height. She knew most of the songs by heart, but liked having the sheet music or chords in front of her just in case, so she always brought her iPad. She taped a print out of the set list to the top of the piano and waited for Fred's signal.

They always started with Cross Roads blues by Robert Johnson, which was an instant warm up for Caitlyn with its fast riffs and steady left-hand rhythm. She had played through most of the songs at home, on her trusty old Yamaha and had quickly found that she couldn't quite bend her knee far enough yet to use the pedal with her right foot. It was awkward to have to use the pedal with her left, almost uncomfortable, like writing with the wrong hand. They moved on to something slightly less bluesy. Caitlyn laughed as Howard, who never cared if a song originally had harmonica parts or not, improvised a little, and clearly messed up a few notes. Halfway a Tab Benoit song Thomas and Ellen came in. Thomas briefly held up a hand to greet her and apologetically motioned at his watch and at Ellen - still in her dark purple hospital scrubs. Caitlyn quickly waved at them and pointed to the table where they could sit down, then turned her head towards the microphone again. She often sang along during the refrains, providing backup vocals for Ayana, together with Fred and Webber. She had a pretty decent voice but was perfectly happy - and much more comfortable - out of the spotlight and safely hidden away behind the keys.

After Ayana's rendition of Me and Bobby McGee, Darryl came back on stage.

"Do we have any guests who want to relieve some of our band members? All instruments, songs and genres are welcome! Come one, you can earn a small discount on your bill!"

Caitlyn made room for a man who offered to play and sing a few Beatles songs on piano, and followed Ayana off the stage, while most of the rest of the band was jamming along with Let it be.

She joined Thomas, Ellen and her parents.

"Wow, you are really good!" Ellen said as she scooted her chair aside to make room for the one Caitlyn had pulled up. "I didn't know you also sang."

"Thanks! A little bit." Caitlyn sat down next to her.

"So sorry we couldn't make it on time," Ellen added, "my shift ran late."

"Don't worry about it, I'm glad you're here."

"Thank god it's warm in here. I was a bit worried when I couldn't go home to change."

"Could have called me, El, I would have picked you out something?" Thomas said.

"Mister who pretty much wears the same dark blue jeans with a T-shirt or a sweater every day?"

"Hey, at least I'm wearing blue, and it's not just the jeans." Thomas rolled back and lifted up his pant legs a bit to show them the vibrant blue socks he was wearing. Caitlyn laughed out loud and motioned to Darryl. "Free drink for him later, please!"

She turned to Ayana.

"So, you and Howard?"

Ayana nodded with a wide smile and a slight blush.

"Congrats. I'm happy for you guys! Oh, no! Man, I just sat down!"

Caitlyn took a few gulps of her water and shoved a quick handful of mini pretzels in her mouth.

"Sorry, looks like I've gotta go back up. The guest player is leaving." Caitlyn didn't like how everyone was staring at her, she still hadn't gotten used to it, and the awkward moment where the Beatles man tried to help her up the steps by grabbing her arm only made it worse. *Is this what it's like for Thomas, when people don't ask first and just start yanking you around?*

They slowed it down with a Keb' Mo' song, then Ayana gave Noah some room for his violin and vocals solo in "The Devil Went Down to Georgia". Caitlyn was having a blast. She loved the rapid fiddle playing, and Noah always impressed her. It had been such a long time since she played with the Blues Crew, but it was effortless and easy to slip back into it. She could look at Webber and time the final chords with him, she loved how Lucy always went all-in and played a passionate and solid, steady beat.

Caitlyn always became somewhat oblivious to what was going on around her when she was really getting into playing music, but at the beginning notes of "I've Got Friends in Low Places" she noticed Thomas perk up and after a while he was drumming along with his fingertips on the table. But the next time she glanced his way, he had stopped, and was looking at something very intently. Caitlyn followed his gaze and almost stopped playing. The five men from the restaurant. Their Rolling Stones, as Thomas had called them. There they were. Standing out like a sore thumb in a sea of people dressed in blue. She snapped her attention back to Thomas and pointed them out with her eyes. He gave her a slight nod. At the end of the song, Caitlyn caught Fred's attention and motioned that she needed a break for her leg.

Fred nodded and turned to the crowd. "Do we have any other piano players in the room? Someone still waiting for their dinner to arrive, maybe? As you can see our own is slightly injured and needs to take a short break." Caitlyn felt a bit uncomfortable, she hadn't intended it to be such a public announcement. But it didn't matter, The Restaurant Five had no doubt already noticed her as soon as they walked in, and she needed to talk to Thomas.

She got back to the table, where her mom looked at her slightly worried.

"Are you OK, honey?"

"What? Yes, I'm fine mom. I just wanted to give that Beatles guy another shot. People seemed to like him. Also, I need a bathroom break. Thomas, did I show you where the accessible restroom is? Here, I'll take you."

Without waiting for Thomas' reply, she grabbed her backpack and crutched off. Thomas followed her through the door into the hallway behind the stage.

"How the hell did they find us?! We never spoke on the phone about this, did we?" Caitlyn asked as soon as the door closed.

"No. I don't think we did. And I don't know how they found us, but I don't like it," Thomas said.

"What do you think they want? I mean, they can't really do much with all these other people around, can they?"

Thomas opened the door a crack and peered out. "Whatever it is, they're definitely looking for us, they're coming this way."

CHAPTER TWENTY-THREE

"Quick, follow me. There really is an accessible toilet." Caitlyn led Thomas through the hallway and swung the door open. She noticed Thomas' look at the sign on the door that read "Changing Room".

"It was the changing room before the break room was built. I guess they never changed the sign."

Thomas followed her in, and she closed the door behind them.

At first all they could hear was the muffled music. Then there were voices walking past them.

"Is that them?" she whispered to Thomas.

He gestured for her to be quiet and leaned his ear against the door.

Caitlyn could hear them opening doors. First the male bathroom, then the break room. She almost grinned as she heard Zach, the chef, loudly tell them off. "Sir, please get out of my kitchen".

The voices came back and stopped in the hallway a few feet away from them.

"Wait Eduard! We can't just storm into the ladies'. We don't want to cause a scene. What do you think will happen when all those girls start screaming at us? Besides, that crippled cop was with her, they wouldn't have gone in there."

Thomas narrowed his eyes.

"So, where did they go?"

"How should I know? Just go look for her!"

Vinny's voice was uncomfortably close to their door, and

Caitlyn held her breath.

One of the other voices turned back in the direction of the kitchen, Caitlyn could hear him talking as he opened the emergency exit. Judging from the slight Hispanic accent she figured it was Jesus.

A voice she guessed was Oscar's came from farther away. It was lower than the others.

"So how the hell do you figure we can follow that chick if we don't even know which car is hers?"

Vinny replied. "We wait for her to leave here, and then we follow. Are you really this stupid?"

Eduard returned and started arguing with Vinny until Jesus came back.

"Hey. Stop that. Remember, we don't want to attract too much attention. Let's go back inside and wait there. They can't have left, she's playing."

When all the men had gone, Caitlyn turned to Thomas.

"So, they're going to follow me home."

"Sounds like it. That means at the moment they still don't know where you live. I checked my security footage by the way, but the side of my house is not covered, so I can't confirm it was them who placed the bug."

Caitlyn thought for a moment and frowned.

"Did you notice them following you on the way here?"

"No." Thomas admitted. "But it was pretty hectic, I was running late myself. I had to get Brad to El's parents, and then pick her up at the hospital. But, no, I didn't see them."

"They said they wanted to know which car was mine, not where I lived. Do you think they'll put a tracker on my car? Do you think they could have put one on yours?"

Thomas' eyes got a little wider. "Remind me to check for one."

Caitlyn was silent for a while.

"Any chance of them wanting to hurt me?"

"Always. But not tonight. At least I don't think so, they're not acting like they planned anything other than following you.

What are you smiling about?"

Caitlyn's mind was racing now and her eyes had started to twinkle with mischief.

"I've got this."

Caitlyn put the crutches against the wall. She limped to the toilet, sat down on the lid, and rummaged through her backpack. She took out a small black box. It was about half the size of a deck of cards and half as thin. The antenna on the side was flush with the box, but Caitlyn turned it so it stuck up at a ninety-degree angle.

"Cellphone and Wi-Fi signal jammer."

"I don't want to know."

"Did you park in the handicap spot?"

Thomas nodded.

"I'll go check for a tracker on your car. I only heard four voices in the hallway, you?"

Thomas nodded again.

"Better check that the fifth one didn't find my parent's car then. We need a diversion so they won't spot me. Let me talk to Darryl. He'll help stall them. He's done it before with drunk creeps. Or, wait, no. You go back in, explain to Darryl there's a *guy problem*. Tell him I'm doing the Wi-Fi thing again, he'll understand.

He's a fan, actually. He's always complaining that people are way too preoccupied with their phones too, that they're not talking to each other, or really listening to the music. Oh, and try not to show that thing to my parents, if you could. They made me throw out the first one I made. I guess I tested it at home a few too many times."

Thomas nodded slowly.

"You can pretend you're getting your free drink or something, so the Restaurant Five won't think it's suspicious that you're talking to Darryl."

"The Restaurant Five?"

Caitlyn shrugged sheepishly. "That's what I've been calling your Rolling Stones in my mind. Give me a few minutes, I need to get my coat from the break room. Then press this button. Press once to block Wi-Fi, but don't press twice or you will block all cell signals too, OK? Not sure if Darryl would be happy about that."

Thomas was staring at her and Caitlyn frowned.

"Once for Wi-Fi, twice for Wi-Fi and cellphone signals. Three times to turn it off." She repeated. "It's a three-way toggle."

"Got it, got it. That's not it. I -. Good plan. Let's do it."

Thomas went back in and Ellen raised her eyebrows at him from across the room.

"Work," Thomas gestured, his face still a little grim.

He wheeled up to the bar, purposely not looking at the five men as they unsuccessfully tried to hide and watch him from a few tables away.

Darryl leaned over the bar and looked down at him.

"Caitlyn's friend, you're wearing blue she said? I'm afraid jeans don't count."

"Socks," Thomas replied, slightly distracted.

"Good enough, man. Just checking. What can I get you?"

Ten minutes later Thomas was back at the table with a drink. He had the black box in his lap under the table and pressed the button. A small red light on top of the box turned on and stayed lit. At first he wasn't sure if it did anything, but it took only a few moments before he could see some people waving their phones around, as if holding them up one extra foot would somehow get them a better internet signal. Soon people started muttering, talking with people at other tables, looking at their phones. Distracted.

Darryl gave Thomas a brief smile and hopped onto the stage at the end of "Don't Stop Believin'".

"Apologies for the inconvenience, we seem to be having a few issues with our internet connection at the moment. We're rebooting the router, it should be fixed shortly."

Darryl pointed to a blackboard on one of the walls. "In the meantime, as you can see, we have some house rules. Most of you should be familiar with this one by now, but for those who hadn't noticed yet, please note rule number seven: if you wear blue on Blues Night you get a free drink."

Darryl pointed at the five men who, to Thomas' amusement, did not at all like to have all the attention turned on them. "These guys obviously are new here. First, let's give them a warm welcome."

A handful of regulars raised their glasses.

"Now about those free drinks, did you know we have some blue T-shirts for sale? Tonight's proceeds will go to MacCowan Middle School."

One of the restaurant five reluctantly drew his wallet.

As soon as Thomas went back inside, Caitlyn got her coat from the break room, then went out through the emergency exit and crutched across the parking lot. She shivered as the bitter cold hit her face and hoped this wouldn't take too long. It was snowing; the ground was slowly but surely turning white. In a flash she was back inside her car, looking out onto the street, at the snow floating down. Stuck...

She shook her head and got rid of the image.

She stopped near Thomas' car and looked back over her shoulder. She was still very much in sight of the diner, and even with the wooden fence she would surely be seen by whoever decided to look her way. And, with the crutches, even from a distance they would immediately know who she was.

Caitlyn leaned the crutches against Thomas' car and awkwardly tried to crouch down, then gave up. She took off her coat, and sat down on top of it with her bad leg stretched out straight. If the phone bug on the outside of Thomas' house was anything to go by, any car bug they had placed would hopefully be just as easy to spot. She used the flashlight on her cellphone and ran her hand along the lower edges of the car. It took a while, but she finally found it, stuck to a wheel well. She wiped her hands, took a picture, then dropped it on the ground next to Thomas' car.

Caitlyn pulled herself up on a door handle and scanned the

parking lot. There were well over a hundred parked cars there, but she quickly found the other car she had hoped to check out. The little red, very beat up Ford from the picture Thomas had texted her, parked in the second row.

She tried to crutch to it as casually as she could. She hoped Darryl would be able to keep the Restaurant Five occupied long enough - hoped with all her might they wouldn't see her. If they did spot her lurking around their car, she would have no plausible explanation.

Caitlyn wasn't completely alone in the parking lot either, in the distance she saw a couple get out of their car. But they were well out of earshot and hopefully gone by the time she would do what she was planning to do.

It was an old model Ford, which meant there was no modern alarm system. She wished she could quickly ping Axl3 to ask him for help. She needed to get the door open, and he'd know exactly how to get in. Maybe she could find some metal, something long and thin, to shimmy the lock? She wished she had lock picks. She wished she had studied and practiced lock picking. Or practiced breaking into cars with coat hangers. Should she break a window with a crutch? But no, that would be a dead giveaway that someone had messed with their car. They were a bit dense, but not to that extent. To her surprise and relief, she lucked out. The passenger side door was unlocked.

Caitlyn put her crutches against the side of the car again, carefully opened the door and cursed under her breath when a very bright dome light flickered on. She very quickly closed the door again, and tried to calm her breath, glanced back over her shoulder and froze.

There was someone standing outside the diner, looking her way. But at the flame of a lighter, followed by the orange glow of the cigarette, she relaxed a little again.

Still, they would surely see her silhouetted against the dome light. Would they be able to tell which car she had opened from this distance? She had to risk it.

Caitlyn ducked into the car again, half laying half leaning over the seats to open the lock on the driver's side door. When she pushed herself back up, she noticed something on the dashboard.

DEAN INVESTIGATIONS, in bold, black letters.

She reached out to pick Thomas' businesscard up, then changed her mind.

Better leave that there, so they don't know anyone was in here.

She limped over to the driver's side door, opened it, and pulled the latch to pop the hood. After that, it only took a few minutes before she was done.

But when she turned to go back, she saw she had left a perfectly clear trail of crutch and limping uneven shoe prints, leading straight from Thomas' car to the red Ford.

Shit!

She couldn't think of any way to quickly fix it, and hoped the snow would cover her tracks by the time the Restaurant Five decided to leave.

Finally, she checked her parent's car, but she didn't find anything there. She quickly crutched back to the diner and slid back in through the emergency exit.

When she had stopped shivering and washed her hands in the break room, she joined Thomas, Ellen and her parents.

"Where did you go?" her mom asked.

"Needed some air. I took some painkillers before we left because I knew I'd be playing for a few hours, and they didn't settle well. But I'm fine again, all good."

She put her bag on the floor next to Thomas and he handed the black box back to her under the table.

She pressed the button until it switched off and gave Darryl a smile and a thumbs up.

Darryl took the microphone again, and while he was telling everyone the Wi-Fi was back in working order, Thomas bent closer to Caitlyn.

"Anything?"

"GPS tracker on your car." Caitlyn whispered back and showed him the picture she took on her phone.

"Well, that explains why they stopped following me." Thomas

commented. "Looks like a cheap one. I usually order the same on Amazon."

"I left it on the floor, so I hope they will think it just fell off. Nothing on my parent's car." She smiled with mischief. "But I also got something else."

She opened her backpack a little and showed Thomas what was inside.

"One of their spark plugs, and some random engine hose that I'm pretty sure they'll miss. Don't worry, they're not going anywhere tonight."

Thomas still looked angry and a little worried. "I should have checked for trackers. I will be more careful in the future." But then he relaxed a little. "I still don't want to know, but did you say you made this black box thing yourself?"

"Not my design, but yes. You can keep this one, it might come in handy again." Caitlyn took the box out of her bag again. "I've got a few versions at home."

Caitlyn went back on stage and got a small applause when Fred reintroduced her. She occasionally glanced at the Restaurant Five. Their behavior hadn't changed. In fact, they seemed more relaxed now that they could see both Caitlyn and Thomas again. She hoped this meant they hadn't spotted her outside. She also noticed the small stack of blue Jimmy's T-shirts on their table, and smiled.

Go Darryl!

They played for another hour.

After the last song Caitlyn joined the rest of the Blues Crew for the applause and a final bow. She felt tired but wired, and thoroughly happy.

Caitlyn invited Thomas and Ellen to join her, her parents and the rest of the musicians backstage in the break room.

Fred counted the total in the tip jar.

"Great result guys, MacCowan Middle School will be happy."

Then he left with a woman with long brown hair that Caitlyn hadn't seen before.

Must be his date, she thought. *I guess she liked us.*

Darryl served everyone drinks, and Lucy handed out disposable chopsticks and paper plates with dumplings.

"Zach warmed them up." Lucy said.

"Mmm, these are good!" Thomas said. "What's in these?"

"Beef, oil, onion, soy sauce. Probably something loaded with MSG?" Lucy said. "I'm not really sure, my mom makes them."

Thomas put Ellen's dumpling in his mouth as well, and declined the drink Darryl offered him.

He noticed the tattoo on Darryl's forearm.

"French foreign legion?"

Darryl paused.

"1980's. You?"

"Marines. Up to 2008."

"Thought you were a cop."

"I was, after. Did Caitlyn tell you?"

"No, you look like one."

"Hah. I'm a P.I. now." Thomas reached into his pocket and handed Darryl a business card.

Caitlyn smiled as she saw Darryl sit down next to Thomas a little later, talking his ear off. She thought those two would hit it off.

Caitlyn was talking with Ellen and Ayana, until Thomas gave Ellen a brief almost imperceptible nod with his head.

"Right." Ellen said as she stood up. "Thank you very much for inviting us. I've had a great evening. But I also have an early start tomorrow, so we'd better be going."

"Good idea," Caitlyn said. "Let me get my parents and I'll walk you guys out."

"Oh, thank god," Caitlyn said as she stepped outside, "it's still snowing."

She was almost shocked by the amount that had fallen in such a short time. But thankful that it had definitely covered all her tracks.

Caitlyn's parents shot her a somewhat confused look.

"Uh, I mean, I thought of how happy Sophie will be," she quickly said. "I'm pretty sure there will be an amazing collection of snowmen on both our lawns by the end of tomorrow."

She couldn't exactly explain the real reason for her relief, but it seemed to satisfy her parents.

"Trails!" Caitlyn mouthed to Thomas, when they said goodbye.

Caitlyn followed her parents to the car. The snow dampened and muffled all sounds, and she enjoyed the stark difference between the noise inside the bar, and the quietness outside.

When they drove away, Caitlyn caught a glimpse of some very agitated men standing next to a tiny dented red car.

CHAPTER TWENTY-FOUR

"I'm sorry to say your PC was beyond repair." Caitlyn waved a hand at the PC on Thomas' kitchen table. "So," she put her backpack down and took out a laptop, "here is your free upgrade."

Thomas started to object, but Caitlyn stopped him.

"I knew you would do this, which is why I didn't tell you. It's an old laptop of mine. It's not top-of-the-line or anything, but it definitely beats what you had."

"That's why I'm paying."

"Nope. I've already taken up way more of your time than I planned to. And I don't think this is making me even either. I'm having a lot of fun figuring out who hit me, except for the part where, you know, it's actually my life and there's a bunch of creeps following us around." Caitlyn paused. "I'm... less jumpy than I was. Well, except for this morning when the snow slid off the roof. That scared me half to death. But it feels good to have some control again. It helps."

Thomas nodded. "Taking control back always does. How are you sleeping?"

Caitlyn gave a noncommittal shrug. "A little better, but I keep crashing, over and over again. Or a dream starts out normal, but then something goes wrong and I'm suddenly back in that car. But like I said, it's getting better, and I'm less jumpy. It's mainly very annoying now."

"Annoying is better than scary," Thomas agreed.

"Remember, calm people live. Scared turns to annoyed, and then the annoyance slowly lessens until you're calm, mostly. And dreams are weird anyway. Like you say, something always goes wrong. I often suddenly collapse, or I'm walking and people start carrying me, or pick me up for no reason. It's weird waking up like that. Those few seconds where you're not fully awake yet and it's like you can just jump out of bed..."

They both were silent for a few seconds, then Caitlyn pushed the laptop a little closer to Thomas. "You may have to get a new battery in a few years, but it's good for now. I transferred the backup we made. I didn't look at any of it by the way."

"Thank you. I appreciate it," Thomas said.

"What should I do with my old one?"

"I don't know, maybe donate it to a museum?"

Thomas actually looked a little hurt.

"Sorry. I mean, if you want to, I could install some Linux version for you. But some of the software you use might not be compatible. You could also turn it into a media server and hook it up to your TV? Or save it for Bradley, so he can play some old DOS or Commodore games with an emulator."

Thomas looked at his old PC a little dazed.

"That all sounds... way too complicated."

"Honestly, I would just completely destroy the hard disk and throw the whole thing out or put it on Craigslist for free pickup or something."

"What do you mean, completely destroy?"

"Overwrite it a few dozen times. Or get a hammer or a drill. Take it apart and scratch it up real good. You don't want any information about old cases landing in the wrong hands."

Thomas looked horrified at the thought.

"I can tell you hadn't considered that. Man, it's good you have me. It's way too easy to recover data from old hard disks if you simply delete the files."

"Right. Well. Now I know. Thank you."

"No problem. And we should take the laptop with us."

Caitlyn slid it back into her backpack. "I've put some extra software on it that will come in handy today."

"I'm not hearing any of this."

Thomas slightly turned and froze with a grimace.

"You OK?"

"It's the weather. It's freezing, then it's warmer, then it's freezing again. Body's acting up. And all this half-melted snow makes it feel like I'm wheeling through a Slushy." Thomas grumbled. Then he admonished himself. "Don't worry about it. Come on, let's go."

Thomas got in the car and typed the address into the GPS. It was Saint Patrick's Day, and traffic moved slowly as they turned onto I-5.

Their route followed the Willamette River and the majority of it consisted of a rolling, hilly landscape with frosty farmland on both sides. After two hours of the same thing it was getting monotonous. They crossed a few bridges, passed a golf course, a huge parking lot at a Best Buy, and a scrap yard full of rusty old cars.

Somewhere near Eastfall, traffic slowed down even more, and they barely crept forward for the next half an hour. Caitlyn looked at the airplanes taking off and landing at the airport in the distance. Thomas took an exit to stop for gas and escape the slow pace for a while.

An attendant filled up their car and Caitlyn got out.

"I'm paying, and I'm getting snacks, what do you want? Wait, are you getting out too?"

Thomas had pushed his seat all the way back.

"No, just stretching. Chips or a salad, maybe some juice, thanks."

Caitlyn went inside the gas station.

The girl behind the counter looked at her disapprovingly when she asked for a plastic bag to put the food and drinks in, but nodded, friendlier, when Caitlyn explained she couldn't carry things while on crutches.

She gathered a few items and waited in line to pay, then got back into the car and handed Thomas a bottle of orange juice and a prepackaged salad with olives, pasta, chicken and rocket salad.

"Hope you like Italian."

Thomas took a pill bottle out of his bag and washed one down with the juice.

"You OK?

"Fine. I hate winter. Stop asking."

He started the car and checked the GPS.

"We should be in Mayfield in forty minutes, it says. Let's see if we can make it in under 2 hours, depending on which direction most of this traffic is going."

They walked into the 24hour photo shop, the first location on their list, and Caitlyn crutched up to the kid behind the counter. He was wearing a bright green shirt and hat, and looked like he hadn't quite gotten through puberty yet.

"Happy Saint Patrick's Day! How can I help you?"

"Thanks. Uh, are you Sam?"

"Sam I am." He laughed at his own play on words.

"Oh... Kay. We were told to meet you here."

"Ah, for the... thing."

"Yes."

"Follow me."

Caitlyn frowned.

Sam walked to a door and Caitlyn and Thomas followed him, then stopped. Caitlyn turned to Thomas who took one look at the staircase leading down and shrugged. "I'm happy to wait here, if you're OK to go alone?"

Caitlyn nodded. "He seems harmless."

Sam had come back up, and for a moment seemed confused that no one had followed him.

"Here, take these." Caitlyn handed him her crutches and quickly hopped down the stairs using the handrails.

Sam looked at her over his shoulder. "Is he coming too?"

"No."

Caitlyn's doubts grew when she saw the basement.

It was cluttered, and seemed to be mainly used for storage. Sam handed her the crutches back, then showed her to a corner where he had set up a white heavy cloth backdrop that needed ironing, some lighting equipment and a point-and-shoot camera on a tripod. There was a small cleared space on a desk, in between stacks of paper, where a laptop and what Caitlyn recognized as a budget model scrapbooking laminating machine stood.

Just to be sure, she asked, "Is this it?"

Sam nodded and flashed her a wide smile.

"This is it. I mainly do fake IDs for high school and college students, but I'm pretty sure I can do licenses too." Caitlyn stared at him, and Sam continued. "You know, take a picture over there, edit it in Photoshop. I can make you really pretty..." Caitlyn was sure he didn't know how insulting that sounded. "... then stick it in a template, print it out upstairs, come back down to laminate and... uh... pay." He gave her a bright smile. "I'm saving for college."

Caitlyn didn't smile back. She was starting to feel sorry for him. This was just an overoptimistic, overconfident kid trying to finance the future he had planned for himself. Not a lot of kids his age were this illegally proactive.

"Do you print everything upstairs?" she asked.

"Uh-huh, my boss is never in, and my colleague is happy to look the other was for a ten percent cut."

Caitlyn had heard enough. "You know what, thanks, but I changed my mind."

Sam's face dropped. "Oh man, are you sure? I mean, I was really excited to try an Oregon license."

"I'm looking for one that can pass inspection. Up close. Not from a distance."

Sam paused, then shrugged and smiled again.

"Right. Too bad. Can I keep the down payment?"

"No. And a quick word of advice," Caitlyn added as she followed him back up the stairs. "You may want to screen your customers. Run some kind of background check before you lead them down here." *Before you tell them every single detail of your operation,* she added in her mind. "For all you know, we could have been cops."

Sam stopped walking and suddenly looked very anxious.

"You're not though, right??"

Caitlyn stopped too, slightly out of breath from hopping up the stairs. "I'm not. Don't worry. Just... If you get caught, college is going to be a hell of a lot harder to get into. Trust me."

At the top of the stairs Sam thanked her and quickly walked back to his spot behind the counter, where a line of customers was waiting for him. Caitlyn scanned the store looking for Thomas. She didn't see him. She walked around for a while, starting to worry, then smiled with relief as she saw him roll up.

"Bathroom." Thomas explained. "And?"

"Remember when you said it was not done by a high school kid on his home printer? Yeah, this is definitely that high school kid, except one with access to the right equipment. Not who we're looking for." Caitlyn filled Thomas in as they walked back to the car. "Completely wrong setup, except for the high-quality printer, and he's not nearly paranoid enough."

Caitlyn waited next to the car while Thomas got in and started dragging wheelchair parts inside. She knew it was quicker and easier for him if he didn't have to be careful not to hit her in the head with anything. But the longer she stood there, the more the cold got to her. She looked through the window at Thomas who sat in the driver's seat, not moving, with his body tense and his eyes closed. The seat of his chair was still outside.

Caitlyn opened the door and hesitated.

"Uh, I know I was not going to ask anymore, but are you OK?"

"Give me a minute."

"Can I do anything?"

Thomas briefly shook his head.

After a moment he visibly relaxed and let out a long breath.

Caitlyn looked at him, still concerned.

Thomas ignored her, picked up his seat and carefully put it inside.

Caitlyn got in and tried a smile. "Maybe you should move to Miami?"

Thomas didn't laugh at her attempt to lighten the mood. "I left

Florida when I was sixteen, and I'm not ever going back unless I have no other choice. This is not your problem, just stop asking and let me deal with it." He jabbed at the GPS, trying to get to the right screen.

"Sorry." Thomas let out another sigh. "Didn't mean to snap at you like that."

He hesitated, then added. "If you could get the chair in and out? That would help."

Caitlyn nodded.

Thomas turned to the GPS again, his finger hovering over the screen. "Where are we going next?"

"Right. Hang on. I wrote down the address."

Caitlyn started digging through her bag, then in frustration tipped the whole thing over in her lap. "What is it with always losing stuff in bags?!"

Thomas stared at her.

"What?" Caitlyn asked, slightly distracted.

Thomas motioned at the heap of electronics.

Caitlyn shrugged. "You never know what you're going to need."

"You would have made a fine, well-prepared boy scout."

Caitlyn separated two cables that had gotten tangled and began to put items back.

"Your laptop, water bottle, Wi-Fi adapter, Wi-Fi scanner, this is an antenna that fits on both, this one is for BlueTooth, this connects to wireless security cameras – depending on what frequency they're running on. Bunch of spare USB cables, small parabolic microphone. Ah! my notebook!" She put it aside on the dashboard. "Phone charger, signal jammer – it's similar to the one you have – TV remote jammer, not sure how this got in here." She held up a few tiny USB flash drives on a key chain. "Universal boot tool for diagnostics, Kali, Xubuntu, latest Ubuntu, Rubber Ducky."

Thomas interrupted her.

"A what?"

Caitlyn took the flash drive with the bright yellow duck logo off the keyring and showed it to him.

"It's like a computer bug, you plug this into a computer you want access to and it does most of the work for you once you've programmed it. It pretends it's a keyboard, so it's really hard for a virus scanner to block it, because then it also blocks all real keyboards. It creates a hidden network, shares the whole C drive, logs keystrokes, and -."

"Stop talking please," Thomas said. He gave her the flash drive back and raised both hands as if warding off some evil spirit, but he was kind of smiling.

Caitlyn flipped to the right page and handed her notebook to Thomas. He copied the address that was scribbled in the corner into the car's GPS, while Caitlyn shoved the remaining gadgets back into her backpack.

"Nice handwriting," Thomas commented as he read the rest of the page. "Anatomy, Biochem. Is this your school planner?"

"Yeah, but it's not like I'm using it for school anytime soon. Figured I'd use it for case notes."

Thomas looked at the schedule.

"At least it explains why you're failing."

"What do you mean?" Caitlyn asked, confused.

"You don't seem to prepare at all, or review, you don't spread out your workload evenly at all. Seriously, you start studying for a test a week before?"

"It's what I've always done," Caitlyn said. "I used to start days before, but I quickly found out I couldn't do that anymore. Doesn't everybody study this way?"

"Really, for someone so smart, you can be amazingly clueless at times. When you go back, we have to have a word about your study skills."

When they entered Douglas County, the barren winter farm fields changed into a welcome but brief stretch of road with pine forest on both sides. One hour later they zigzagged through Camellia. Thomas parked on a side street right next to the store on the corner.

Caitlyn handed Thomas his wheels and the wheelchair seat and checked her watch. "If all goes well we should be home before dinner."

Thomas nodded and got out.

They rounded the corner and went into Engelhardt Print & Photo.

It was a small print store, with narrow aisles that did not feel nearly as cramped as they could have, thanks to the brightly lit and meticulously clean environment. It reminded Caitlyn of a research lab where everything had to be sterile and well organized, to avoid contamination.

A short, thin man looked up from a desk behind the counter and immediately zeroed in on Thomas with a slightly hostile sounding "What do you want?"

Caitlyn bent closer to Thomas and whispered. "That's more like it."

She straightened up and answered the man. "I have an appointment."

The man took her in for a few seconds before turning to Thomas again. "Doubt it. I don't do appointments. It's a store. You can walk in whenever you want."

Thomas stopped, not liking the hostile reception. He looked at his chair and Caitlyn's crutches, then slowly looked back up at the man. It didn't rattle the man at all, but after a brief second, he waved a hand in a half apologetic gesture and added with fake politeness. "In a manner of speaking".

Caitlyn walked closer and tried to take a subtle peek at his computer monitor, noticing the almost empty desk with only a keyboard and mouse on it. A mental image of her own desk flashed through her mind; it was nowhere close to her dad's chaos, but nowhere close to this minimalist setup either.

How do people manage to be this neat, where do they leave all their stuff?

"I made an appointment with you on Monday. I transferred the down payment, and you agreed to meet me here. There's no one else here, it's you."

The man stood up and positioned himself between Caitlyn and his desk, still with his eyes on Thomas, but also physically blocking her from seeing his screen, Caitlyn thought. This was going to be even more difficult than she had expected.

"I'm sorry about the mess by the way." Thomas was browsing the aisles and motioned at the wet tracks he was leaving all over the store. Caitlyn saw the man's face twitch briefly.

"But with all the wet snow outside…"

"Look, we're OK." Caitlyn tried again. "We're not looking to cause you any trouble, we're just looking for information on a man named Dino Augeri –"

This got the man's full attention. "You-, what?"

Caitlyn took a folded piece of paper out of her pocket. "We're looking for a man, someone I think you… rendered some services for? I don't actually need those services, but I will pay you the same for some information. I brought a paper wallet, you can check the Bitcoin balance –."

"That's it! Both of you. Out! Now! I don't know who you think I am, I don't know what you're talking about, and unless you have a warrant," he looked at Thomas again. "Don't come back!"

"Fine, fine," Thomas said loudly from one of the isles. "We're leaving and… Oops!"

Thomas took a turn a bit too wide and bumped into one of the shelves. A dozen small cardboard boxes with printer inks came tumbling down in a waterfall of colorful packaging.

Thomas began putting boxes back on the shelf in random order. Caitlyn was sure even Bradley would have managed a neater stack.

"No! Just… leave!" The man rushed over to him. He only briefly hesitated before he grabbed the backrest of Thomas' chair and started to physically push him out of the store. Thomas quickly put his brakes on and held on to a push rim. "Please, let me help you clean up, I insist."

Caitlyn took her chance, and – making sure the man wasn't looking at her – bent over.

"I *hate* it when people push me," Thomas muttered under his breath when they were outside. "Did it work?"

"Perfect distraction, thanks!"

Thomas got in the car and took a towel out of the door compartment to dry his hands while Caitlyn followed Thomas' instructions.

"If you can pick up the whole chair and tip it? Yes, like that, then it fits through the door and you can drop it on the back seat if you angle it."

"Wow, I thought it would be a lot heavier!"

"It's pretty lightweight." Thomas agreed.

Caitlyn got in the car and glanced at the storefront.

"You know, that name doesn't suit him at all."

"What do you mean?"

"Engelhardt. It's Dutch, or probably German. It means 'heart of an angel'."

Caitlyn got Thomas' laptop out of her bag, plugged a Wi-Fi adapter in, and turned it on.

"So, I put the Ducky in his computer, and now I can connect to the same network he's on, and with a bit of luck I can remote in and we can see what he's doing. If that doesn't work, we'll have to use the screenshots it's sending to my server."

"You know none of this means anything to me, right?"

Caitlyn waited for her laptop to connect, then opened a command line window and started typing, occasionally pausing to read the output in one of the tabs.

She felt Thomas stare at her and glanced at him.

"What?"

"You type really fast."

"Pianist," Caitlyn said, distracted. She smiled with pride and satisfaction when the browser window she was watching changed from black to video, then gasped when she realized what she was looking at.

"That's him! That's Dino! Here, this is the store owner's monitor, and he's looking at him right now! We've actually found him! Look at the picture!"

She turned the laptop so Thomas could see the screen.

"Huh!" he said.

"Paranoid but predictable. He logged on to his computer to

check for Dino in his records as soon as he got rid of us."

Caitlyn switched to another window. "And look, here… Uh-oh."

"Uh-oh, what?"

"I don't know. I lost the connection." Caitlyn changed the angle of the antenna on the Wi-Fi adapter, then checked the screen to see if that had any effect.

"I thought you were supposed to be this super hacker?" Thomas teased her.

"It's your fault you know, I could have been a lot better if you hadn't been called in to my high school!" Caitlyn teased back. "Hold on, let me try…"

Thomas glanced at the screen again, and the commands Caitlyn was typing.

"Like I said, magic."

He leaned back and looked out the window, then his tone changed.

"Caitlyn. Quick!"

Caitlyn half looked up. "What?"

She had just enough time to take her fingers off the keyboard before Thomas slammed the laptop lid shut. He started the car and pointed at the store owner who came running at them, rounding the corner.

"Looks like he found your duck thing. Put your seatbelt on."

Thomas pushed the lever next to his steering wheel down and they sped off.

Inside a small restaurant that, according to a weathered wooden sign, looked out over Beverly Lake they stopped for some hot coffee and tea.

The lake was frozen solid and a few teenagers were fooling around on the ice. They were sliding around on their shoes and laughed as they were falling over.

Caitlyn had Thomas' laptop open again and was looking through the screenshots that had started uploading to her server a few seconds after she had plugged the Rubber Ducky into the store's computer. She looked at Thomas, feeling elated.

"We've got them, both. It looks like this Engelhardt guy keeps meticulous records, he has this whole program that keeps track of everything."

She showed Thomas the screenshots.

"See, this is the first one when I plugged the Rubber Ducky in and it connected. Here's when he logged on." She pressed the right arrow a couple of times. "And here he's typing in a password. Looks like he encrypted his whole drive, smart, but of course when you're taking screenshots that doesn't matter."

Caitlyn copied two of the images to a different folder and opened them side by side.

"And here are our unsubs."

"Unsubs, eh? You watch too much TV, Harry."

Caitlyn ignored him.

"Dino and Donna Augeri."

Caitlyn looked at the picture of the woman with the brown curly hair. It looked like the woman in the pictures IRC had found for her.

"She's actually kind of pretty. Do you think she's involved too?"

"Possibly," Thomas said, studying the pictures and sipping his coffee.

"At least we've got a lot of new information now. We have a city, an email address and a phone number."

Caitlyn opened Notepad and typed out the phone number she saw in the screenshots.

"He used a throwaway email address, as instructed by Engelhardt. It's one that expires after a day, so that's pretty useless, but it's the same phone number for both of them, let me check… "

She clicked on the PhonePhinder shortcut on her desktop, checked some settings, and pasted the phone number into a search bar at the top. It didn't take long for a map to appear on the screen. Caitlyn turned it to show Thomas.

"See all these dots? This is every single cell phone tower that this phone has pinged in the last 6 months. If you mouse over one of the dots, it will show you the date and time, see?"

"That's really impressive," Thomas said. "This is on my laptop?"

"Officer Dean!" Caitlyn gently elbowed him and laughed. "What happened to *'I don't want to know'*?"

"Very useful." Thomas added.

"Welcome to the dark side." Caitlyn laughed

While they waited for the program to finish, Caitlyn explained how it worked to Thomas.

"Google does something similar, it creates a map using your phone's locations over time, if you're logged in. This program is based on that. Except you can do it with any phone number you want, not just your own. It's pulling information from several databases with cell tower IDs and known Wi-Fi networks. It can take a while and it doesn't always work, but when it does, it's really good. You know, I could even put an app on your phone that can connect to this. So you don't have to always bring the laptop?"

"One step at a time please, this is enough new technology for me for at least the rest of the month. "

Caitlyn studied the map for a while.

"It looks like he got this phone at the end of September, it's probably a cheap burner that he activated then. Nothing is showing up before then. If you let it play - like this - and set all the dots to show a different color for each day," she changed a few settings and clicked the play button again, "then it's pretty easy to spot the pattern." She pointed at the map. "He thinks he's smart by turning off his phone when he gets close to home and only turning it back on when he leaves. Like they can't track him home that way. Except, as you can see, it creates this giant blind spot."

Caitlyn leaned back and beamed at Thomas, who nodded and smiled.

"We know where he lives."

CHAPTER TWENTY-FIVE

"Brrr!" Caitlyn shivered as she entered Thomas' home. She had almost forgotten how cold it could get before the sun had a chance to chase some of the early morning chill away.

"Don't worry, it's supposed to warm up today. And at least it's much better than all that snow and slush," Thomas said, "thank God for that."

"I'm so ready for spring!" Caitlyn said. "You really don't mind driving me again? I know it's going to take almost a full day again, I could ask my mom, or –"

"No. Really, it's fine. I love to drive, and I don't have any other cases. And someone needs to keep an eye on you, and all your electronics." His blue eyes twinkled at her. "Besides, we've gotten this far, I want to see it through. It's fun for me too, to not work alone for a change. In the Marines I was part of a team, when I was a cop I almost always had a partner. I never really got used to flying solo."

Thomas held on to a push rim and reached back to grab his coat from a kitchen chair.

"Doing better?" Caitlyn asked.

"Yes."

"You know next time *that* happens, you can just call me to cancel or reschedule. Even if it's on very short notice."

"Thanks. But keeping busy actually helps."

Thomas turned off the lights and locked the door behind them.

By now they had their routine down. Caitlyn threw the crutches on the backseat, got in the car, and put the parts Thomas handed her in their place while they were talking.

"Are we still going to Donna's work first?" Caitlyn asked.

"Yes, why?"

"Her work is pretty far from where their house should be. I thought maybe it was better to go door to door, where that blind spot is, show some pictures to people until we find them?"

Thomas shook his head. "Too risky. If you find the wrong neighbor, they will tip them off. It's much better to go to her work first, confirm it's her, and see if we can get an address."

Caitlyn nodded. "Makes sense if you put it like that."

Thomas stopped at a light.

"Have you given any thought to what you're going to say when we actually find him?" he asked.

"Yes." Caitlyn replied. "I want to ask him what happened, what caused the crash. I want to know why he left."

They drove in silence for a while. Caitlyn looked out the window as they crossed the second bridge and drove past the golf course again. A watery sun was breaking through the clouds. It made the few bits of early morning frost that were clinging to the dried-out wheat in the fields sparkle.

Close to Eastfall Thomas had to slow down until it was stop and go.

"Did we miss another national holiday?" Caitlyn asked.

"I don't think so." Thomas looked unsure.

Then Caitlyn noticed a small billboard on the side of the road and pointed at it. "There. Looks like there's some event. Hockey and an ice-skating race on Reynold's Pond?"

"Huh."

"Did your parents take you skating when you were a kid?"

"I grew up in Miami. It doesn't really freeze there."

"My parents always dragged me and my sister along in winter."

"Sounds like fun."

"Mmm. I mainly remember half freezing to death and drinking hot chocolate at the end. That was the best part, finally warming up again. It was always outdoors on some frozen lake or pond, preferably in the middle of nowhere. My mom is not a fan of ice-skating rinks, says they're too crowded and she wants to hear the ice sing or something. You know that sound you get when you skate on real ice?"

Thomas shook his head.

"Oh, right. Well, it always made me think it was going to crack any second. It's this eerie hollow yet clear tone, a bit like when you wiggle a sheet of metal? It's hard to explain. My mom grew up in the Netherlands where apparently as soon as there's a tiny bit of ice, they measure if it's thick enough, and then half the population switch their clogs for a pair of ice skates and jump on top of a canal. They've got a hundred-mile-long race in the north that apparently is a big deal, but they haven't been able to hold it for years now. Global warming, probably."

"Have you ever been?"

"The Netherlands? Not in winter, not skating. Definitely not that race, different province. But we did spend a lot of summers with my grandparents when I was growing up. They still live in the Netherlands, in the house my mom grew up in. But it's only oma now. Opa, my granddad, passed away a few years ago. I haven't been back after the funeral. My parents and sister have though. Have you ever been?"

"Not to the Netherlands, but I've seen several places all over Europe when I was in the military. Spent some time in Germany, I think that was the closest I ever came. Trained with Dutch soldiers once, too. Organized and disciplined bunch. Good men."

As soon as they passed the exit, traffic cleared up a little and the sun fully broke through the clouds. Caitlyn angled her face to soak up some of the light.

A few miles later she was still half looking out of the window, and half dozing off, but she immediately jerked awake when Thomas exclaimed.

"You've got to be kidding me!"

"What, what??"

"Look. Behind us! They're back! I thought I noticed them

before. I wasn't sure, but it's them. I can't believe I missed them, they must have been following us all the way from my house!

Caitlyn checked the rear-view mirror, and then her side mirror. "Where are they? I don't see them."

"Gray Impala."

"I don't know what an Impala looks like."

"Four cars behind us, behind that black one."

Caitlyn peered at her side mirror, pressing her cheek and nose against the window.

"Are you sure it's them? It's not the station wagon, or that red dented one."

"I'm positive. Look at the guy next to the driver, with the long hair. It's Jesus."

"Well, shit! Sorry. Now what?"

Thomas' face turned grim.

"They've been tailing us for long enough I'd say. Time to shake things up. Hang on."

He waited for an exit to come up, then suddenly sped up and turned onto the off ramp at the last second. Caitlyn looked back over her shoulder. The gray car was still following them, farther away now, but rapidly closing in.

Thomas turned onto a side street and parked behind another car. When the Impala had passed them, he turned and drove off in the other direction. Caitlyn could see the red brake lights flashing on the gray car behind them, as they turned the corner.

Meanwhile the voice on the GPS kept sounding off instructions at them. "Recalculating... Continue point seven miles, then turn left –.

"Could you shut that woman up?!" Thomas asked as he took over two other cars at what Caitlyn felt was well past the speed limit. Caitlyn fumbled around until she found the power button and pressed it down until the unit powered off. Thomas turned into a parking garage, only to exit again at the other end. Caitlyn had been holding on to the door handle, but quickly changed to the grab handle above the door when Thomas increased his speed even more and swerved through some of the narrow city streets.

He checked his rear-view mirror to see if they were still being followed, then pulled the car around a corner, made the quickest U-turn Caitlyn had ever experienced, and finally stopped the car on the berm.

"Whoohooo!" Thomas exclaimed. He kept looking outside to see if the gray Impala would drive past, then he glanced at Caitlyn who was sitting next to him, motionless, and with her eyes closed.

"Oh no, are you OK, did I hurt your leg?"

"Leg's fine. Best if I don't talk."

Thomas instantly caught on and eyed her suspiciously.

"You're not going to puke in my car, are you?"

"Don't say the P word." Caitlyn mumbled. She cracked her window open and stuck her face into the very chilly breeze that blew in.

Thomas kept checking the road and his mirrors, but didn't see the other car.

"I think we lost them," he said after a few minutes. "How are you doing?"

"Better." Caitlyn sighed and opened her eyes. "I think it's safe to drive again, but can I leave this window open for a while?"

"Sure. Let me know if I need to pull over, OK?" Thomas shot another slightly weary glance at her, eased onto the road and turned the GPS on again.

"Sorry about that," Caitlyn said after a while. "I used to always get car sick when I was a kid. I thought I was over it now; sitting in the passenger seat usually works well enough."

She took another deep breath of cold air, then closed the window again. "I think I'm good. That was really impressive though, how you got rid of them. I didn't know you could drive like that."

"I didn't know I still could, either." Thomas grinned, more to himself. "I took a few courses in evasive driving in the military, and then again after I joined the police force. I guess the hand controls don't make that much of a difference."

Caitlyn turned in her chair and looked behind them for a few seconds. "It also worked. They're definitely gone."

Thomas parked in front of a large mall.

Caitlyn crutched slowly towards the entrance, then sped up when Thomas had caught up with her. She could walk at an almost normal speed by now.

"Remember," Thomas warned her. "We don't want to spook her."

Caitlyn paused, she realized she hadn't given this part much thought at all. She had mainly worried about what to do and say when she finally stood face to face with Dino. But what did she expect? That she could just walk up to his wife, and tell her she wanted a word with her husband?

She turned to Thomas.

"So, what do we do?"

"Recon," Thomas replied. "Once we know she's in there, we'll go in and see if she's willing to talk to us."

They found the floor plan on a large board near the mall entrance and walked to where the nail salon was located. Paullished was nestled in between a Body Shop and a place called Taqueria Jalis that sold burritos and tamales.

The odd mixture of musky perfume and Mexican food was almost enough to turn Caitlyn's stomach again.

The front of Paullished consisted of a large glass wall with a door in the center.

"Too risky to walk in, she's going to remember us. Crutches, wheelchair. Best to not let her see us for now," Thomas said as he scanned the area.

"Perfect. Hang tight. I'll be right back."

Caitlyn sat down at a table near the Taqueria, where she could hide behind some browning, unrecognizable plants that looked like they could really do with some watering.

She watched as Thomas rolled up to a group of teenagers that were fooling around near a drinking fountain. There was a small puddle of water on the floor, their coats were zipped open, and they were trying to splash each other.

Thomas wheeled around the puddle and asked them something Caitlyn couldn't hear. It led to a short discussion between the boys after which one of them half stepped, half got pushed forward by the others. Thomas pointed at the nail salon and showed the boy something on his phone. After another short conversation the boy nodded. Thomas got his wallet out and offered him a few bills.

Caitlyn guessed the boy was around fifteen or sixteen. He had on a beanie that covered most of his dark hair. He reminded her a little of Ralph Macchio in the original Karate Kid movies.

Thomas came back and pulled a chair away from the table so he could join Caitlyn.

Together they watched as the boy confidently strolled past them. Thomas gave the kid a nod.

"What's happening?" Caitlyn asked Thomas.

"I asked if one of them would be willing to go in and check if Donna was working today," Thomas explained. "Robert over there got volunteered by his friends."

Robert walked into the nail salon without hesitation.

For a while nothing happened at all, no one went into the salon, no one came out. They couldn't tell what was going on inside.

"Just in case, what happens if she suspects something's up?" Caitlyn asked nervously.

"Then we run, so to speak," Thomas said. "Don't worry. I showed him my PI license, told him I was working a case and needed help. He seemed like the type of kid that really doesn't want to lose face in front of his friends and thinks all this secret PI stuff is incredibly cool."

Thomas was right. A couple of long minutes later Robert came walking out of the nail salon, turned the corner and gave Thomas two thumbs up, followed by a rolling arm gesture and a very theatrical bow.

"Arrogant little dude," Thomas grinned, "but at least he made sure he was out of sight first."

Robert walked over to them, briefly looked at Caitlyn, then spoke to Thomas.

"Lady you're looking for is definitely working there," he said. "I walked around until I found her. Her name is Donna. Her hair is a bit shorter, and darker. But it's her, from the picture."

"And you didn't tell her about me?" Thomas checked.

"Of course not! Told her I wanted to buy something nice for my mom, like you suggested. She got me some kind of manicure kit. Here," he dug in his pocket and pulled out a few bills and coins. "Your change."

"Keep it."

Robert looked pleasantly surprised.

"A small tip for the extra flair you added," Thomas said. "Thank you for your help."

Robert smiled back. "Hey, thanks man!"

He walked back to his friends.

"It's her! It's really her!" Caitlyn said excitedly.

"Yes. Let's go in," Thomas said.

But Caitlyn stopped him.

"Hang on, I've got a better idea."

Caitlyn googled the nail salon and dialed the number using the IncogniDial app on her phone.

"Hi, could I speak to Donna please?"

Caitlyn waited, then shot Thomas a slightly nervous glance.

"Hi Donna, this is Leslie, from UPS. I've got a package for you, but part of the address label is ripped off. Could you please confirm your last name and your address?"

Another pause as Donna answered.

"I'm sorry ma'am, but we are not allowed to open packages. I don't know what's in it."

Caitlyn listened to the reply with a panicky look on her face.

"Look I'm busy working, I know you must be busy too, I could always have it returned to the sender so you can arrange for them to ship it to you again?"

Caitlyn's panic faded. She smiled, then started writing.

"Yes, I will make sure. Thank you. Have a nice day."

Caitlyn hung up.

"Phew, that was close. She asked how I got her work phone

number. Should have just told her it was on the shipping label. Either way." She showed her notebook page to Thomas. "I got it."

"3165 Porter Drive," Thomas read.

"My social engineering lessons are finally paying off," Caitlyn joked.

"Huh?"

"Manipulating people into doing what you want, without them catching on that you're doing it. A bit like acting, a bit like deceiving. One of my online friends is really into it, he gets himself into events for free all the time."

Thomas parked the car on Hanover Street twenty-five minutes later.

"Uh," Caitlyn said, looking at the GPS. "We're still a block away?"

"Never park right in front of the house you're going to visit," Thomas said. "Don't want to give them a heads up so they can run, or toss their drugs, or... "

"Right. I didn't think of that."

"It looks just like a regular house," Caitlyn said, quickening her pace a little.

"I know. They often do," Thomas said. "And remember, no hasty decisions, you can't go storming in without a plan. Always do recon before you enter unknown territory."

They watched the house from a short distance for a few minutes.

Caitlyn was growing increasingly impatient.

"That's long enough, " she decided. She didn't even wait for Thomas' to reply and crutched up to the house, trying to control her nerves.

Caitlyn rang the doorbell and waited. After a few seconds a male voice sounded from behind the door.

"Who are you and what do you want?"

Not the friendliest of welcomes, Caitlyn thought. It occurred to her that Donna could have called ahead.

"Good day, sir. UPS. I've got a package that you need to sign for."

The door opened, and for the first time Caitlyn got a good look at him up close.

Average height, with a Mediterranean tan. Jeans and a light pink pullover. Strong, confident posture. He looked fit, like he worked out. He had a neatly trimmed short beard and mustache. And very dark brown eyes.

She shuddered in recognition, but he didn't seem to notice, or recognize her back.

"I don't see any package. Where's your uniform? Who are you??"

Just then Thomas joined them and Dino narrowed his eyes.

"And who's the cop?"

Caitlyn decided to drop the act.

"OK, fine. My name is Caitlyn Harrison. Three months ago, a car hit me. I think you were the one driving it."

The door slammed shut.

"Hello?" Caitlyn tried.

Silence.

"He's not a cop anymore!" she said loudly.

Nothing.

"I don't want to cause any trouble, I only want to know what happened!"

More silence. Caitlyn felt tears welling up and tried to suppress them.

"Mr. Augeri? Please, I need to know."

This got a very stressed sounding response from behind the door, his voice tighter and higher pitched.

"How do you know that name?! Who sent you?!"

"What? No one sent me, I... It's a long story. Just... Can you please open the door?"

"Go away!" The pitch went up a few more notches.

"Please, can we just talk? Was it you?"

There was a sharp click from behind the door, and Thomas sprang into action.

He grabbed Caitlyn's arm and said with urgency. "We have to leave. Now!"

He pulled her sleeve, insisting she move. When that didn't work he started to physically push her along. When he finally got her moving in the direction of the car, Thomas let go and grabbed something from underneath his seat.

Caitlyn turned her head and gaped at him. "You've got a gun?!"

"Of course I've got a gun. And so does he. Go!"

"He– what??"

"GO!"

Back in the car Caitlyn was trying not to cry.

"Sorry," she sniffed. "It's just, I was so close. I don't know what happened. This wasn't how I planned it to go at all. It's him though."

"He definitely didn't want to talk," Thomas said grimly. "He pulled a gun on us."

Caitlyn looked up at him. "A gun, are you sure?"

"Pretty distinctive sound."

Caitlyn let that sink in for a minute.

"So, what do we do now?"

"Regroup. Go back home, come up with Plan B."

Thomas noticed how disappointed Caitlyn looked. "This just went from *possibly* very dangerous to *actually* very dangerous. Do you still want to do this, or do you want to hand it over to the police?"

Caitlyn was silent for a while, but quickly made up her mind.

"We still have no proof. We have to try again."

Thomas gave a curt nod.

"Let's take a little time to think over our options, come up with the best approach and go back next week."

He too thought for a while.

"He knows I'm a cop. Maybe Rubino warned him?" Thomas ran a hand through his hair. "Do you think it's my haircut?"

"I think it's your everything," Caitlyn replied.

"We found him." Caitlyn and her mom were sitting at the dinner table while her dad was cleaning up in the kitchen. "The first meeting didn't go well though, he... freaked out a little. We're going back next week."

"Are you OK?" Anne asked.

"Yes, mom, just disappointed. But we're very close now. We need to get him to confirm, or confess, and then we'll hand everything we have over to the police. Let's hope it's enough to reopen the case and convince insurance. The police report already said I wasn't at fault, and with a confession as extra proof they'd have no other option than to pay out."

"That would be great," Anne said. "Hey, I've got a conference coming up, I might ask dad to come with me, make it a long weekend."

"Sounds great, where are you going?"

"Orange County."

"Ooh, nice! Have fun!"

"Are you sure you'll be OK? By yourself I mean?"

"It's fine mom. I can cook, I've got a TV, I can almost walk again, and I've got a phone. Don't worry, go, enjoy! Get some sun!"

Over what should have been a lazy long week with the cats, Caitlyn grew more and more restless. Thomas called to thank her again for the laptop and to get a quick PhonePhinder refresher course, so he could track the non-cheating husband. They planned another trip to Dino for the upcoming Saturday.

Caitlyn watched Netflix, baked some bread and tried walking with only one crutch.

Not quite there yet, but soon. Progress!

She kept going over the encounter with Dino in her mind. The more she thought about it, the more she thought Dino had been scared, not murderous. He had actually seemed pretty harmless before she told him who she was. And she never saw a gun. Could Thomas really be that sure that he had had one?

Don't let the fear guide you, she reminded herself.

She considered calling Thomas, but felt like she had been imposing enough already and didn't want to make him waste another full day. Not for a man who would probably still refuse to talk to them.

And now that she thought about it, Dino had only gotten scared when he had seen Thomas and made him as a cop. Without Thomas there, he might be a lot calmer, and more willing to talk? And the longer she waited, the bigger the chances of Dino vanishing again, a little better and farther away this time, disappearing forever.

Caitlyn's parents were gone and Michelle and Jess both had to work, so she couldn't ask them to drive her either. Driving herself was definitely not a good idea. Yet the more convinced herself this was the right thing to do, the surer she felt.

She checked her bank balance, decided any amount of money was worth finally getting answers, and booked a Lyft.

CHAPTER TWENTY-SIX

"Come on, lady, you've gotta make up your mind!" The Lyft driver who had picked Caitlyn up that morning had been very accommodating at first, but now was quickly losing his patience, and his temper.

Caitlyn was directing him through Camellia, zigzagging through random streets, basically making him drive like an idiot. She was trying to remember the surveillance lessons Thomas had taught her, while at the same time making sure no one was following them.

She knew she had stretched her driver's patience too thin, and directed him straight to Dino's house. It was only after they had stopped that she remembered Thomas told her to never park in front of the house you're visiting. But after a quick look at the very annoyed driver next to her, she kept her mouth shut.

"Thanks. Can you wait for me here, please?"

"Are you going to be quick about it?"

"Yes," Caitlyn reassured him.

"Don't be too long, I've got other things to do today."

"Isn't all of this included in the fare?"

"There's no money in the world that's worth all this hassle. Just hurry up."

Caitlyn's phone buzzed as she got out of the car. It was a text from Thomas.

Bugged me that we were followed.
Checked again.

Found a GPS tracker under my car.
Well hidden this time.
They must have used a creeper.

She stared at it for a few seconds.
What the hell is a creeper? And... does this change anything?
She looked at the house and decided.
No, I don't think it does.

She texted Thomas back.

That explains it!
Went back to Dino alone, but don't worry, was not
followed. Took a Lyft. Made sure.
Thought he might be more willing to talk without you
there? Sorry :) C.

Caitlyn put her phone on silent and clicked the button that turned the screen off, she didn't want to be interrupted while she tried to talk to Dino.

She knocked on the front door. A familiar man opened almost immediately, as if he had been expecting her, and roughly pulled her inside.

Caitlyn almost lost her balance when he dragged her over the doorstep and felt a sharp twinge in her ankle when she put her right foot down.

She held her leg up in a protective reflex and took a couple of deep breaths as she steadied herself. Her first instinct was to give in to the flash of anger. But when she turned to face the man all that changed.

She stood face to face with Jesus, with his long hair in a ponytail, and a gun in his hand that he was pointing straight at her. Her heart was already racing and now upped its tempo to about a million beats a minute from the surge of extra adrenaline.

"What–", she took a small step back on her crutches. "... You?"

Jesus was almost as surprised as she was, but it took him much less time to get over the shock.

"You." A statement, not a question, as he looked down his nose at her.

Jesus opened the door and peered through the crack.

"Is that cop with you?"

"What? No." Caitlyn instantly realized how stupid she had been to come back alone, without Thomas to back her up. Stupid to be so naïve to think Dino would be willing to talk to her alone. Stupid to ignore all possible danger, blinded by the possibility of – finally after all these months – finding out what happened.

She also realized how stupid it was to answer Jesus. Now he knew she came alone.

Shut up! She told herself.

Jesus pushed her to his right, further into a wide hallway. Caitlyn barely noticed the framed family photographs on the walls. She kept her right foot up, intentionally slowing down. To give herself some time to gather her thoughts and come up with an escape plan. But also because she didn't yet want to test how much weight her ankle could hold, not sure if she re-injured it. She was pretty sure she could feel a tingle in her back, right where the gun was pointing.

At the end of the hallway Jesus stopped her in front of a door.

"Phone." After a brief pause he added. "Crutches too."

"I need these to–"

"I don't care. Phone. Or I will get it myself."

Caitlyn did not like the sly smile he gave her. She reached into the back pocket of her jeans and handed over her phone and, reluctantly, her crutches.

Jesus briefly checked her phone, saw the black screen, and put it in his pocket.

He unlocked the door and pushed Caitlyn in.

The door locked behind her, and she found out she wasn't alone when a sharp and slightly nasally voice on her right addressed her in a demanding tone.

"Who the hell are you?"

Caitlyn immediately recognized the woman on the bed as Donna even though she looked a lot more disheveled than she did in her pictures. She had a hint of a New York accent. One, Caitlyn thought, her husband lacked. The color of her foundation didn't match the rest of her, and she had clearly been crying, because there were light streaks where the caked-on layer had been washed away. Her mascara had run halfway down both cheeks. She pointed at Caitlyn with a long pink and black panther patterned nail.

"Who are you," Donna asked again, "and what are you doing in my house?"

Before Caitlyn could answer, Donna suddenly sat up a little straighter and looked at her with a hopeful half smile.

"Wait, did you come to rescue me?"

But her smile fell as quickly as it had appeared.

"No, because how could you know they locked me up in here?"

She was clearly thinking out loud, and not really expecting Caitlyn to answer. So Caitlyn stood there, silent, and waiting for the monologue to end. It gave her some time to calm down.

Donna finished her ramble with a final exclamation. "I don't know what's going on!"

That makes two of us, Caitlyn thought.

She half hopped, half limped to the bed and sat down next to Donna. Her ankle was protesting, but her knee was holding up.

"My name is Caitlyn. You don't know me, but I came to talk to your husband."

"Dino?"

Caitlyn nodded. "Is he here, too? In the house I mean."

Donna promptly burst out in tears.

"No, they're waiting for him. They keep asking me what time he will be home, but I don't know!"

Caitlyn awkwardly put a hand on Donna's leg in an attempt to comfort her.

"If they only want your husband, at least we are safe here. Don't worry. If they wanted to kill you, or me, I'm sure they would have done so already, instead of locking us up in here."

"Kill us?! I don't want to die! Oh God! And we've seen their faces too!"

"I, uh, actually already knew who they were before I came here," Caitlyn said.

Donna's head snapped up. "You know them? You mean, you're with them?!"

"No, no..!" Caitlyn quickly reassured her. "They've been following me–"

"You led them here?! Why would you do that?!"

"No, I mean, I don't know, maybe?"

I am sure I wasn't followed, Caitlyn thought, *but the GPS tracker Thomas just found must have led Rubino and his men straight to this house. This* is *my fault.*

Donna pushed herself backwards. "Get away from me!"

Caitlyn got up again and limped the few steps to the other side of the room. She tried to tune out the hysterical sobbing and hoped the Lyft driver would call someone when she didn't come back. She looked out the window, but couldn't see the street from here. Couldn't signal for help.

She sat down on a chair behind a small white wooden desk. There were burglar bars in front of the window. Even with two good legs, jumping out of it would have been impossible.

Caitlyn's attention turned to her ankle. There still was a sharp twinge, but it was not as bad as she feared, and she knew it would be fine in a week or so. Assuming she lived.

"I am not with them." Caitlyn told Donna again. "Really. Why would they lock me in here with you if I was?"

Donna wiped her eyes, and smeared more of the makeup across her face in the process. She took one last big sniff and seemed to collect herself.

"Do you know how many men there are?" Caitlyn asked.

"Three." Donna said. "Three men. And they all have guns."

Donna told her how they had pushed their way in when she opened the door and Caitlyn matched their names to the descriptions Donna gave her.

"I think the first one was Vinny, Jesus was the one who opened the door for me, with the ponytail. The other one is probably Eduard."

Caitlyn stood up and limped to the door. She tried the handle, but it was definitely locked. She put her ear against the door and listened. She could hear voices in the hallway, but they were too far away for her to tell what was being said.

"I don't know what they want!" Donna said.

"I thought we already agreed they want your husband."

Some panic started to creep back into Donna's voice. "We need to find a way to warn him."

"We need to find a way out," Caitlyn said. "I'm guessing they took your phone too?"

Donna nodded.

"Jesus is probably waiting behind the front door again. No way he wouldn't see us, even if we could open this door to get out." Caitlyn thought and looked at the window. "These bars, can they be removed from the inside?"

Donna shook her head. "I don't think so."

"Why do you have bars on your guest bedroom window, anyway?" Caitlyn asked. Donna shrugged. "Dino, my husband... Something happened last year, and he's been a little over the top when it comes to security since then."

Caitlyn double checked, but couldn't see any way to use the window as an exit.

"What's wrong with your leg, anyway?" Donna asked.

Caitlyn turned her attention from the window back to Donna. "Car accident."

"Actually," she added, "That's what I wanted to talk to your husband about. I'm –."

Suddenly there were loud voices in the hallway. Men were shouting. Then someone started screaming. "Donna! Where's Donna?! What did you do to her?!"

"Dino!" Donna gasped. She jumped up and pressed her ear against the door, next to Caitlyn's. There was more shouting and screaming. The front door was slammed shut, and they heard the sound of loud stumbling footsteps and voices going up the stairs. Caitlyn guessed they were dragging Dino along, and judging by all the noise, he was putting up a hell of fight.

Donna sat back down on the bed, visibly trembling, and Caitlyn sat down on the chair behind the desk. Both of them instinctively moved as far away from the door as they could. Away from the danger.

Caitlyn could hear one of the men shout in a room upstairs, somewhere above her head, a little towards the front of the house. "Where is it?!"

Judging by the dull thuds and moans that followed, Dino didn't know, or wasn't talking.

When the noise stopped, the footsteps moved around again. For a few seconds there was total silence, followed by an unintelligible conversation as the men talked to each other. Caitlyn heard someone come down the stairs, turn into the hallway, and held her breath as the footsteps stopped in front of their door.

Caitlyn and Donna briefly glanced at each other, but when they heard the key turn, their focus turned back on the door.

Jesus came back in, followed by Eduard. Both men were holding a gun.

Eduard dragged Donna off the bed, and Jesus grabbed Caitlyn by her elbow.

"Get up!"

Caitlyn complied, but Donna was screaming at Eduard, who was a good few inches shorter than her. "Let me go! What did you do to my husband?! Dino!"

Muffled sounds came from upstairs. Dino must have heard his wife.

"Shut up!" Eduard roughly shook Donna, and she fell silent.

Jesus pushed Caitlyn forward, and she grabbed his arm in order to keep her balance. She wasn't sure how much weight her right leg could hold, but it also occurred to her that the weaker and slower she seemed, the better her chances of escaping would be, if an opportunity presented itself.

Jesus shook her off as if she was something wet that he had to peel off. "Walk."

"I can't."

He squinted his eyes at her knee brace, then said. "Ed, watch them."

Eduard lazily waved his gun from Donna to Caitlyn, as if he was playing a very slow game of Pong, until Jesus came back with the crutches.

Stay calm. Caitlyn told herself. *Calm people live, think this through!*

The Lyft driver was still outside, maybe she could signal him for help?

Also, she thought as they started moving, it was possibly a good sign, Jesus bringing her the crutches. Not something he would have done if he wanted to hurt her, or didn't care if she would live or not. It calmed her a little more

"Thanks," she said.

It got her an extra shove.

Vinny was waiting at the front door, holding leading Dino. Dino's nose was bleeding and one of his eyes was rapidly swelling shut.

Caitlyn saw Dino briefly shake his head at Donna, after which Donna stopped protesting and quietly let Eduard hold her.

A fourth man came in. Tall, shaved head.

Oscar. That makes four. Caitlyn thought. *Great counting, Donna.*

"Did you check the street?" Vinny asked.

Oscar nodded. "We're clear."

That meant her Lyft driver had left, Caitlyn thought, despair creeping in. Her hopes of getting rescued were fading by the second.

"Let's go," Vinny said.

Jesus hissed in Caitlyn's ear as he pushed her outside.

"If you make a sound, I will shoot you."

There were three cars parked in front of Dino's house.

A gray Impala, a black BMW and a black van with a green Basil leaf logo on the side panel.

Caitlyn, Donna and Dino were pushed into the back of the van. There was a low and narrow wooden bench on both sides, over the wheel wells, that they all sat down on.

Caitlyn had to suppress a badly timed nervous giggle as a thought flashed through her mind.

Did they do this on such a regular basis, that they installed a place to sit? Was this their kidnapping van?

Eduard watched them, his gun pointed at Dino, while Oscar tied their wrists behind their backs with zip-ties. He put a pillowcase over each of their heads.

Caitlyn couldn't see much, could only tell what direction the light was coming from. She turned her head towards the sound and felt someone move her left leg, then the right by grabbing hold of the knee brace. Oscar zip-tied her ankles together and from the sound she could tell he did the same to Dino and Donna.

TV and movie scenes of freshly dug graves flashed through her mind.

Going back alone had been a really, really bad idea.

The van's doors closed, and she was instantly surrounded by darkness. She could clearly hear the four men talking on the other side of the van's side panel.

"Make sure you leave nothing behind that could prove we were ever here. Roy will send a cleaning crew over later."

So they definitely were following Rubino's orders.

"I know. I put all their stuff in the trunk for now."

"Good, we'll deal with it later."

Caitlyn leaned her shoulders back against the side of the van, trying to find the most comfortable position for her arms and legs. Outside the ring tone of a phone sounded. It was quickly cut off when someone answered the call.

"No boss, he won't talk…"

"I know, but we're in a residential area, we can't make that much noise here."

"Yeah, his wife, and also the girl on crutches.

"Yes, her."

"I don't know."

"Right. On our way. See you in a few, boss."

Caitlyn heard the doors of the other car open, and two more men got into their van.

They started driving.

CHAPTER TWENTY-SEVEN

Thomas stared at his phone.

Sorry. Don't worry.

Went back alone?!

And what on earth is a Lyft?!

He pressed the dial button. It rang until it went to voicemail.

Dammit Harrison!

He thought for a moment, then scrolled through his phone's contacts and dialed another number.

"Martin? Hi. This is Thomas Dean."

"Hi Thomas," Martin replied, surprised.

"Have you heard from Caitlyn today?"

"No, she should be home, why?"

"Just checking."

"Anne and I went up to Anaheim for a few days. Anne for work, me for vacation and wine."

"Sounds nice," Thomas said, distracted.

"It's raining," Martin grumbled with a smile in his voice. "But at least it's warm."

"I thought I called your home phone?"

"Caitlyn forwarded it to my cell. We talked to her last night, to check on her. You know we worry ever since... Anyway, she said she'd be heading out to – what was it?"

Thomas heard him put his hand over the phone and briefly talk to Anne.

"She took one of those cab services to Camellia this morning, said she had to go back? Didn't you go with her?"

"No, I was out most of the morning."

"Oh, well, she said she'd probably be back home in time for dinner. We're flying back in an hour. Is it urgent?"

"Not really. I'll try her again later."

"OK." Martin paused. "She's safe, right?"

Thomas, too, paused. "I'm pretty sure where she went. Just wanted to check with you before I jumped in my car. I'll let you know. Don't worry, I'm sure she's fine."

Three hours later Thomas cautiously wheeled up the short path that led to Dino's front door. He had dropped Bradley off at Ellen's parents', texted Ellen a quick explanation, and had arrived at Dino's house in record time. There was a black Beamer parked in the driveway that he guessed belonged to Dino.

Good cover in case bullets start flying. And if it's Dino shooting, let's hope he loves his car.

Two visible exits. Probably more at the back.

He rang the doorbell and waited, mentally reprimanding Caitlyn for going back, for going back alone. Mentally reprimanding himself, too, because he should have known she would do this. He remembered being just as brazen when he was working his first couple of cases, when he knew he was this close to all the answers he needed, and ignoring all safety protocols as a result. He should never have expected her to wait another week.

Nothing happened.

He rang the bell again, and rapped his knuckles against the wooden door. Still nothing.

Thomas felt a faint hint of anxiety and worry start to rise in his chest. He was pretty sure this was where Caitlyn had gone back to, but what if she had meant the ID maker, or any of the other locations?

He leaned a bit closer to the door and listened.

There was no shuffling of feet, no sound of a door opening inside the house, no sharp clicks of magazines being checked and pushed back into a gun.

Dead silence.

He knocked again and called out.

"Hello?"

Thomas rolled back and checked out Dino's car. It was unlocked.

Bad sign, or bad habit?

He checked the glove compartment and all the junk and pieces of paper that were stuffed into the driver's side door, but he found nothing that could help him.

Thomas pushed himself over to the side of the house and checked all the windows he could reach, slightly flattening a few frosty perennials in the process.

He saw nothing. No movement. No people.

At the back of the house were two large sliding glass doors.

Thomas popped his chair up onto the deck and got his Glock out of the holster that was velcro'd under his seat. He pressed his face against the large glass panes, cupping one hand around his eyes so he could see into the living room. He tapped the butt of his gun against the glass, hoping for movement inside at the sharp sound it made.

Still nothing.

He shouted "Hello! Dino?", and banged on the glass with his fist.

Absolute silence. The place was deserted.

Thomas cursed.

Stay calm, focus! Caitlyn told herself. *Come up with a plan.*

The comfortable position she had found had stopped being comfortable after about the second turn they made. The pillowcase over her head smelled strongly of a popular brand of fabric softener, too strong to be pleasant.

Probably from Donna's linen closet, she thought.

It did nothing to help the disorientation.

After the fifth sharp turn a slight and familiar queasiness was setting in.

She tried to keep track of time, so she could figure out how far they had driven.

Sixty seconds. Two minutes. Five minutes... Or was that six? Dammit. Lost it.

Math was not going to get her out of this anyway.

What would Thomas do?

Stay calm and escape.

Come on, think!

At least the pillowcase means they are worried about us seeing them, or where they're taking us.

Donna broke the silence in a whisper that was loud enough to cut through the pillowcase and the road noise.

"Are you OK?"

"Fine, though my nose is still bleeding." That was Dino.

"Do you know where we're going?" Caitlyn asked.

A harsh "Shut up!" from the front of the car made everyone jump.

Caitlyn went over the options in her mind.

She could wait until they got to where they were going, and run.

Or she could make such a scene in the back of the van that they'd have to pull over, and then she could run.

Or...

She sighed in frustration as she tried to reposition her legs.

Any plans she could come up with involved running like hell, and she knew that was not going to happen. If only she had been tied up in the back of a car four months earlier, and they didn't have any guns. Or, if she was wishing for a more ideal situation, not abducted at all, and still in med school. Or, maybe not med school.

A sharp sudden turn made her fall sideways, and she landed half on top of what by the sounds of the low grunt was Dino's leg.

"Sorry", she said as she straightened up again.

"It's fine." Dino muttered.

"Any suggestions on how we're going to get out of this?"

"Shut up or we will gag you!"

Caitlyn was not looking forward to getting some dirty handkerchief stuffed in her mouth, and decided that, at least for now, coming up with a collective escape plan was too risky.

The longer they drove, the more the starts and stops and turns taken slightly too fast were turning her queasiness into full nausea. The bumpy vibrations combined with keeping her balance as the van rounded corners, weren't exactly having a therapeutic effect on her leg either.

A few more sharp turns later Caitlyn's focus shifted from trying to get out alive, to not throwing up.

Don't move. Calm, easy breathing.

She tried to turn her body sideways so she at least was facing the direction they were traveling in.

Breathe in, breathe out. Don't puke. Don't move. Don't think about puking. Whatever you do, do not throw up inside this freshly laundered pillowcase.

Being tied up in the back of a moving van with a pillowcase over your head was like riding a roller coaster in the dark. Like a poor man's version of Space Mountain.

A violent almost 360 turn sent another big wave of nausea through her. But it also made her pause and sit up a little straighter, and forget about not-puking for a second.

The turn they just made, she knew it... If she was right, they would...

Caitlyn smiled. The sound of the wheels on the road changed, and she could feel the van climb a little.

Relief crept in between the nausea.

She knew exactly where she was.

They had just turned onto the Chandler Island Bridge. And it was much closer to the safety of home than she had been when this car ride from hell had started. After they came off the bridge she tried to follow the route the car was taking, but where she always turned right going further into the city, the van took a left.

She wasn't familiar with this part of town.

Doesn't matter. Don't puke.

Maybe now that they were in the city she could signal someone for help? Or shout, or... But the guns...

By the time the car finally slowed, turned and parked, she could feel something rise in the back of her throat. She longed for home, for safety, and for some cool, fresh winter air. But when the doors opened and she took a big inhale, she was hit by a wave of car exhaust fumes that mixed with the detergent smell.

Someone roughly pulled the pillowcase off and cut the zip ties around her ankles. She blinked at the light, ignored the gun that was pointed at her, and as quickly as she could, half scooted, half rolled to the edge of the van and started retching.

"Christ!" The man with the gun jumped backwards, his nose wrinkled in disgust.

Caitlyn spit one last time and tried to straighten up. The man roughly pulled her upright, and Caitlyn had to suppress another wave of nausea at the sudden jerky movement.

He dragged her to the edge of the van and she sat there, one leg dangling over the edge of the van, the other one sticking out at the angle of the knee brace, while he tried to clean the spatter off his shoes.

Caitlyn took a careful deep breath in. Cool, fresh winter air this time. *Relief.*

She looked up. She didn't recognize the man who was holding her at gunpoint.

"You done?" he snapped.

"I think so." One more breath. "Tell your buddy his driving sucks."

The man said nothing but waved his gun at her and she slid off the edge.

Dino and Donna followed.

Caitlyn looked around. They were in an industrial area with lots of concrete buildings. There was a dark warehouse looming at the end of an asphalt driveway, past the red and white barrier they were parked in front of.

She could see some gray, similar looking buildings in the distance, but with darkness rapidly falling they were fading into black. And anyway, there were no people nearby that she could see. No one to call for, or signal for help. No one, and nowhere, to run to for safety.

Oscar punched in a code on the keypad next to the barrier, and the striped pole slowly moved up.

The man who was holding Caitlyn at gunpoint pushed her forward.

"Wait!" Caitlyn protested.

"Do you need to hurl again?!"

"No, but I need my crutches."

"Hey!" the man shouted after a brief glance at Caitlyn's knee brace. "This one says she's on crutches?"

"In the trunk," Jesus waved at the gray car as he pushed Donna forward, "it's unlocked."

A good sign, Caitlyn thought, *if it still means they don't plan on hurting or killing me.*

The man cut the zip ties around her wrists.

Slightly less of a good sign, they know I'm not a threat.

Caitlyn rubbed her wrists and checked her watch. It was close to six p.m.

She carefully tested her ankle after accepting the crutches, then everyone half ducked under the barrier and the string of hostages and men with guns headed towards the building.

Caitlyn's leg was stiff and sore from the long car ride, and she hoped the walking would loosen up the muscles.

A big flood light came on as they neared it.

Thomas went back to his car and got in. He tried to think of what to do next.

Should I call the police?

Then he remembered. *The laptop, the program!* With a mix of relief and hope he got the laptop from his backpack. He clicked the PhonePhinder icon, typed Caitlyn's number in the field, hit the 'Phind' button, and waited.

At first nothing seemed to happen, and he was worried he hadn't done it right. He thought he remembered everything Caitlyn had explained to him correctly, was he missing a step?

But when he zoomed out he saw dots had appeared on the map, all the way up in … Washington? Surely she hadn't driven all the way up north? The dots stayed close to Spokane for a long time, then came a long line of dots that went down into Oregon. They briefly stopped past Haweville, then went north where nothing happened for a while. He thought the program was done, but then saw more appear at Caitlyn's parents' house, several locations in the city, and even his own house.

Thomas realized it was showing him every place Caitlyn had been to in at least the last six months. The crash site, the hospital. He looked at the screen, and found the red stop button. He clicked it, and to his relief the map cleared.

He tried again, but this time set the date range to today only.

Thomas waited, as the map was generated again, much quicker this time. It showed Caitlyn's house, with a line of dots closing in on Camellia. Thomas laughed as a whole lot of zigzaggy lines followed.

Countersurveillance. Well done Harry!

Except, of course, this time it hadn't helped, The Restaurant Five had already known where to go, because he hadn't found the GPS tracker sooner.

As the dots stopped at Dino's house, a thought made Thomas panic a little.

What if she had turned off her phone?

But to his relief, seconds later more appeared. They moved from Dino, back up to… Haweville? Why would she drive back to Haweville and not go back home?

And why wasn't she answering her phone? If her battery ran out, why not just borrow a phone? Martin had said Caitlyn had forwarded their landline to his cell. She could have called him too, if something was wrong.

Thomas looked at the screen, and at the keyboard, but couldn't for the life of him remember what Caitlyn had done to make the timestamps appear for each dot. He had way of knowing when she had arrived at Dino's house, or when she had left.

He noticed the time in the lower right corner of the laptop screen and double checked his watch. It was a little after 17:00. From Haweville to Camellia was a three hour drive. Martin told him Caitlyn had left around 11:00.

Thomas zoomed in on Haweville and frowned. It was not, like he had guessed, Rubino's restaurant. It was much farther west.

Wait, was this the warehouse he had followed the whole crew to?

But Caitlyn didn't know where that was.

He cursed as he realized.

They definitely took her.

He looked at the screen, hoping for some dots that would show Caitlyn heading home from the warehouse.

But instead a short message popped up at the bottom of the window.

"Phone trace DONE!".

Just to be sure he called Martin

"Has she called you back yet?"

"No, we're getting a bit worried."

"I'll let you know as soon as I know more." He almost hung up, then added, "Don't worry."

CHAPTER TWENTY-EIGHT

The warehouse door opened and a man Caitlyn recognized as Joseph motioned them inside. "Hurry up." He quickly scanned the area then closed the door behind them.

Inside, Caitlyn looked around. There was a staircase leading up on the left, with a thin wall next to it that separated the stairway from the main storage area. They walked through a second door that was permanently held open by a concrete block. The same ones her dad used under his bee boxes, Caitlyn thought.

There were rows of tall racks on her left, all the way up to the ceiling. From what she could see they held large boxes and bags of pasta, tomato sauce, and other restaurant supplies. She could see part of an open attic above the racks, with what looked like a makeshift wooden fence in front of it, that was supposed to keep people from falling down. Along the right wall was a row of small rooms. All the doors were closed, except for the first one which had a sign on it that read 'Main Office'. At the far wall Caitlyn noticed a lit green Emergency Exit sign.

Joseph motioned everyone into the second to last room. The man Caitlyn didn't know took her crutches again and re-zip-tied her wrists.

The room was clearly used to store packaging material and trash. There were stacks of empty boxes, bubble-wrap, a shelf with shipping labels and rolls of packing tape.

No chairs, no table.

No landline to call home on. Just a bare light bulb and lots of flattened cardboard on a dirty carpet.

The door closed behind them.

Caitlyn looked around the room once more, but didn't see anything she could use to escape or fight. She pushed a stack of cardboard against the wall and sat down on her makeshift chair. Donna and Dino did the same.

The big space on the other side of the door acted like an echo chamber, amplifying the sounds. She caught part of a short phone conversation that ended with an "understood". Caitlyn heard the men talk about calling the boss before they walked off.

From the occasional shuffling sounds outside the door, it was clear that one of them had stayed behind to guard them. Footsteps came closer again, and when the door opened, Oscar and Eduard came in and took Dino away.

It took a while for Donna to calm down after that, but eventually she asked Caitlyn. "What should we do?"

She sounded just as scared as Caitlyn felt.

"I don't know," Caitlyn replied. "We're back to where we were at your place. Except this time," she gestured at the small window high up in the outside facing wall, "there are no bars in front of the window."

"But we can't climb out of this one either," Donna sighed. "It's too small."

"I know."

"We could break the light bulb and cut them with glass?" Donna suggested.

"There's too many of them. And they have guns. It won't work. And it would be dark."

Donna clearly didn't like the idea of darkness either.

"As soon as we can, we have to try and escape though."

Caitlyn nodded in agreement.

They listened to the conversation outside, hoping to overhear something they could use.

"The boss said he was on his way. Told me to get started."

They could hear someone shout up in the attic. "Where is the money?!" When Dino didn't answer, they beat him.

Caitlyn had to reach out her arm to stop Donna.

"Don't, they will shoot you."

Donna reluctantly sat down, and they both tried to ignore Dino's screams.

"Hey, can you hand me that roll of packing tape?" Caitlyn asked Donna.

She used her teeth to cut long strips of tape off, and wrapped them around her sock, like a makeshift ankle brace. She put her shoe back on and tried a few steps.

"Better?" Donna asked.

Caitlyn nodded. It felt more stable. "Good enough, I can walk on this."

She figured her chances of successful escape had just gone up, and immediately felt better.

After a while, footsteps came closer again, and Joseph opened the door. Eduard and Oscar pushed Dino in. He had a bleeding lip, and squinted at them through two swollen eyes. He was clutching his ribs and moved very slowly.

Donna guided him onto a cardboard stack chair and started fussing over him.

"I got a few good punches in before they pinned me down," Dino grumbled. "Donna, leave it, it's fine."

Caitlyn could tell he was taking quick and shallow breaths. "Ribs?" she asked.

Dino glanced at her and nodded.

Caitlyn held up the roll of packing tape. "Strap them?"

"No use, they're not done with me yet."

"Deep, slow breaths are better."

"What are you, a doctor?"

"Medical student. It prevents pneumonia."

"I don't think it's pneumonia I have to worry about," Dino grunted, but he tried to breathe in better. He turned to Donna. "Don't worry, love, I won't talk. If I do, we're dead." He glanced at Caitlyn. "All of us."

Caitlyn felt fear start to take over again.

"Wait, why would they kill me too? I just got caught up in the middle of whatever this is."

"So you don't know?" Dino said.

"That you hit me?" Caitlyn asked.

"No; about the drugs." Dino gestured at the lasagna boxes in the corner and lowered his voice. "There's a freezer room in the back that's not holding any frozen food. I mean, it looks like it is, and they keep it nice and cold, but they're putting cocaine in empty lasagna boxes."

"Wait, what?" Caitlyn blurted out.

"Coke." Dino replied. "Blow. Dust. Snow."

Caitlyn suddenly remembered the conversation she overheard at the restaurant the first time she and Thomas met Rubino. She had assumed the men had been talking about the weather. How naive.

"Roy orders most of his restaurant supplies from Italy, " Dino continued. "You know, the authentic stuff, lots of dried pasta and tomato sauce. Everything arrives at the Port every month or so. I'm pretty sure he bribed the port authority to look the other way. He's got cops on the payroll, too. They unload the shipping containers and drive the cocaine straight into the warehouse."

There was shuffling on the other side of the door, and Dino briefly paused.

"Those wooden benches in the back of all the vans, the hard-ass ones we just sat on, they're hollow. They use the vans to distribute the cocaine to their dealers. I already had my suspicions when there were so many junkies knocking on the back door of the kitchen when I was a chef, but they always bought small quantities. It happens. I can look the other way. But then I found a box full of the stuff. Someone," Dino motioned at the door, "had taken the wrong box into the kitchen. At first I thought I'd just pretend I hadn't seen anything, keep my mouth shut, you know. But somehow Roy, my boss, knew I'd seen it."

Dino repositioned himself with a grunt.

"At first he thought I wanted in. He knows my family, my brothers. But that's not me." Dino was getting worked up,

"I'm nothing like them!"

Donna shushed him. "I know, baby."

"I wanted out. We've got our first grandchild on the way, "he smiled at Donna, "and I just couldn't do it. But I couldn't turn him in either, he's not the type of man who forgives and forgets. And then I thought, WITSEC, but like a DIY version, you know? Buy a new identity, move someplace nice, retire from cooking. Clean slate. But to do that, I needed money. And where there's drugs there's lots of money, so I went looking for it. "

"Why didn't you go to the cops?" Caitlyn asked.

Dino's face said it all.

"Psh! Are you nuts? I may not be like my family, but I sure as hell ain't no snitch either."

Dino winced and paused to catch his breath.

"I found the safe, and once I had the code, I took some of Roy's money. Well. A lot of it, since it was just laying there."

Dino paused again. "I got greedy. I guess that makes me a little like my family after all, but I wanted a better life for us." He looked at Donna.

"And Rubino found out and wants his money back," Caitlyn said, more a conclusion than a question.

Dino nodded. "We've been moving around, renting a small house in a new city every month. I paid for Donna's beautician training, got myself into community college, learned to weld. And now Roy wants it back. All of it, with interest."

"And I'm guessing you can't just...?"

"Definitely not. I've got a good chunk still stashed away, so we can all move when the baby gets here. Roy is going to kill me as soon as I tell him where it is. He's going to kill Donna, and probably you too. I'm not telling them shit!"

Then he looked at Caitlyn. "How did you get caught up in all of this anyway, if you didn't know about the drugs?"

"I came back to talk to you, about when you hit my car," Caitlyn said sheepishly.

"Wrong place, wrong time. I know what that is like." He turned to his wife. "I was going to tell you to pack your bags again Donna.

I'm so sorry."

"As long as we're together I can live anywhere," Donna said. Then she frowned. "Did you really hit her?"

"I did. It was the first night we left. I wanted to go back to the restaurant one last time. Get my knives, my stuff. Sentimental value. So stupid. I waited for everyone but Roy to leave and tried to sneak in while he was busy cleaning up in front. Except he saw me. I barely got away in time. I was driving fast, too fast. The weather was bad. He called me, tried to convince me he would pretend all of this never happened. But I knew he already had the others looking for me. Chasing me." Dino turned to Caitlyn. "I'm sorry I didn't stay. It wasn't safe, I couldn't risk him finding me. He would have killed me. I checked to make sure you were OK before I left, though, I called an ambulance."

"I broke my femur, it was bleeding internally."

"I didn't know."

Caitlyn let it all sink in for a while, then looked at Dino.

"Why did you move to Camellia? It's so close to Haweville."

"None of this was Donna's fault, I didn't want to punish her for my mistakes. She deserves to be close to her family. And I know Roy hardly ever drives south. A different gang runs the cocaine business there, and they wouldn't want him in their territory. I thought the risk would be minimal. How did you find me anyway?"

Caitlyn explained that she and Thomas had been looking for him for a long time.

She abruptly stopped talking when voices and footsteps came closer.

The door swung open. It was Roy Rubino.

CHAPTER TWENTY-NINE

It was just after 20:00. when Thomas arrived at the warehouse. Darkness had set in when he crossed the bridge into Haweville. He parked out of sight and checked the laptop one last time. The dot hadn't moved for the past hour. He hoped to God Caitlyn was still in there.

He put on his shoulder holster, tucked his Glock 22 inside and put a black coat on top that he left unzipped. The coat was too thin for this kind of weather, but it would conceal him much better than the reflective stripes on his winter coat.

Thomas leaned over to open the glove compartment and got out some FlexiCuffs. Just when he was about to close the compartment again, his eye fell on a small black box. He smiled, and put it in his pocket, then transferred into his chair to assess the situation.

Thomas was thankful for the darkness outside. At least this time he had a chance to investigate without being seen.

He ducked under the barrier and slowly wheeled up the slight incline of the driveway, careful to avoid any big holes that would make his front casters rattle and possibly give him away to anyone outside.

He could see two doors from here, both closed. There was a row of small windows across the top of the left wall, unevenly spaced out, with light coming through most of them. He could see a security camera on the outside wall and another one along the driveway.

He needed to know if Caitlyn was inside, if she was OK. Needed to know how many other people were inside, and if they were armed.

And he had to hurry. There were only some very twiggy bushes on the side of the asphalt that would be very noisy to wheel through. A dumpster stood against the wall, too close to one of the doors. Neither would be very good to hide behind. He was a sitting duck, an easy target in plain sight, and he didn't like it one bit.

Thomas crept closer, keeping an eye on all the doors. He listened for any sounds that would indicate that someone was coming out, trying his very best to stay out of the line of sight of the cameras.

He didn't notice the huge flood light until it sprang to life.

"The floodlight just came on, and the camera shows there's an extra car parked up front. No, it's not Mr. Marino. Go check it out." Caitlyn could hear it was Rubino giving orders.

An extra car? She felt a tiny glimmer of hope.

Dino's shouts had started again, up in the attic.

Caitlyn looked at Donna who was sitting on a cardboard box stack, slightly trembling with a mix of anger and fear.

"They're talking about a car that doesn't belong to them, I think my Lyft driver might have followed us here, since I didn't pay him yet. This is our chance! I'll distract whoever is guarding our door, and you can run for help. It's probably the best chance we have."

"There's the door we came in through," Caitlyn nodded her head at the wall in the right direction, "and there's an emergency exit on that side."

"I saw another door opposite us," Donna said. "If that's open, it's the closest one. There were stairs on the outside, so there must be a door on the second level somewhere as well."

"Dino and at least one other man are upstairs, better not risk it. But the emergency exit or the side door might work?"

They both fell silent when they heard someone walk up to

Rubino outside the door.

"Boss, I need to leave for my shift."

"Right, take Joe too, it's busy. Come back after."

A few seconds passed and they heard Rubino swear.

"Vinny!"

A pause.

"Where's Vinny?... Chris!"

Footsteps.

"I can't get a damn signal and I need to take a call. Put those two in the freezer room."

"Uh, boss? The freezer door can be opened from the inside."

"Then watch this door until I'm back. Oscar and Joe just left for their shift. Vinny's outside checking on that car. I need to call Mr. Marino about the deliveries."

Caitlyn counted in her head. Rubino, Jesus, Eduard, Chris. Vinny outside. Were there others she hadn't seen yet?

"Four men still inside, I think," she whispered to Donna.

Thomas wheeled up to the building at full speed, stopped behind the dumpster in the shadows, and held his breath. There was a small parking lot at the back of the building, with a dense row of fir trees separating the two.

There was also another door, and a few large windows. Thomas waited for a while, then carefully wheeled closer, trying to keep his adrenaline in check as he looked inside. He could see Rubino standing in front of a door, watching as his men loaded boxes into the backs of two black restaurant vans.

Clearly standing guard.

There were two restaurant vans parked outside, and with the extra two inside that meant there were at least four people. Probably more, considering the lights were on everywhere. A lot more.

Too many to shoot, if it came to that.

He continued, slowly circling around, slowly losing feeling in his hands.

Not good, when it came to shooting.

Somewhere behind him a door opened and Vinny walked out.

Thomas quickly turned around the corner. He heard the footsteps come closer and waited.

An arm appeared, a hand holding a gun.

Thomas grabbed the arm and twisted the hand up so that Vinny was forced to drop his gun. In one fluid motion, Thomas twisted Vinny's arm behind his back and rotated the palm outward and up. Vinny fell to his knees with a short grunt.

Thomas hooked his left elbow around the man's neck as soon as he could reach it, and anchored his hold with his right arm. He tried to ignore the shooting pain in his back.

Vinny didn't make a sound as Thomas slowly counted to ten. His army instructor's voice echoed in his mind.

Never more than ten seconds if you want them to live.

He wasn't completely sure.

When Thomas eased off, Vinny quietly stayed down. Thomas held on to one of his push rims, balancing as he leaned far sideways. He rolled Vinny over and Flexicuffed his wrists behind his back, then tied his ankles together as well.

One down. Not sure how many more to go.

He knew it wouldn't be long before Vinny would regain consciousness, and he shoved one of his gloves in Vinny's mouth to keep him silent.

Thomas wished he could drag Vinny out of sight, but this would have to do.

He quickly scanned the area, but no one else was trying to sneak up on him.

He took his cell phone out of his pocket, opened the IncogniDial app, and dialed three digits.

Way overdue, he thought, feeling guilty.

Thomas knew exactly what he was going to say.

When he was done, he took the black box out of his pocket, pressed the button once, and placed it on the ground against the wall, with the red light facing down. He covered it with some dirt, so it wouldn't be noticed in the dark.

Caitlyn heard Rubino curse as he came back.

"Chris, do you have a signal?"

A short silence, followed by "No, boss." on the other side of the door.

"Fucking Vinny's disappeared. Phone's not working, and Augeri's still not talking."

Caitlyn heard Rubino cursed some more as he walked away again.

There's no cell signal here.

She hadn't even thought of trying to steal a cellphone to call for help. But wait, the car, Vinny missing, no phones...

Caitlyn gasped.

Thomas!

Should she risk yelling, or banging on the outside wall? But that would only put herself, Donna and Thomas in danger. And it would tip off Rubino's men that someone had come to save her and was outside. Then her eyes fell on the lamp again.

Light.

Thank you, dad!

A plan formed in her mind, and she started whispering to Donna.

CHAPTER THIRTY

Thomas checked another window and added one more to the head count. He grinned as he saw Rubino and another man holding up their phones.

Thomas circled the building once more, then saw one of the room lights flickering on and off. The room Rubino had been guarding.

On and off it turned, in the classic dot dot dot dash dash dash dot dot dot pattern of SOS, in a repeating loop.

Caitlyn!

He resisted the urge to bang on the outside of the wall in reply. He was too vulnerable here. And out-manned.

He made up his mind and rolled back down the slope. This time he was careful to avoid the floodlight.

He opened the car door, reached in and honked, long short long short.

C.

The light stopped, then started again.

T-E-N-M

Ten. Ten... what? Minutes? Men?

He honked once and waited.

L-O-A-D-E-X-I-T .

10 minutes. Loading dock exit.

Got it.

He honked twice and got in the car. Wishing that for once he could skip the hassle of having to drag his chair in after him. He had made way too much noise and had no doubts someone else would come outside to check on him. He needed to get to the back parking lot, to where he could see the exit, but would be hidden from sight by the trees.

He drove fast and slammed the car in park. He checked his watch as he got out again. Six minutes left. He hoped Caitlyn knew what she was doing. He fought some branches and pushed into the row of trees.

Caitlyn checked her watch, she could hear Rubino giving orders to check out who honked. She waited ten minutes, then banged on the door until someone opened it. It was Chris, not Rubino. She felt a little of the nervousness disappear.

"I need to use the restroom."

"Hold it."

"I've been holding it. I really gotta go! It's been hours!" Caitlyn pleaded. "And, if I can't hold it any longer, who do you think will have to clean it up? Surely not your boss himself."

That got Chris thinking. He turned to Donna. "Do you need to go too?"

Donna anxiously shook her head.

"Fine." He gestured with his gun for Caitlyn to follow him.

"I'm gonna need my crutches."

Chris turned his head and talked to someone inside one of the delivery vans. Caitlyn peeked past him and saw stacks of frozen lasagna boxes.

"Can you watch the door? This one needs the bathroom."

"Sure, I'll keep an eye out." It was Jesus. "I'm almost done loading up."

The door closed and Chris came back with her crutches and cut the zipties around her wrists loose.

"I'm sorry for puking on your shoes." Caitlyn said, rubbing her wrists.

Chris grunted.

And for what I'll do next.

Chris directed Caitlyn along the row of offices, keeping his gun pointed at her back.

Caitlyn glanced around, but didn't see anyone other than Chris watching her. Phew!

The first part of her plan went really well. Chris followed her into the bathroom. But before she went into the stall, he took both of the crutches from her.

Shit, shit, shit! This was a lousy plan, hitting him with the crutches. I this how I'm going to die? And Donna, and probably Thomas too. And then Ellen has to raise Bradley alone, and...
Don't panic. Breathe. Calm down! Think!

An image of Ellen and Thomas popped into her mind. Laughing at the kitchen table at a story Ellen had told, about rehab, about guys whacking each other with wheelchair parts...

Caitlyn looked down. *Please, let this work!*

She took off her knee brace and took a deep breath. Hoping her leg would hold for what she was about to do, and for what would follow. Hoping she could swing hard enough in this cramped space. She flushed the toilet, unlocked the bathroom stall door, then let out a sort of squeaky moan, and waited.

"You done?" she heard Chris ask.

She didn't reply. She was gripping the knee brace so tightly she thought her fingers would leave indentations. Her heart was beating out of her chest.

"Hey, you hear me? You done?"

What seemed like minutes later, she heard the shuffling of his feet as he came closer.

As soon as the bathroom stall door opened, she swung the knee brace as hard as she could.

"Fuck!"

Chris jumped back and put his hands over his nose, dropping his gun on the floor.

"You bitch! You–"

Before he could finish his sentence, Caitlyn swung the brace again, this time landing a blow on the top of his head. He groaned as the hard metal connected. His eyes rolled back, and Chris collapsed against the side of the stall.

Caitlyn was buzzing with adrenalin as she climbed over him. She hoped the noise hadn't alerted anyone else. She dropped the knee brace on the floor, there was no time to put it back on, and grabbed her crutches.

Caitlyn eased the door open and peered through the crack, eying the distance to the Emergency Exit and wishing with all her might that it was unlocked. She took one more deep breath, gathered all her courage, and went for it.

Thomas heard shouts coming from inside and pulled his Glock from his holster in one effortless fluent motion, like he had done a thousand times before, and pointed it at the figure that came stumbling out of the building.

As soon as he recognized who it was, he aimed his gun behind her.

"Caitlyn! Thank god! Are you OK?"

"I'm fine! I don't think they saw me escape. They'd have heard this though. Where's your car?"

Thomas pointed behind him with his free hand and rolled backwards for a few seconds before he turned around. Caitlyn half crutched half ran towards the row of fir trees.

They only made it halfway when a voice made them turn and look.

It was Rubino, holding his gun to Donna's temple.

"Stop." He ordered. He looked at Thomas. "Drop your gun."

Calm, cold, and calculated, Caitlyn thought.

And definitely creepy!

Thomas lowered his gun, but then hesitated.

Caitlyn glanced at him sideways and saw him... Smile?

Then she heard it. The sirens approaching in the distance. Getting closer, getting louder. She could already see the red and blue lights flashing in the dark.

Roy snapped his head towards the sound, and too saw the lights. He paused for only a few seconds, then let go of Donna and ran back inside.

"Clear out! Cops incoming! Get those vans away from here!

Quick, hurry!" he yelled.

"Let's go!" Thomas led the way through the row of trees, with Caitlyn and Donna in tow, and pressed the button on his car key that unlocked the doors.

"You saved us!" Donna sounded stunned.

"Well," Thomas said modestly. He reached into the glove box and cut Donna's zipties.

"But, I mean –", she gestured.

Thomas squinted at her and swung a wheel slightly too close to her head.

"Brain still works, lady."

He kept an eagle eye on the row of trees in front of him, but there was no one else coming through.

Thomas closed his door and looked at Caitlyn, his expression changed when he saw her face. "You OK, you hurt?"

"I'm OK. Leg hurts. But it's fine. I've never been so happy to see you! I knew it was you with the phones!"

"Very useful."

Thomas drove off, circling back to the front of the warehouse.

"Did you get Vinny?" Caitlyn asked.

Thomas smirked. "He's gonna have a bit of headache."

"My guy too," Caitlyn grinned. "I got him with the knee brace." Then her smile faded again, and she looked behind them. "They've got a lot of drugs packed into their vans. Cocaine. I don't think they'll follow us, they're getting out as soon as they can, before the cops arrive."

"We should, too," Thomas said.

Caitlyn frowned. "Why?"

"They don't like me. I don't like them. And I may have called in with that app of yours saying I heard people talking about a bomb threat. I know what to say to make it sound like domestic terrorism. I'm sure they're coming in full force, SWAT should follow in an hour, tops, for what basically is an empty warehouse. They'll establish a perimeter, we should leave before they do."

"I hope they check the freezer room," Caitlyn said.

The adrenalin was wearing off, and she suddenly felt

exhausted.

They passed the red barrier and Thomas slammed on the brakes when Donna suddenly shrieked into his ear.

"Stop! Stop the car!"

"Christ, what is your problem!?"

Donna pointed at the dark figure that came stumbling onto the road, clutching his ribs with one arm.

"Dino!"

Donna flung the door open and Dino squeezed himself in next to her with a grunt of pain. Thomas sped off again while Donna started fussing over Dino until he lovingly but firmly told her: "Enough!"

Dino took a better look at the wheelchair parts on the backseat that took up most of the available space. "Wait, you're that crippled cop?"

"Former cop. And I don't like the C word. Come to think of it, I don't like either of you." Thomas looked at Dino in the rearview mirror. "Do you have friends here in the city? Where can I drop you off?"

Dino thought for a second. "The subway station will do. You the one who called the co- sorry, police?"

Thomas frowned but nodded.

"Don't like 'em, but... saved my ass. Rubino's guys all high-tailed it out of there. Thank you."

After Thomas dropped Donna and Dino, Caitlyn explained everything that happened. Apologizing several times for going back alone.

When she was done, Thomas dialed a number.

"Lawrence, buddy. You know how I owe you one?"

"Right. How do you feel about a possible promotion in your future?"

Caitlyn listened as Thomas gave his cop friend a quick summary of what he would find in the warehouse freezer and Rubino's vans and smiled when he finished with. "Oh, and if you come across a knee brace, I'd like to give that back to its owner.

You know my situation, we had to leave in a bit of a hurry. I didn't want to run into the sergeant."

When he hung up, he turned to Caitlyn.

"He says thank you... Did you get all the answers you were looking for?"

Caitlyn thought, then nodded. "I think so."

CHAPTER THIRTY-ONE

Thomas stopped in front of Caitlyn's parents' house.

Martin and Anne clearly had been watching the street, because they soon came out of the front door.

"Is everything OK? We were worried, we thought you would be home well before us. Why didn't you call?! And where is your knee brace?"

"Lost it. Someone took my phone. It got a bit dicey, but Thomas rescued me. Don't worry, I'm fine, really."

Anne hugged her tightly.

"Dankje, mams," Caitlyn said in Dutch.

"Come in, come in." Martin waved his hand. "It's too cold and dark out here to stand and talk."

He looked at Thomas as he, again, briefly struggled with the high threshold.

"Coffee, tea? Something stronger?"

Thomas thought, then declined. "Thank you, but I should be going soon, Ellen is waiting for me at home, too. Just wanted to drop Caitlyn off."

Anne bent down and hugged him. "Thank you."

Caitlyn turned to her parents. "We found the guy who hit me. He didn't want to talk at first, so I went back alone. Not the best idea I ever had... but he was not nearly as scary as I made him out to be in my mind. We talked. It was good. It was... closure." She briefly glanced at Thomas. "The people he used to work for were... a lot scarier, and I sort of got caught up in the middle."

"And I apologize for letting that happen," Thomas said.

Then he turned to Caitlyn and tried to break the uncomfortable silence that followed.

"You're pretty good at this though, I'd hire you any day."

Martin shot Thomas a curious look.

"Thanks." Caitlyn yawned. "Guys. I'm beat. I'm going to bed. I'll tell you everything tomorrow." *Or maybe not everything,* she thought, deciding there was no need to worry her parents more than she already had.

Michelle came over later that week, waving around a newspaper.

"Did you see this!? They're writing about you! I mean, not by name, but... They're saying a disabled former cop who started his own PI firm helped the police roll up a huge cocaine smuggling ring. They mention his company, Dean Investigations. That's your friend, right?"

Caitlyn nodded.

"He came to rescue me, we kind of found out about the drugs thing by accident."

They talked for a while, about everything that happened.

After Michelle left, Caitlyn sat on the couch with Volta on her lap. She got a mini black-light and read the note Sophie had written to her in invisible ink.

Her life was back to normal, or at least her normal, post-car-crash. Her knee was doing better, her ankle didn't hurt anymore. There was no lasting damage from that final inelegant sprint to the car. She was back to where she had been two weeks before, once again on her way to normal walking. And to her surprise, despite the whole abduction ordeal, she hadn't had any more nightmares.

Maybe escaping under her own power, had made all the difference. She now knew that – as long as she was conscious, and with a little help from a friend – she could trust herself to get out of a difficult and scary situation. She was not as helpless and injured as she had been back in her car. For the first time in a long time she felt... capable again. And grateful for it.

She thought about her future, about finding a job and

eventually going back to medical school. But she mainly thought about what Thomas had so jokingly said. *"I'd hire you."*

Caitlyn got up and crutched to the shed. A watery sun was trying its best to brighten the day, and green bits of new grass were poking through the dark soil in the strawberry planter pots. Her mom had to start weeding again soon.

Martin was inside his shed, hammering away at a wooden construction, talking with Fenton, one of his beekeeper friends.

Caitlyn waited. She knew Fenton never stayed long.

And indeed, after a few minutes she heard him say his default phrase.

"I shouldn't overstay my welcome."

She smiled as Fenton walked past, then turned to her dad.

"What are you making?

Martin had just stuck some nails in his mouth, and mumbled something Caitlyn couldn't make out.

"Hey Dad?"

"U-huh?"

"I... think I'm going to take Thomas up on his offer."

Martin straightened up and took the nails out of his mouth.

"That's not entirely unexpected. So, no medical school?"

"I've given it a lot of thought. And I don't think it's for me. The long hours, the focus on illness. I'd like a break from all of that. I still want to help people, but I think this will make me a lot happier. I've had more than enough of hospitals for a while.

I'd have a lot more freedom, and less stress. And knowing I can take care of myself, it's a good feeling."

"Like I said, not unexpected." Her dad smiled reassuringly. "I've seen your mood improve every week since you started this investigation, and you know how this family feels about working a job that you actually like doing. It's such a big part of your life, it's no use wasting that much time on something you hate, just for the paycheck. But I won't lie, I'll worry. Your mom will definitely worry. It's a lot more dangerous than I would like - I'm pretty sure you haven't told us everything that happened."

Caitlyn felt her cheeks flush and felt a little guilty, but also certain. And this was an argument she had prepared for.

"People risk their lives every day. Cops, military, firefighters. And even in the medical field you are one needle stick or super bug away from a small disaster. There are risks everywhere. You know what they say, you could get hit by a car any day." Caitlyn half grinned and lifted a crutch.

"True, true."Martin paused. "Are you really sure?"

Caitlyn nodded.

"My daughter the PI." Martin smiled. "I will talk to your mom."

Caitlyn went back inside and called Thomas.

"Dean Investigations, this is Thomas speaking."

"Wow. That's... formal."

"Oh, Harry, hi! Sorry, I didn't see it was you. It's been really busy."

Caitlyn paused, suddenly a little nervous.

"Is everything OK?"

"Yes. Yes. I... Were you serious, when you said you'd hire me?"

Thomas was silent for a beat, but then answered without hesitation.

"Yes."

"Because I think I could be good at this. And apart from the whole kidnap hostage situation, it was actually a lot of fun. And..."

Thomas interrupted her.

"And I will pay you. I'm not sure how much I can afford, but we'll figure something out. Ever since the article appeared in the paper this morning, my phone has been ringing non-stop. I've got more prospective clients than I can handle on my own. It's probably going to die down soon, but for now it's enough to get me... to get us started. I've enjoyed working with you. So yes, my offer stands."

"I would love to accept it." Caitlyn felt the nervousness make place for excitement.

"Good. I'm glad," Thomas replied. "That said, I'm not sure if working from home is the safest option. This time we got lucky, but I don't want to put our families at risk like this again. We'll have to figure something out."

"OK... So... When can I start?"

"Rehab that leg first. We need you running, get you some self-defense and martial arts training –"

Thomas clearly had given the possibility of Caitlyn working with him some serious thought too.

"Also," Caitlyn interrupted him, "I can fix your whole IT situation, get you some new software."

Thomas laughed. "That's definitely going to be your department! How about I come over on Saturday, and we'll discuss all the details?"

"Great!" Caitlyn said. "Come have lunch here, I'll bake bread. Bring Ellen and Bradley."

By the time Thomas arrived, Anne had adjusted to her daughter's change in career plans.

Jess had called her to congratulate her on her new job, Sophie was working on a card, and Caitlyn was getting used to the idea herself as well.

Martin motioned to Thomas as he got out of his car. "Follow me."

There was a wooden ramp leading up to the kitchen door.

"I... Thank you," Thomas said, visibly moved.

"I figured we'd be seeing more of you. I know my daughter, I've seen her eyes light up when she's talking about working with you. I remembered you told me last time that you couldn't come in."

Thomas looked at him, slightly puzzled and confused. Then it clicked, and he laughed.

"You mean when you gave me the honey? I meant I had to get back home before El had to leave for work, or Bradley would have been alone! But really, this is very thoughtful. Thank you."

"It was either this, or I'd have to start chipping away at the front door threshold. I made some calculations, how's the incline?" Martin asked, proudly looking at his creation and clearly eager for Thomas to test it.

Thomas pushed up with ease. "Perfect, feels very solid too."

"My dad's a physics teacher," Caitlyn explained.

Thomas made a face.

"Not a fan, eh?" Martin chuckled. "Don't worry, I'll get you there."

Inside, Ellen sat down and kept an eye on Bradley who began to play with the toy fire truck they had brought with them. Thomas transferred to the couch and pushed his chair to the side. Seconds later Newton jumped on top, sat down, and started grooming himself.

"Is that OK?" Caitlyn asked.

Thomas hesitated. "I'm a little worried about the nails. It's an air cushion."

Caitlyn looked at her cat. "I can get him off if you like, but he should be fine. I'll keep an eye on him." Bradley walked over to Newton. "Uh... but he can scratch sometimes, hang on, mom?"

Anne took Bradley over to Volta, who was always very tolerant with kids, and showed him how to carefully pet her, stroking the fur in the right direction and being gentle with her.

Thomas reached for his bag and handed Caitlyn a piece of paper.

"I brought a contract. Oh, and this came for you too." He handed her padded envelope.

Caitlyn put the envelope on the table and quickly read through the contract.

"60/40 division, going to 50/50 once I'm licensed?"

"Sounds fair?"

"Definitely!"

"Take your time going over it," Thomas said. "Also," he added, "about our future office. A certain restaurant in the city closed down. The tenant went to jail for a long time, big drug bust. The owner of the building had been trying to get rid of Rubino for a while. He called me, he is very grateful. If we want it, we can get a great deal on a small office space close to Haweville's city center.

If that works for you, I'd like to sign a one year lease."

"Perfect!" Caitlyn said. "I can easily drive there, once I get a new car."

Anne brought in sandwiches. Caitlyn turned to Ellen, "Nut free everything, we made sure," and got a grateful smile in return. Soon everyone was talking.

"I know you're probably a little worried about your daughter, after this first case got... a bit more exciting than we bargained for," Thomas said. "But please, let me reassure you. With most cases we'll be watching people go about their day. We follow them, take some pictures. That's it. And we'll get Caitlyn to where she can properly defend herself when she needs to."

"Yes, some training would be good," Martin nodded.

"And," Thomas turned to him with a smile, "as you know the Morse code you taught her really came in handy."

"Really?" Martin raised his eyebrows. "She hasn't mentioned that. It's a lost art, really. Are you a HAM too?"

"I took Advance Long Range Communication once."

After Thomas, Ellen and Bradley had left, Caitlyn opened the envelope Thomas had brought. Inside was another envelope and a postcard from PDX airport.

She read the back.

```
I saw the article in the paper.
I don't know your address, but I'm sure the cop will
give it to you.
We are safe. I am very sorry I hit you and hurt you.
Insurance leaves a paper trail.
Wish I could give more, but I hope this helps.

Sincerest apologies,
Dino Augeri.

PS - This is not from the freezer. This is from me.
```

Caitlyn counted the bills in the envelope. It was more than enough money to replace her car. She could even start paying her parents back for her medical bills. And use some of it to get Thomas a decent computer. She knew he would refuse any cash she tried to give him.

Later that evening Caitlyn gave Newton a quick scratch on his head and got into bed.

For the first time in a long time she had a solid plan: Rehab her leg, get fit, work alongside Thomas, pay off her parents, get an apartment in the city...

She closed her eyes and smiled.

She was looking forward to the future.